A FAMILY SECRET

"Mummy," Jane said, "is my father alive?"

A strange, dreadful hush suddenly fell over the room. A light like a sword flashed into grandmother's blue eyes. Aunt Sylvia gasped and Aunt Gertrude turned an unbecoming purple. But mother's face was as if snow had fallen over it.

"*Is he?*" said Jane.

"Yes," said mother. She said nothing more. Jane asked nothing more. She turned and went out and up the stairs blindly. In her own room she shut the door and lay down very softly on the big white bearskin rug by the bed, her face buried in the soft fur. Heavy black waves of pain seemed rolling over her.

So it was true. All her life she had thought her father dead while he was living . . . on that far-away dot on the map which she had been told was the province of Prince Edward Island. But he and mother did not like each other and she had not been wanted. She was sure that all the rest of her life she would hear Agnes' voice saying, "You should never have been born."

Jane wondered if she would live to be as old as grandmother and how she could bear it if she did.

JANE
OF
LANTERN HILL

L. M. Montgomery

BANTAM BOOKS
NEW YORK · TORONTO · LONDON · SYDNEY · AUCKLAND

RL 6, IL age 10 and up

JANE OF LANTERN HILL
*A Bantam Book / published by arrangement with
the author's estate*

PRINTING HISTORY
Copyright 1937 by McClelland and Stewart Limited
Canadian Favourites Edition (McClelland and Stewart) 1977
Bantam edition / June 1989

*The Starfire logo is a registered trademark of Bantam Books,
a division of Bantam Doubleday Dell Publishing Group, Inc.
Registered in U.S. Patent and Trademark Office and elsewhere*

ISBN 0-553-28049-X

*Bantam Books are published by Bantam Books, a division of Bantam
Doubleday Dell Publishing Group, Inc. Its trademark, consisting
of the words "Bantam Books" and the portrayal of a rooster, is
Registered in U.S. Patent and Trademark Office and in other
countries. Marca Registrada. Bantam Books, 666 Fifth Avenue,
New York, New York 10103.*

PRINTED IN CANADA
COVER PRINTED IN U.S.A.

U   0 9 8 7 6 5 4 3 2 1

To the memory of "LUCKY"
the charming affectionate comrade
of fourteen years

1

GAY Street, so Jane always thought, did not live up to its name. It was, she felt certain, the most melancholy street in Toronto . . . though, to be sure, she had not seen a great many of the Toronto streets in her circumscribed comings and goings of eleven years.

Gay Street should be a *gay* street, thought Jane, with gay, friendly houses, set amid flowers, that cried out, "How do you do?" to you as you passed them, with trees that waved hands at you and windows that winked at you in the twilights. Instead of that, Gay Street was dark and dingy, lined with forbidding, old-fashioned brick houses, grimy with age, whose tall, shuttered, blinded windows could never have thought of winking at anybody. The trees that lined Gay Street were so old and huge and stately that it was difficult to think of them as trees at all, any more than those forlorn little things in the green pails by the doors of the filling station on the opposite corner. Grandmother had been furious when the old Adams house on that corner had been torn down and the new white-and-red filling station built in its place. She would never let Frank get gas there. But at that, Jane thought, it was the only gay place on the street.

Jane lived at 60 Gay. It was a huge, castellated structure of brick, with a pillared entrance porch, high, arched Georgian windows, and towers and turrets wherever a tower or turret could be wedged in. It was surrounded by a high iron fence with wrought-iron gates . . . those gates had been famous in the Toronto of an earlier day . . . that were always closed and locked by Frank at night, thus giving Jane a very nasty feeling that she was a prisoner being locked in.

There was more space around 60 Gay than around most of the houses on the street. It had quite a bit of lawn in front, though the grass never grew well because of the row of old trees just inside the fence . . . and quite a respectable space between the side of the house and Bloor Street; but it was not nearly wide enough to dim the unceasing clatter and clang of Bloor, which was especially noisy and busy where Gay Street joined it. People wondered why old Mrs. Robert Kennedy continued to live there when she had oodles of money and could buy one of those lovely new houses in Forest Hill or in the Kingsway. The taxes on a lot as big as 60 Gay must be ruinous, and the house was hopelessly out of date. Mrs. Kennedy merely smiled contemptuously when things like this were said to her, even by her son, William Anderson, the only one of her first family whom she respected, because he had been succesful in business and was rich in his own right. She had never loved him, but he had compelled her to respect him.

Mrs. Kennedy was perfectly satisfied with 60 Gay. She had come there as the bride of Robert Kennedy when Gay Street was the last word in streets and 60 Gay, built by Robert's father, one of the finest "mansions" in Toronto. It had never ceased to be so in her eyes. She had lived there for forty-five years and she would live there the rest of her life. Those who did not like it need not stay there. This, with a satirically amused glance at Jane, who had never *said* she didn't like Gay Street. But grandmother, as Jane had long ago discovered, had an uncanny knack of reading your mind.

Once, when Jane had been sitting in the Cadillac, one dark, dingy morning in a snowy world, waiting for Frank to take her to St. Agatha's, as he did every day, she had heard two women, who were standing on the street-corner, talking about it.

"Did you ever see such a *dead* house?" said the younger. "It looks as if it had been dead for years."

"That house died thirty years ago, when Robert Kennedy died," said the older woman. "Before that it was a lively place. Nobody in Toronto entertained more. Robert

2

Kennedy liked social life. He was a very handsome, friendly man. People could never understand how he came to marry Mrs. James Anderson . . . a widow with three children. She was Victoria Moore to begin with, you know, old Colonel Moore's daughter . . . a very aristocratic family. But she was pretty as a picture then and was she crazy about him! My dear, she worshipped him. People said she was never willing to let him out of her sight for a moment. And they said she hadn't cared for her first husband at all. Robert Kennedy died when they had been married about fifteen years . . . died just after his first baby was born, I've heard."

"Does she live all alone in that castle?"

"Oh, no. Her two daughters live with her. One of them is a widow or something . . . and there's a granddaughter, I believe. They say old Mrs. Kennedy is a terrible tyrant, but the younger daughter . . . the widow . . . is gay enough and goes to everything you see reported in *Saturday Evening*. Very pretty . . . and can she dress! She was the Kennedy one and took after her father. She must hate having all her fine friends coming to Gay Street. It's worse than dead . . . it's decayed. But I can remember when Gay Street was one of the most fashionable residential streets in town. Look at it now."

"Shabby genteel."

"Hardly even that. Why, 58 Gay is a boarding-house. But old Mrs. Kennedy keeps 60 up very well, though the paint is beginning to peel off the balconies, you notice."

"Well, I'm glad I don't live on Gay Street," giggled the other, as they ran to catch the car.

"You may well be," thought Jane. Though, if she had been put to it, she could hardly have told you where she would have liked to live if not at 60 Gay. Most of the streets through which she drove to St. Agatha's were mean and uninviting, for St. Agatha's, that very expensive and exclusive private school to which grandmother sent Jane, now found itself in an unfashionable and outgrown locality also. But St. Agatha's didn't mind that . . . St. Agatha's would have been St. Agatha's, you must understand, in the desert of Sahara.

Uncle William Anderson's house in Forest Hill was

very handsome, with landscaped lawns and rock gardens, but she wouldn't like to live there. One was almost terrified to walk over the lawn lest one do something to Uncle William's cherished velvet. You had to keep to the flat stepping-stones path. And Jane wanted to *run*. You couldn't run at St. Agatha's either, except when you were playing games. And Jane was not very good at games. She always felt awkward in them. At eleven she was as tall as most girls of thirteen. She towered above the girls of her class. They did not like it and it made Jane feel that she fitted in nowhere.

As for running at 60 Gay . . . *had* anybody ever run at 60 Gay? Jane felt as if mother must have . . . mother stepped so lightly and gaily yet that you thought her feet had wings. But once, when Jane had dared to run from the front door to the back door, straight through the long house that was almost half the length of the city block, singing at the top of her voice, grandmother, who she had thought was out, had emerged from the breakfast-room and looked at her with the smile on her dead-white face that Jane hated.

"What," she said in the silky voice that Jane hated still more, "is responsible for this outburst, Victoria?"

"I was running just for the fun of it," explained Jane. It seemed so very simple. But grandmother had just smiled and said, as only grandmother could say things,

"I wouldn't do it again if I were you, Victoria."

Jane never did it again. That was the effect grandmother had on you, though she was so tiny and wrinkled . . . so tiny that lanky, long-legged Jane was almost as tall as she was.

Jane hated to be called Victoria. Yet everybody called her that, except mother, who called her Jane Victoria. Jane knew somehow that grandmother resented that . . . knew that for some reason unknown to her, grandmother hated the name of Jane. Jane liked it . . . always had liked it . . . always thought of herself as Jane. She understood that she had been named Victoria after grandmother, but she did not know where the Jane had come from. There were no Janes in the Kennedys or Andersons. In her eleventh year she had begun to suspect that it might have come from the

Stuart side. And Jane was sorry for that, because she did not want to think she owed her favourite name to her father. Jane hated her father in so far as hatred could find place in a little heart that was not made for hating anybody, even grandmother. There were times Jane was afraid she did hate grandmother, which was dreadful, because grandmother was feeding and clothing and educating her. Jane knew she ought to love grandmother, but it seemed a very hard thing to do. Apparently mother found it easy; but, then, grandmother loved mother, which made a difference. Loved her as she loved nobody else in the world. And grandmother did not love Jane. Jane had always known that. And Jane felt, if she did not yet know, that grandmother did not like mother loving her so much.

"You fuss entirely too much about her," grandmother had once said contemptuously, when mother was worried about Jane's sore throat.

"She's all I have," said mother.

And then grandmother's old white face had flushed.

"I am nothing, I suppose," she said.

"Oh, mother, you know I didn't mean *that*," mother had said piteously, fluttering her hands in a way she had which always made Jane think of two little white butterflies. "I meant . . . I meant . . . she's my only child. . . ."

"And you love that child . . . *his* child . . . better than you love me!"

"Not better . . . only differently," said mother pleadingly.

"Ingrate!" said grandmother. It was only one word, but what venom she could put into a word. Then she had gone out of the room, still with that flush on her face and her pale blue eyes smouldering under her frosty hair.

2

"MUMMY," said Jane, as well as her swelled tonsils would let her, "why doesn't grandmother want you to love me?"

"Darling, it isn't like that," said mother, bending over Jane, her face like a rose in the light of the rose-shaded lamp.

But Jane knew it was like that. She knew why mother seldom kissed her or petted her in grandmother's presence. It made grandmother angry with a still, cold, terrible anger that seemed to freeze the air about her. Jane was glad mother didn't often do it. She made up for it when they were alone together . . . but then they were so seldom alone together. Even now they would not have very long together, for mother was going out to a dinner party. Mother went out almost every evening to something or other and almost every afternoon too. Jane always loved to get a glimpse of her before she went out. Mother knew this and generally contrived that Jane should. She always wore such pretty dresses and looked so lovely. Jane was sure she had the most beautiful mother in the whole world. She was beginning to wonder how any one so lovely as mother could have a daughter so plain and awkward as herself.

"You'll never be pretty . . . your mouth is too big," one of the girls at St. Agatha's had told her.

Mother's mouth was like a rosebud, small and red, with dimples tucked away at the corners. Her eyes were blue . . . but not an icy blue like grandmother's. There is such a difference in blue eyes. Mother's were just the colour of the sky on a summer morning between the great masses of white clouds. Her hair was a warm, wavy gold and to-night she was wearing it brushed away from her forehead,

6

with little bunches of curls behind her ears and a row of them at the nape of her white neck. She wore a dress of pale yellow taffeta, with a great rose of deeper yellow velvet at one of her beautiful shoulders. Jane thought she looked like a lovely golden princess, with the slender flame of the diamond bracelet on the creamy satin of her arm. Grandmother had given her the bracelet last week for her birthday. Grandmother was always giving mother such lovely things. And she picked out all her clothes for her . . . wonderful dresses and hats and wraps. Jane did not know that people said Mrs. Stuart was always rather overdressed, but she had an idea that mother really liked simpler clothes and only pretended to like better the gorgeous things grandmother bought for her for fear of hurting grandmother's feelings.

Jane was very proud of mother's beauty. She thrilled with delight when she heard people whisper, "Isn't she lovely?" She almost forgot her aching throat as she watched mother put on the rich brocaded wrap, just the colour of her eyes, with its big collar of grey fox.

"Oh, but you're sweet, mummy," she said, putting up her hand and touching mother's cheek as mother bent down and kissed her. It was like touching a rose-leaf. And mother's lashes lay on her cheeks like silken fans. Some people, Jane knew, looked better further off; but the nearer you were to mother, the prettier she was.

"Darling, do you feel very sick? I hate to leave you but . . ."

Mother didn't finish her sentence but Jane knew she meant, "Grandmother wouldn't like it if I didn't go."

"I don't feel very sick at all," said Jane gallantly. "Mary will look after me."

But after mother had gone, with a swish of taffeta, Jane felt a horrible lump in her throat that had nothing to do with her tonsils. It would be so easy to cry . . . but Jane would not let herself cry. Years ago, when she had been no more than five, she had heard mother say very proudly, "Jane never cries. She never cried even when she was a tiny baby." From that day Jane had been careful never to let

7

herself cry, even when she was alone in bed at night. Mother had so few things to be proud of in her: she must not let her down on one of those few things.

But it was dreadfully lonely. The wind was howling along the street outside. The tall windows rattled drearily and the big house seemed full of unfriendly noises and whispers. Jane wished Jody could come in and sit with her for a while. But Jane knew it was useless to wish for that. She could never forget the only time Jody had come to 60 Gay.

"Well, anyhow," said Jane, trying to look on the bright side of things in spite of her sore throat and aching head, "I won't have to read the Bible to them tonight."

"Them" were grandmother and Aunt Gertrude. Very seldom mother, because mother was nearly always out. But every night before Jane went to bed she had to read a chapter in the Bible to grandmother and Aunt Gertrude. There was nothing in the whole twenty-four hours that Jane hated doing more than that. And she knew quite well that that was just why grandmother made her do it.

They always went into the drawing room for the reading and Jane invariably shivered as she entered it. That huge, elaborate room, so full of things that you could hardly move about in it without knocking something over, always seemed cold even on the hottest night in summer. And on winter nights it *was* cold. Aunt Gertrude took the huge family Bible, with its heavy silver clasp, from the marble-topped center table and laid it on a little table between the windows. Then she and grandmother sat, one at each end of the table, and Jane sat between them at the side, with Great-grandfather Kennedy scowling down at her from the dim old painting in its heavy, tarnished gilt frame, flanked by the dark blue velvet curtains. That woman on the street had said that Grandfather Kennedy was a nice friendly man, but his father couldn't have been. Jane always thought candidly that he looked as if he would enjoy biting a nail in two.

"Turn to the fourteenth chapter of *Exodus*," grandmother would say. The chapter varied every night, of course, but the tone never did. It always rattled Jane so that she generally made a muddle of finding the right place. And grandmother, with the hateful little smile which seemed to say, "So you can't even do this as it should be done," would put out her lean, crêpey hand, with its rich old-fashioned rings, and turn to the right place with uncanny precision. Jane would stumble through the chapter, mispronouncing words she knew perfectly well just because she was so nervous. Sometimes grandmother would say, "A little louder, if you please, Victoria. I thought when I sent you to St. Agatha's they would at least teach you to open your mouth when reading even if they couldn't teach you geography and history." And Jane would raise her voice so suddenly that Aunt Gertrude would jump. But the next evening it might be, "Not quite so loud, Victoria, *if* you please. We are not deaf." And poor Jane's voice would die away to little more than a whisper.

When she had finished, grandmother and Aunt Gertrude would bow their heads and repeat the Lord's Prayer. Jane would try to say it with them, which was a difficult thing, because grandmother was generally two words ahead of Aunt Gertrude. Jane always said, "Amen," thankfully. The beautiful prayer, haloed with all the loveliness of agelong worship, had become a sort of horror to Jane.

Then Aunt Gertrude would close the Bible and put it back in exactly the same place, to the fraction of a hair, on the centre table. Finally Jane had to kiss her and grandmother good-night. Grandmother would always remain sitting in her chair and Jane would stoop and kiss her forehead.

"Good night, grandmother."

"Good night, Victoria."

But Aunt Gertrude would be standing by the centre table and Jane would have to reach up to her, for Aunt Gertrude was tall. Aunt Gertrude would stoop just a little and Jane would kiss her narrow grey face.

"Good night, Aunt Gertrude."

"Good night, Victoria," Aunt Gertrude would say in her thin, cold voice.

And Jane would get herself out of the room, sometimes lucky enough not to knock anything over.

"When I grow up I'll never, never read the Bible or say that prayer," she would whisper to herself as she climbed the long, magnificent staircase which had once been the talk of Toronto.

One night grandmother had smiled and said, "What do you think of the Bible, Victoria?"

"I think it is very dull," said Jane truthfully. The reading had been a chapter full of "knops" and "taches," and Jane had not the least idea what knops and taches were.

"Ah! But do you think your opinion counts for a great deal?" said grandmother, smiling with paper-thin lips.

"Why did you ask me for it then?" said Jane, and had been icily rebuked for impertinence when she had not had the least intention of being impertinent. Was it any wonder she went up the staircase that night fairly loathing 60 Gay? And she did not want to loathe it. She wanted to love it . . . to be friends with it . . . to do things for it. But she could not love it . . . it *wouldn't* be friendly . . . and there was nothing it wanted done. Aunt Gertrude and Mary Price, the cook, and Frank Davis, the houseman and chauffeur, did everything for it. Aunt Gertrude would not let grandmother keep a housemaid because she preferred to attend to the house herself. Tall, shadowy, reserved Aunt Gertrude, who was so totally unlike mother that Jane found it hard to believe they were even half-sisters, was a martinet for order and system. At 60 Gay everything had to be done in a certain way on a certain day. The house was really frightfully clean. Aunt Gertrude's cold grey eyes could not tolerate a speck of dust anywhere. She was always going about the house putting things in their places and she attended to everything. Even mother never did anything except arrange the flowers for the table when they had company and light the candles for dinner. Jane would have liked the fun of doing that. And Jane would have liked to polish the silver and cook. More than anything else Jane would have liked to cook. Now and then, when grandmother was out, she hung about the kitchen and watched good-natured Mary Price cook the meals. It all seemed so easy . . . Jane was sure she could do it perfectly if she were allowed. It must be such fun to cook a meal. The smell of it was almost as good as the eating of it.

But Mary Price never let her. She knew the old lady didn't approve of Miss Victoria talking to the servants.

"Victoria fancies herself as domestic," grandmother had once said at the midday Sunday dinner where, as usual, Uncle William Anderson and Aunt Minnie and Uncle David Coleman and Aunt Sylvia Coleman and their daughter Phyllis were present. Grandmother had such a knack of making you feel ridiculous and silly in company. All the same, Jane wondered what grandmother would say if she knew that Mary Price, being somewhat rushed that day, had let Jane wash and arrange the lettuce for the salad. Jane knew what grandmother would do. She would refuse to touch a leaf of it.

"Well, shouldn't a girl be domestic?" said Uncle William, not because he wanted to take Jane's part but because he never lost an opportunity of announcing his belief that a woman's place was in the home. "Every girl should know how to cook."

"I don't think Victoria wants very much to learn how to cook," said grandmother. "It is just that she likes to hang about kitchens and places like that."

Grandmother's voice implied that Victoria had low tastes and that kitchens were barely respectable. Jane wondered why mother's face flushed so suddenly and why a strange, rebellious look gleamed for a moment in her eyes. But only for a moment.

"How are you geting on at St. Agatha's, Victoria?" asked Uncle William. "Going to get your grade?"

Jane did not know whether she was going to get her grade or not. The fear haunted her night and day. She knew her monthly reports had not been very good . . . grandmother had been very angry over them and even mother had asked her piteously if she couldn't do a little better. Jane had done the best she could, but history and geography were so dull and drab. Arithmetic and spelling were easier. Jane was really quite brilliant in arithmetic.

"Victoria can write wonderful compositions, I hear,"

said grandmother sarcastically. For some reason Jane couldn't fathom at all, her ability to write good compositions had never pleased grandmother.

"Tut, tut," said Uncle William. "Victoria could get her grade easily enough if she wanted to. The thing to do is study hard. She's getting to be a big girl now and ought to realize that. What is the capital of Canada, Victoria?"

Jane knew perfectly well what the capital of Canada was, but Uncle William fired the question at her so unexpectedly and all the guests stopped eating to listen . . . and for the moment she couldn't remember for her life what the name was. She blushed . . . stammered . . . squirmed. If she had looked at mother she would have seen that mother was forming the word silently on her lips, but she could not look at anyone. She was ready to die of shame and mortification.

"Phyllis," said Uncle William, "tell Victoria what the capital of Canada is."

Phyllis promptly responded.

"Ottawa."

"O-t-t-a-w-a," said Uncle William to Jane.

Jane felt that they were all, except mother, watching her for something to find fault with, and now Aunt Sylvia Coleman put on a pair of nose-glasses attached to a long black ribbon and looked at Jane through them as if wishing to be sure what a girl who didn't know the capital of her country was really like. Jane, under the paralysing influence of that stare, dropped her fork, and writhed in anguish when she caught grandmother's eye. Grandmother touched her little silver bell.

"Will you bring Miss Victoria *another* fork, Davis?" she said in a tone implying that Jane had had several forks already.

Uncle William put the piece of white chicken meat he had just carved off on the side of the platter. Jane had been hoping he would give it to her. She did not often get white meat. When Uncle William was not there to carve, Mary carved the fowls in the kitchen and Frank passed the platter around. Jane seldom dared to help herself to white meat because she knew grandmother was watching her. On one occasion when she had helped herself to two tiny pieces of breast grandmother had said,

"Don't forget, my dear Victoria, that there are other people who might like a breast slice too."

At present Jane reflected that she was lucky to get a drumstick. Uncle William was quite capable of giving her the neck by way of rebuking her for not knowing the capital of Canada. However, Aunt Sylvia very kindly gave her a double portion of turnip. Jane loathed turnip.

"You don't seem to have much appetite, Victoria," said Aunt Sylvia reproachfully when the mound of turnip had not decreased much.

"Oh, I think Victoria's *appetite* is all right," said grandmother, as if it were the only thing about her that *was* all right. Jane always felt that there was far more in what grandmother said than in the words themselves. Jane might have broken her record for never crying then and there, she felt so utterly wretched, had she not looked at mother. And mother was looking so tender and sympathetic and understanding that Jane spunked up at once and simply made no effort to eat any more turnip.

Aunt Sylvia's daughter Phyllis, who did not go to St. Agatha's but to Hillwood Hall, a much newer but even more expensive school, could have named not only the capital of Canada but the capital of every province in the Dominion. Jane did not like Phyllis. Sometimes Jane thought drearily that there must be something the matter with her when there were so many people she didn't like. But Phyllis was so condescending . . . and Jane hated to be condescended to.

"Why don't you like Phyllis?" grandmother had asked once, looking at Jane with those eyes that, Jane felt, could see through walls, doors, everything, right into your inmost soul. "She is pretty, lady-like, well-behaved and clever. . . . everything that you are not," Jane felt sure grandmother wanted to add.

"She patronises me," said Jane.

"Do you really know the meaning of all the big words you use, my dear Victoria?" said grandmother. "And don't you think that . . . possibly . . . you are a little jealous of Phyllis?"

"No, I don't think so," said Jane firmly. She knew she was not jealous of Phyllis.

"Of course, I must admit she is very different from that Jody of yours," said grandmother. The sneer in her voice brought an angry sparkle into Jane's eyes. She could not bear to hear any one sneer at Jody. And yet what could she do about it?

3

SHE and Jody had been pals for a year. Jody matched Jane's eleven years of life and was tall for her age too . . . though not with Jane's sturdy tallness. Jody was thin and weedy and looked as if she had never had enough to eat in her life . . . which was very likely the case, although she lived in a boarding house . . . 58 Gay, which had once been a fashionable residence and was now just a dingy three-story boarding house.

One evening in the spring of the preceding year Jane was out in the back yard of 60 Gay, sitting on a rustic bench in an old disused summer-house. Mother and grandmother were both away and Aunt Gertrude was in bed with a bad cold, or else Jane would not have been sitting in the back yard. She had crept out to have a good look at the full moon . . . (Jane had her own particular reasons for liking to look at the moon) . . . and the white-blossoming cherry tree over in the yard of 58. The cherry tree, with the moon hanging over it like a great pearl, was so beautiful that Jane felt a queer lump in her throat when she looked at it . . . almost as if she wanted to cry. And then . . . somebody really was crying over in the yard of 58. The stifled, piteous sounds came clearly on the still, crystal air of the spring evening.

Jane got up and walked out of the summer-house and around the garage, past the lonely dog-house that had never had a dog in it . . . at least, in Jane's recollection . . . and so to the fence that had ceased to be iron and become wooden paling between 60 and 58. There was a gap in it behind the dog-house where a slat had been broken off amid a tangle of creeper, and Jane, squeezing through it, found herself in the untidy yard of 58. It was still quite light, and Jane could see a girl huddled at the root of the cherry tree, sobbing bitterly, her face in her hands.

"Can I help you?" said Jane.

Though Jane herself had no inkling of it, those words were the keynote of her character. Any one else would probably have said, "What is the matter?" But Jane always wanted to help: and, though she was too young to realise it, the tragedy of her little existence was that nobody ever wanted her help . . . not even mother, who had everything heart could wish.

The child under the cherry tree stopped sobbing and got on her feet. She looked at Jane and Jane looked at her and something happened to both of them. Long afterwards Jane said, "I knew we were the same kind of folks." Jane saw a girl of about her own age, with a very white little face under a thick bang of black hair cut straight across her forehead. The hair looked as if it had not been washed for a long time but the eyes underneath it were brown and beautiful, though of quite a different brown from Jane's. Jane's were goldy-brown like a marigold, with laughter lurking in them, but this girl's were very dark and very sad . . . so sad that Jane's heart did something queer inside of her. She knew quite well that it wasn't right that anybody so young should have such sad eyes.

The girl wore a dreadful old blue dress that had certainly never been made for her. It was too long and too elaborate and it was dirty and grease-spotted. It hung on the thin little shoulders like a gaudy rag on a scarecrow. But the dress mattered nothing to Jane. All she was conscious of was those appealing eyes.

"Can I help?" she asked again.

The girl shook her head and the tears welled up in her big eyes.

"Look," she pointed.

Jane looked and saw between the cherry tree and the fence what seemed like a rudely made flower-bed strewn over with roses that were ground into the earth.

"Dick did that," said the girl. "He did it on purpose . . . because it was my garden. Miss Summers had them roses sent her last week . . . twelve great big red ones for her birthday . . . and this morning she said they were done and told me to throw them in the garbage pail. But I couldn't . . . they were still so pretty. I come out here and made that bed and stuck the roses all over it. I knew they wouldn't last long . . . but they looked pretty and I pretended I had a garden of my own . . . and now . . . Dick just come out and stomped all over it . . . and *laughed*."

She sobbed again. Jane didn't know who Dick was, but at that moment she could cheerfully have wrung his neck with her strong, capable little hands. She put her arm about the girl.

"Never mind. Don't cry any more. See, we'll break off a lot of little cherry boughs and stick them all over your bed. They're fresher than the roses . . . and think how lovely they'll look in the moonlight."

"I'm scared to do that," said the girl. "Miss West might be mad."

Again Jane felt a thrill of understanding. So this girl was afraid of people too.

"Well, we'll just climb up on that big bough that stretches out and sit there and admire it," said Jane. "I suppose that won't make Miss West mad, will it?"

"I guess she won't mind that. Of course she's mad at me anyhow to-night because I stumbled with a tray of tumblers when I was waiting on the supper table and broke three of them. She said if I kept on like that . . . I spilled soup on Miss Thatcher's silk dress last night . . . she'd have to send me away."

"Where would she send you?"

"I don't know. I haven't anywhere to go. But she says I'm not worth my salt and she's only keeping me out of charity."

"What is your name?" asked Jane. They had scrambled up into the cherry tree as nimbly as pussy cats and its whiteness enclosed and enfolded them, shutting them away into a fragrant world all their own.

"Josephine Turner. But everyone calls me Jody."

Jody! Jane liked that.

"Mine's Jane Stuart."

"I thought it was Victoria," said Jody. "Miss West said it was."

"It's Jane," said Jane firmly. "At least it's Jane Victoria but *I* am Jane. And now" . . . briskly . . . "let's get acquainted."

Before Jane went back through the gap that night she knew practically all there was to be known about Jody. Jody's father and mother were dead . . . had been dead ever since Jody was a baby. Jody's mother's cousin, who had been the cook at 58, had taken her and was permitted to keep her at 58 if she never let her out of the kitchen. Two years ago Cousin Millie had died and Jody had just "stayed on." She helped the new cook . . . peeling potatoes, washing dishes, sweeping, dusting, running errands, scouring knives . . . and lately had been promoted to waiting on the table. She slept in a little attic cubby-hole which was hot in summer and cold in winter, she wore cast-off things the boarders gave her and went to school every day there was no extra rush. Nobody ever gave her a kind word or took any notice of her . . . except Dick, who was Miss West's nephew and pet, and who teased and tormented her and called her "charity child." Jody hated Dick. Once when everybody was out she had slipped into the parlor and picked out a little tune on the piano, but Dick had told Miss West and Jody had been sternly informed that she must never touch the piano again.

"And I'd love to be able to play," she said wistfully. "That and a garden's the only things I want. I do wish I could have a garden."

Jane wondered again why things were so criss-cross. She did not like playing on the piano, but grandmother had insisted on her taking music lessons and she practised faithfully to please mother. And here was poor Jody, hankering for music and with no chance at all of getting it.

"Don't you think you could have a bit of a garden?" said Jane. "There's plenty of room here and it's not too shady, like our yard. I'd help you make a bed and I'm sure mother would give us some seeds. . . ."

"It wouldn't be any use," said Jody drearily. "Dick would just stomp on it too."

"Then I'll tell you," said Jane resolutely, "we'll get a seed catalogue . . . Frank will get me one . . . and have an *imaginary* garden."

"Ain't you the one for thinking of things?" said Jody admiringly. Jane tasted happiness. It was the first time any one had ever admired her.

4

OF course it was no time before grandmother knew about Jody. She made a great many sweetly sarcastic speeches about her but she never actually forbade Jane going over to play with her in the yard of 58. Jane was to be a good many years older before she understood the reason for that . . . understood that grandmother wanted to show anyone who might question it that Jane had common tastes and liked low people.

"Darling, is this Jody of yours a nice little girl?" mother had asked doubtfully.

"She is a *very* nice little girl," said Jane emphatically.

"But she looks so uncared for . . . positively dirty. . . ."

"Her face is always clean and she *never* forgets to wash behind her ears, mummy. I'm going to show her how to wash her hair. Her hair would be lovely if it was clean . . . it's so fine and black and silky. And may I give her one of my jars of cold cream . . . I've two, you know . . . for her hands? They're so red and chapped because she has to work so hard and wash so many dishes."

"But her clothes . . ."

"She can't help her clothes. She just has to wear what's given her and she never has more than two dresses at a time . . . one to wear every day and one to go to Sunday School in. Even the Sunday School one isn't very clean . . . it was Mrs. Bellew's Ethel's old pink one and she spilled coffee on it. And she has to work so hard . . . she's a regular little slave, Mary says. I like Jody very much, mummy. She's *sweet*."

"Well" . . . mother sighed and gave way. Mother always gave way if you were firm enough. Jane had already discovered that. She adored mother but she had unerringly laid her finger on the weak spot in her character. Mother couldn't "stand up to" people. Jane had heard Mary say that to Frank one time when they didn't think she heard and she knew it was true.

"She'll go with the last one that talks to her," said Mary. "And that's always the old lady."

"Well, the old lady's mighty good to her." said Frank. "She's a gay little piece."

"Gay enough. But is she happy?" said Mary.

"Happy? Of course, mummy is happy," Jane had thought indignantly . . . all the more indignantly because, away back in her mind, there was lurking a queer suspicion that mother, in spite of her dances and dinners and furs and dresses and jewels and friends, wasn't happy. Jane couldn't imagine why she had this idea. Perhaps a look in mother's eyes now and then . . . like something shut up in a cage.

Jane could go over and play in the yard of 58 in the spring and summer evenings after Jody had finished washing stacks of dishes. They made their "imaginary" garden, they fed crumbs to the robins and the black and grey squirrels, they sat up in the cherry tree and watched the evening star together. And talked! Jane, who could never find anything to say to Phyllis, found plenty to say to Jody.

There was never any question of Jody coming to play in the yard of 60. Once, early in their friendship, Jane had asked Jody to come over. She had found Jody crying under the cherry tree again and discovered that it was because Miss West had insisted on her putting her old teddy bear in the garbage pail. It was, Miss West said, utterly worn out. It had been patched until there was no more room for patches and even shoe buttons couldn't be sewn any more into its worn-out eye-sockets. Besides, she was too old to be playing with Teddy Bears.

"But I've nothing else," sobbed Jody. "If I had a doll, I wouldn't mind. I've always wanted a doll . . . but now I'll have to sleep alone away up there . . . and it's so lonesome."

"Come over to our house and I'll give you a doll," said Jane.

Jane had never cared much for dolls because they were not alive. She had a very nice one which Aunt Sylvia had given her the Christmas she was seven but it was so flawless and well dressed that it never needed to have anything done for it and Jane had never loved it. She would have loved better a teddy bear that needed a new patch every day.

She took Jody, wide-eyed and enraptured, through the splendours of 60 Gay and gave her the doll, which had reposed undisturbed for a long time in the lower drawer of the huge black wardrobe in Jane's room. Then she had taken her into mother's room to show her the things on mother's table . . . the silver-backed brushes, the perfume bottles with the cut-glass stoppers that made rainbows, the wonderful rings on the little gold tray. Grandmother found them there.

She stood in the doorway and looked at them. You could feel the silence spreading through the room like a cold, smothering wave.

"What does this mean, Victoria . . . if I am allowed to ask?"

"This is . . . Jody," faltered Jane. "I brought her over to give her my doll. She hasn't any."

"Indeed? And you have given her the one your Aunt Sylvia gave you?"

Jane at once realised that she had done something quite unpardonable. It had never occurred to her that she was not at liberty to give away her own doll.

"I have not," said grandmother, "forbidden you to play with this . . . this *Jody* in her own lot. What is in the blood is bound to come out sooner or later. But . . . if you don't mind . . . please don't bring your riff-raff here, my dear Victoria."

Her dear Victoria got herself and poor hurt Jody away as best she could, leaving the doll behind them. But grandmother did not get off scot-free for all that. For the first time the worm turned. Jane paused for a moment before she went out of the door and looked straight at grandmother with intent, judging brown eyes.

"You are not fair," she said. Her voice trembled a little but she felt she *had* to say it, no matter how impertinent grandmother thought her. Then she followed Jody down and out with a strange feeling of satisfaction in her heart.

"I ain't riff-raff," said Jody, her lips quivering. "Of course I'm not like you . . . Miss West says you're *people* . . . but my folks were respectable. Cousin Millie told me so. She said they always paid their way while they were alive. And *I* work hard enough for Miss West to pay *my* way."

"You aren't riff-raff and I love you," said Jane. "You and mother are the only people in the whole world I love."

Even as she said it, a queer little pang wrung Jane's heart. It suddenly occurred to her that two people out of all the millions in the world . . . Jane never could remember the exact number of millions, but she knew it was enormous . . . were very few to love.

"And I like loving people," thought Jane. "It's *nice*."

"I don't love anybody but you," said Jody, who forgot her hurt feelings as soon as Jane got her interested in building a castle out of all the old tin cans in the corner of the yard. Miss West hoarded her tin cans for a country cousin who made some mysterious use of them. He had not been in all winter, and there were enough cans to build a towering structure. Dick kicked it down next day, of course, but they had had the fun of building it. They never knew that Mr. Torrey, one of the 58 boarders who was a budding architect, saw the castle, gleaming in the moonlight, when he was putting his car in the garage and whistled over it.

"That's rather an amazing thing for those two kids to build," he said.

Jane, who should have been asleep, was lying wide awake that very moment, going on with the story of her life in the moon, which she could see through her window.

Jane's "moon secret," as she called it, was the one thing she hadn't shared with mother and Jody. She couldn't, somehow. It was her very own. To tell about it would be to destroy it. For three years now Jane had been going on dream voyages to the moon. It was a shimmering world of fancy where she lived very splendidly and sated some deep thirst in her soul at unknown, enchanted springs among its shining silver hills. Before she had found the trick of going to the moon, Jane had longed to get into the looking glass as *Alice* did. She used to stand so long before her mirror hoping for the miracle to happen that Aunt Gertrude said Victoria was the vainest child she had ever seen.

"Really?" said grandmother, as if mildly inquiring what Jane could possible have to be vain about.

Eventually Jane had sadly concluded that she could never get into the looking-glass world, and then one night, when she was lying alone in her big unfriendly room, she saw the moon looking in at her through one of the windows . . . the calm, beautiful moon that was never in a hurry; and she began to build for herself an existence in the moon, where she ate fairy food and wandered through fairy fields, full of strange white moon-blossoms, with the companions of her fancy.

But even in the moon Jane's dreams ran true to the

ruling passion. Since the moon was all silver it had to be polished every night. Jane and her moon friends had no end of fun polishing up the moon, with an elaborate system of rewards and punishments for extra good polishers and lazy ones. The lazy ones were generally banished to the other side of the moon . . . which Jane had read was very dark and very cold. When they were allowed back, chilled to the bone, they were glad to warm themselves up by rubbing as hard as they could. Those were the nights when the moon seemed brighter than usual. Oh, it was fun! Jane was never lonely in bed now except on nights when there was no moon. The dearest sight Jane knew was the thin crescent in the western sky that told her her friend was back. She was supported through many a dreary day by the hope of going on a moon spree at night.

5

Up to the age of ten Jane had believed her father was dead. She could not recall that anybody had ever told her so, but if she had thought about it at all she would have felt quite sure of it. She just did not think about it . . . nobody ever mentioned him. All she knew about him was that his name must have been Andrew Stuart, because mother was Mrs. Andrew Stuart. For anything else, he might as well never have existed as far as Jane was concerned. She did not know much about fathers. The only one she was really acquainted with was Phyllis' father, Uncle David Coleman, a handsome, oldish man with pouches under his eyes, who grunted at her occasionally when he came to Sunday dinners. Jane had an idea his grunts were meant to be friendly and she did not dislike him, but there was nothing about him that made her envy Phyllis for having a father. With a mother so sweet and adorable and loving, what did one want of a father?

Then Agnes Ripley came to St. Agatha's. Jane liked Agnes well enough at first, though Agnes had stuck her tongue out at Jane rather derisively on the occasion of their first meeting. She was the daughter of somebody who was called "the great Thomas Ripley" . . . he had built "railroads and things" . . . and most of the St. Agatha's girls paid court to her and plumed themselves if she noticed them. She was much given to "secrets," and it came to be thought a great honour among the St. Agathians if Agnes told you a secret. Therefore Jane was conscious of a decided thrill when one afternoon on the playground Agnes came up to her and said, darkly and mysteriously, "I know a secret."

"I know a secret" is probably the most intriguing phrase in the world. Jane surrendered to its allure.

"Oh, tell me," she implored. She wanted to be admitted to that charmed inner circle of girls who had been told one of Agnes' secrets; and she wanted to know the secret for its own sake. Secrets must always be wonderful, beautiful things.

Agnes wrinkled up her fat little nose and looked important.

"Oh, I'll tell you some other time."

"I don't want to hear it some other time. I want to hear it *now*," pleaded Jane, her marigold eyes full of eager radiance.

Agnes' little elfish face, framed in its straight brown hair, was alive with mischief. She winked one of her green eyes at Jane.

"All right. Don't blame *me* if you don't like it when you hear it. Listen."

Jane listened. The towers of St. Agatha's listened. The shabby streets beyond listened. It seemed to Jane that the whole world listened. She was one of the chosen . . . Agnes was going to tell her a secret.

"Your father and mother don't live together."

Jane stared at Agnes. What she had said didn't make any sense.

"Of course they don't live together," she said. "My father is dead."

"Oh, no, he isn't," said Agnes. "He's living down in Prince Edward Island. Your mother left him when you were three years old."

Jane felt as if some big cold hand were beginning to squeeze her heart.

"That . . . isn't. . . true," she gasped.

"Tis too. I heard Aunt Dora telling mother all about it. She said your mother married him just after he came back from the war, one summer when your grandmother took her down to the Maritimes. Your grandmother didn't want her to. Aunt Dora said everybody knew it wouldn't last long. He was poor. But it was you that made the most trouble. You should never have been born. Neither of them wanted you, Aunt Dora said. They fought like cat and dog after that, and at last your mother just up and left him. Aunt Dora said she would likely have divorced him, only divorces are awful hard to get in Canada, and anyhow all the Kennedys think divorce is a dreadful thing."

The hand was gripping Jane's heart so tightly now that she could hardly breathe.

"I . . . I don't believe it," she said.

"If that's how you're going to talk when I tell you a secret, I'll never tell you another one, Miss Victoria Stuart," said Agnes, reddening with rage.

"I don't want to hear any more," said Jane.

She would never forget what she had heard. It couldn't be true . . . it couldn't. Jane thought the afternoon would never end. St. Agatha's was a nightmare. Frank had never driven so slowly home. The snow had never looked so grimy and dirty along the dingy streets. The wind had never been so grey. The moon, floating high in the sky, was all faded and paper-white but Jane didn't care if it was never polished again.

An afternoon tea was in progress at 60 Gay when she

arrived there. The big drawing-room, decorated lavishly with pale pink snap-dragons and tulips and maidenhair fern, was full of people. Mother, in orchid chiffon, with loose, trailing lace sleeves, was laughing and chatting. Grandmother, with blue-white diamonds sparkling in her hair, was sitting on her favorite needlepoint chair, looking, so one lady said, "Such an utterly sweet silver-haired thing, just like a Whistler mother." Aunt Gertrude and Aunt Sylvia were pouring tea at a table covered with Venetian lace, where tall pink tapers were burning.

Straight through them all Jane marched to mother. She did not care how many people were there . . . she had one question to ask and it must be answered at once. At once. Jane could not bear her suspense another moment.

"Mummy," she said, "is my father alive?"

A strange, dreadful hush suddenly fell over the room. A light like a sword flashed into grandmother's blue eyes. Aunt Sylvia gasped and Aunt Gertrude turned an unbecoming purple. But mother's face was as if snow had fallen over it.

"*Is he?*" said Jane.

"Yes," said mother. She said nothing more. Jane asked nothing more. She turned and went out and up the stairs blindly. In her own room she shut the door and lay down very softly on the big white bearskin rug by the bed, her face buried in the soft fur. Heavy black waves of pain seemed rolling over her.

So it was true. All her life she had thought her father dead while he was living . . . on that faraway dot on the map which she had been told was the province of Prince Edward Island. But he and mother did not like each other and she had not been wanted. Jane found that it was a very curious and unpleasant sensation to feel that your parents hadn't wanted you. She was sure that all the rest of her life she would hear Agnes' voice saying, "You should never have been born." She hated Agnes Ripley . . . she would always hate her. Jane wondered if she would live to be as old as grandmother and how she could bear it if she did.

Mother and grandmother found her there when everybody had gone.

"Victoria, get up."

Jane did not move.

"Victoria, I am accustomed to being obeyed when I speak."

Jane got up. She had not cried . . . hadn't somebody ages ago said that "Jane never cried?" . . . but her face was stamped with an expression that might have wrung anybody's heart. Perhaps it touched even grandmother, for she said, quite gently for her.

"I have always told your mother, Victoria, that she ought to tell you the truth. I told her you were sure to hear it from someone sooner or later. Your father *is* living. Your mother married him against my wish and lived to repent it. I forgave her and welcomed her back gladly when she came to her senses. That is all. And in future when you feel an irresistible urge to make a scene while we are entertaining, will you be good enough to control the impulse until our guests are gone?"

"Why didn't he like me?" asked Jane dully.

When all was said and done, that seemed to be what was hurting most. Her mother might not have wanted her either, to begin with, but Jane knew that mother loved her now.

Mother suddenly gave a little laugh so sad that it nearly broke Jane's heart.

"He was jealous of you, I think," she said.

"He made your mother's life wretched," said grandmother, her voice hardening.

"Oh, I was to blame, too," cried mother chokingly.

Jane, looking from one to the other, saw the swift change that came over grandmother's face.

"You will never mention your father's name in my hearing or in your mother's hearing again," said grandmother. "As far as we are concerned . . . as far as *you* are concerned . . . he *is* dead."

The prohibition was unnecessary. Jane didn't want to

27

mention her father's name again. He had made mother unhappy, and so Jane hated him and put him out of her thoughts completely. There were just some things that didn't bear thinking of, and father was one of them. But the most terrible thing about it all was that there was something now that could not be talked over with mother. Jane felt it between them, indefinable but there. The old perfect confidence was gone. There was a subject that must never be mentioned, and it poisoned everything.

She could never bear Agnes Ripley and her cult of "secrets" again, and was glad when Agnes left the school, the great Thomas having decided that it was not quite up-to-date enough for his daughter. Agnes wanted to learn tapdancing.

6

IT was a year now since Jane had learned that she had a father . . . a year in which Jane had just scraped through as far as her grade was concerned . . . Phyllis had taken the prize for general proficiency in her year and did Jane hear of it! . . . had continued to be driven to and from St. Agatha's, had tried her best to like Phyllis and had not made any great headway at it, had trysted with Jody in the backyard twilights and had practised her scales as faithfully as if she liked it.

"Such a pity you are not fonder of music," said grandmother. "But of course, how could you be?"

It was not so much what grandmother said as how she said it. She made wounds that rankled and festered. And Jane *was* fond of music . . . she loved to listen to it. When Mr. Ransome, the musical boarder at 58, played on his violin in his room in the evenings, he never dreamed of the two

enraptured listeners he had in the backyard cherry tree.
Jane and Jody sat there, their hands clasped, their hearts
filled with some nameless ecstasy. When winter came and
the bedroom window was shut, Jane felt the loss keenly.
The moon was her only escape then, and she slipped away
to it oftener than ever, in long visitations of silence which
grandmother called "sulks."

"She has a very sulky disposition," said grandmother.

"Oh, I don't think so," faltered mother. The only times
she ever dared to contradict grandmother were in defence
of Jane. "She's just rather . . . sensitive."

"Sensitive!" Grandmother laughed. Grandmother did
not often laugh, which Jane thought was just as well. As for
Aunt Gertrude, if she had ever laughed or jested it must
have been so long ago that nobody remembered it. Mother
laughed when people were about . . . little tinkling laughs
that Jane could never feel were *real*. No, there was not
much real laughter at 60 Gay, though Jane, with her con-
cealed gift for seeing the funny side of things, could have
filled even that big house with laughter. But Jane had
known very early that grandmother resented laughter. Even
Mary and Frank had to giggle very discreetly in the
kitchen.

Jane had shot up appallingly in that year. She was
rather more angular and awkward. Her chin was square and
cleft.

"It gets more like *his* every day," she once heard grandmother saying bitterly to Aunt Gertrude. Jane winced. In
her bitter new wisdom she suspected that "his" was her
father's chin, and she straightway detested hers. Why
couldn't it have been a pretty rounded one like mother's?

The year was very uneventful. Jane would have called it
monotonous if she had not as yet been unacquainted with
the word. There were only three things in it that made
much impression on her . . . the incident of the kitten, the
mysterious affair of Kenneth Howard's picture, and the unlucky recitation.

Jane had picked the kitten up on the street. One afternoon Frank had been in a big hurry to get somewhere on

time for grandmother and mother and he had let Jane walk home from the beginning of Gay Street when he was bringing her from St. Agatha's. Jane walked along happily, savouring this rare moment of independence. It was very seldom she was allowed to walk anywhere alone . . . to walk anywhere at all, indeed. And Jane loved walking. She would have liked to walk to and from St. Agatha's or, since that really was too far, she would have liked to go by street-car. Jane loved travelling on a street car. It was so fascinating to look at the people in it and speculate about them. Who was that lady with the lovely shimmering hair? What was the angry old woman muttering to herself about? Did that little boy *like* having his mother clean his face with her handkerchief in public? Did that jolly looking little girl have trouble getting her grade? Did that man have toothache and did he ever look pleasant when he hadn't it? She would have liked to know all about them and sympathise or rejoice as occasion required. But it was very seldom any resident of 60 Gay had a chance to go on a street-car. There was always Frank with the limousine.

Jane walked slowly to prolong the pleasure. It was a cold day in late autumn. It had been miserly of its light from the beginning, with a dim ghost of sun peering through the dull grey clouds, and now it was getting dark and spitting snow. The lights gleamed out: even the grim windows of Victorian Gay were abloom. Jane did not mind the bitter wind, but something else did. Jane heard the most pitiful, despairing little cry and looked down to see the kitten, huddled miserably against an iron fence. She bent and picked it up and held it against her face. The little creature, a handful of tiny bones in its fluffed-out maltese fur, licked her cheek with an eager tongue. It was cold, starving, forsaken. Jane knew it did not belong to Gay Street. She could not leave it there to perish in the oncoming stormy night.

"Goodness' sake, Miss Victoria, wherever did you get that?" exclaimed Mary, when Jane entered the kitchen. "You shouldn't have brought it in. You know your grandmother doesn't like cats. Your Aunt Gertrude got one once but it clawed all the tassels off the furniture and it had to go. Better put that kitten right out, Miss Victoria."

Jane hated to be called "Miss Victoria," but grandmother insisted on the servants addressing her so.

"I *can't* put it out in the cold, Mary. Let me give it some supper and leave it here till after dinner. I'll ask grandmother to let me keep it. Perhaps she will if I promise to keep it out here and in the yard. *You* wouldn't mind it round, would you, Mary?"

"I'd like it," said Mary. "I've often thought a cat would be great company . . . or a dog. Your mother had a dog once but it got poisoned and she would never have another."

Mary did not tell Jane that she firmly believed the old lady had poisoned the dog. You didn't tell children things like that, and anyway, she couldn't be dead sure of it. All she was sure of was that old Mrs. Kennedy had been bitterly jealous of her daughter's love for the dog.

"How she used to look at it when she didn't know I saw her," thought Mary.

Grandmother and Aunt Gertrude and mother were taking in a couple of teas that day, so Jane knew she could count on at least an hour yet. It was a pleasant hour. The kitten was happy and frolicsome, having drunk milk until its little sides tubbed out almost to the bursting point. The kitchen was warm and cosy. Mary let Jane chop the nuts that were to be sprinkled over the cake and cut the pears into slim segments for the salad.

"Oh, Mary, blueberry pie! Why don't we have it oftener? You can make such delicious blueberry pie."

"There's some who can make pies and some who can't," said Mary complacently. "As for having it oftener, you know your grandmother doesn't care much for any kind of pie. She says they're indigestible . . . and my father lived to be ninety and had pie for breakfast every morning of his life! I just make it occasional for your mother."

"After dinner I'll tell grandmother about the kitten and ask her if I may keep it," said Jane.

"I think you'll have your trouble for your pains, you

poor child," said Mary as the door closed behind Jane. "Miss Robin ought to stand up for you more than she does . . . but there, she's always been under the thumb of her mother. Anyway, I hope the dinner will go well and keep the old dame in good humour. I wisht I hadn't made the blueberry pie after all. It's lucky she won't know Miss Victoria fixed the salad . . . what folks don't know never hurts them."

The dinner did not go well. There was a tension in the air. Grandmother did not talk . . . evidently some occurrence of the afternoon had put her out. Aunt Gertrude never talked at any time. And mother seemed uneasy and never once tried to pass Jane any of the little signals they had . . . the touched lip . . . the lifted eyebrow . . . the crooked finger . . . that all meant "honey darling" or "I love you" or "consider yourself kissed."

Jane, burdened by her secret, was even more awkward than usual, and when she was eating her blueberry pie she dropped a forkful of it on the table.

"This," said grandmother, "might have been excused in a child of five. It is absolutely inexcusable in a girl of your age. Blueberry stain is almost impossible to get out, and this is one of my best tablecloths. But of course *that* is a matter of small importance."

Jane gazed at the table in dismay. How such a little bit of pie could have spread itself over so much territory she could not understand. And of course it had to be at this inauspicious moment that a little purry, furry creature escaped the pursuing Mary, skittered across the dining room and bounded into Jane's lap. Jane's heart descended to her boots.

"Where did that cat come from?" demanded grandmother.

"I mustn't be a coward," thought Jane desperately.

"I found it on the street and brought it in," she said bravely . . . defiantly, grandmother thought. "It was so cold and hungry . . . look how thin it is, grandmother. Please may I keep it? It's such a darling. I won't let it trouble you . . . I'll . . ."

"My dear Victoria, don't be ridiculous. I really supposed you knew we do not keep cats here. Be good enough to put that creature out at once."

"Oh, not out on the street, grandmother, *please*. Listen to the sleet . . . it would die."

"I expect you to obey me without argument, Victoria. You cannot have your own way *all* the time. Other people's wishes must be considered occasionally. Please oblige me by making no further fuss over a trifle."

"Grandmother," began Jane passionately. But grandmother lifted a little, wrinkled, sparkling hand.

"Now, now, don't work yourself into a state, Victoria. Take that thing out at once."

Jane took the kitten to the kitchen.

"Don't worry, Miss Victoria. I'll get Frank to put it in the garage with a rug to lie on. It will be quite comfy. And tomorrow I'll find a good home for it at my sister's. She's fond of cats."

Jane never cried, so she was not crying when mother slipped rather stealthily into her room for a good-night kiss. She was only tense with rebellion.

"Mummy, I wish we could get away . . . just you and I. I hate this place, mummy, I hate it."

Mother said a strange thing and said it bitterly. "There is no escape for either of us now."

7

JANE could never understand the affair of the picture. After her hurt and anger passed away she was just hopelessly puzzled. Why . . . *why* . . should the picture of a perfect stranger matter to anybody at 60 Gay . . . and to mother, least of all?

She had come across it one day when she was visiting Phyllis. Every once in so long Jane had to spend an afternoon with Phyllis. This one was no more of a success than the former ones had been. Phyllis was a conscientious hostess. She had shown Jane all her new dolls, her new dresses, her new slippers, her new pearl necklace, her new china pig. Phyllis was collecting china pigs and apparently thought any one "dumb" who was not interested in china pigs. She had patronised and condescended even more than usual. Consequently, Jane was stiffer than usual and both of them were in agonies of boredom. It was a relief to all concerned when Jane picked up a *Saturday Evening* and buried herself in it, though she was not in the least interested in the society pages, the photographs of brides and débutantes, the stock market, or even in the article, *Peaceful Readjustment of International Difficulties*, by Kenneth Howard, which was given the place of honour on the front page. Jane had a vague idea that she ought not to be reading *Saturday Evening*. For some unknown reason grandmother did not approve of it. She would not have a copy of it in her house.

But what Jane did like was the picture of Kenneth Howard on the front page. The moment she looked at it she was conscious of its fascination. She had never seen Kenneth Howard . . . she had no idea who he was or where he lived . . . but she felt as if it were the picture of someone she knew very well and liked very much. She liked everything about it . . . his odd, peaked eyebrows . . . the way his thick, rather unruly hair sprang back from his forehead . . . the way his firm mouth tucked in at the corners . . . the slightly stern look in the eyes which yet had such jolly wrinkles at the corners . . . and the square, cleft chin which reminded Jane so strongly of something, she couldn't remember just what. That chin seemed like an old friend. Jane looked at the face and drew a long breath. She knew, right off, that if she had loved her father instead of hating him she would have wanted him to look like Kenneth Howard.

Jane stared at the picture so long that Phyllis became curious.

"What are you looking at, Jane?"

Jane suddenly came to life.

"May I have this picture, Phyllis . . . please?"

"Whose picture? Why . . . that? Do you know him?"

"No. I never heard of him before. But I like the picture."

"I don't." Phyllis looked at it contemptuously. "Why . . . he's *old*. And he isn't a bit handsome. There's a lovely picture of Norman Tait on the next page, Jane . . . let me show it to you."

Jane was not interested in Norman Tait nor any other screen star. Grandmother did not approve of children going to the movies.

"I'd like this picture if I may have it," she said firmly.

"I guess you can have it," condescended Phyllis. She thought Jane "dumber" than ever. How she did pity such a dumb girl! "I guess nobody here wants *that* picture. I don't like it a bit. He looks as if he was laughing at you behind his eyes."

Which was a bit of surprising insight on the part of Phyllis. That was just how Kenneth Howard did look. Only it was nice laughter. Jane felt she wouldn't mind a bit being laughed at like that. She cut the picture carefully out, carried it home, and hid it under the pile of handkerchiefs in her top bureau drawer. She could hardly have told why she did not want to show it to anybody. Perhaps she did not want anyone to ridicule the picture as Phyllis had done. Perhaps it was just because there seemed some strange bond between her and it . . . something too beautiful to be talked about to anyone, even mother. Not that there was much chance of talking to mother about anything just now. Never had mother been so brilliant, so gay, so beautifully dressed, so constantly on the go to parties and teas and bridges. Even the good-night kiss had become a rare thing . . . or Jane thought it had. She did not know that always, when her mother came in late, she tiptoed into Jane's room and dropped a kiss on Jane's russet hair . . . lightly so as not to waken her. Sometimes she cried when she went back to her own room but not often, because it might show at breakfast and old Mrs. Robert Kennedy did not like people who cried o' nights in her house.

For three weeks the picture and Jane were the best of friends. She took it out and looked at it whenever she could . . . she told it all about Jody and about her tribulations with her homework and about her love for mother. She even told it her moon secret. When she lay lonely in her bed, the thought of it was company. She kissed it good-night and took a peep at it the first thing in the morning.

Then Aunt Gertrude found it.

The moment Jane came in from St. Agatha's that day she knew something was wrong. The house, which always seemed to be watching her, was watching her more closely than ever, with a mocking, triumphant malice. Great-grandfather Kennedy scowled more darkly than ever at her from the drawing-room wall. And grandmother was sitting bolt-upright in her chair, flanked by mother and Aunt Gertrude. Mother was twisting a lovely red rose to pieces in her little white hands, but Aunt Gertrude was staring at the picture grandmother was holding.

"*My* picture!" cried Jane aloud.

Grandmother looked at Jane. For once her cold blue eyes were on fire.

"Where did you get this?" she said.

'"It's mine," cried Jane. "Who took it out of my drawer? Nobody had any business to do that."

"I don't think I like your manner, Victoria. And we are not discussing a problem in ethics. I asked a question."

Jane looked down at the floor. She had no earthly idea why it seemed such a crime to have Kenneth Howard's picture but she knew she was not going to be allowed to have it anymore. And it seemed to Jane that she just could not bear that.

"Will you be kind enough to look at me, Victoria? And to answer my question? You are not tongue-tied, by any chance, I suppose."

Jane looked up with stormy and mutinous eyes.

"I cut it out of a paper . . . out of *Saturday Evening*."

"That rag!" Grandmother's tone consigned *Saturday Evening* to unfathomable depths of contempt. "Where did you see it?"

"At Aunt Sylvia's," retorted Jane, plucking up spirit.

"Why did you cut *this* out?"

"Because I liked it."

"Do you know who Kenneth Howard is?"

"No."

"'No, grandmother,' if you please. Well, I think it is hardly necessary to keep the picture of a man you don't know in your bureau drawer. Let us have no more of such absurdity."

Grandmother lifted the picture in both hands. Jane sprang forward and caught her arm.

"Oh, grandmother, don't tear it up. You *mustn't*. I want it terribly."

The moment she said it, she knew she had made a mistake. There had never been much chance of getting the picture back but what little there had been was now gone.

"Have you gone completely mad, Victoria?" said grandmother . . . to whom nobody had ever said, "You mustn't," in her whole life before. "Take your hand off my arm, please. As for *this* . . ." Grandmother tore the picture deliberately into four pieces and threw them on the fire. Jane, who felt as if her heart were being torn with it, was on the point of a rebellious outburst when she happened to glance at mother. Mother was pale as ashes, standing there with the leaves of the rose she had torn to pieces strewing the carpet around her feet. There was such a dreadful look of pain in her eyes that Jane shuddered. The look was gone in a moment but Jane could never forget that it had been there. And she knew she could not ask mother to explain the mystery of the picture. For some reason she could not guess at, Kenneth Howard meant suffering to mother. And somehow that fact stained and spoiled all her beautiful memories of communion with the picture.

"No sulks now. Go to your room and stay there till I send for you," said grandmother, not altogether liking Jane's expression. "And remember that people who belong here do not read *Saturday Evening*."

Jane had to say it. It really said itself.

"I don't belong here," said Jane. Then she went to her room, which was huge and lonely again, with no Kenneth Howard smiling at her from under the handkerchiefs.

And this was another thing she could not talk over with mother. She felt just like one big ache as she stood at her window for a long time. It was a cruel world . . . with the very stars laughing at you . . . twinkling mockingly at you.

"I wonder," said Jane slowly, "if *anyone* was ever happy in this house."

Then she saw the moon . . . the new moon, but not the thin silver crescent the new moon usually was. This was just on the point of sinking into a dark cloud on the horizon and it was large and dull-red. If ever a moon needed polishing up, this one did. In a moment Jane had slipped away from all her sorrows . . . two hundred and thirty thousand miles away. Luckily grandmother had no power over the moon.

8

THEN there was the affair of the recitation.

They were getting up a school programme at St. Agatha's to which only the families of the girls were invited. There was to be a short play, some music and a reading or two. Jane had secretly hoped to be given a part in the play, even if it were only one of the many angels who came and went in it, with wings and trailing white robes and home-made haloes. But no such good luck. She suspected that it was because she was rather bony and awkward for an angel.

Then Miss Semple asked her if she would recite.

Jane jumped at the idea. She knew she could recite

rather well. Here was a chance to make mother proud of her and show grandmother that all the money she was spending on Jane's education was not being wholly wasted.

Jane picked a poem she had long liked in spite . . . or perhaps because . . . of its *habitant* English, *The Little Baby of Mathieu*, and plunged enthusiastically into learning it. She practised it in her room . . . she murmured lines of it everywhere until grandmother asked her sharply what she was muttering about all the time. Then Jane shut up like a clam. Nobody must suspect . . . it was to be a "surprise" to them all. A proud and glad surprise for mother. And perhaps even grandmother might feel a little pleased with her if she did well. Jane knew she would meet with no mercy if she didn't do well.

Grandmother took Jane down to a room in Marlborough's big department store . . . a room that had panelled walls, velvety carpets and muted voices . . . a room that Jane didn't like, somehow. She always felt smothered in it. And grandmother got her a new dress for the concert. It was a very pretty dress . . . you had to admit grandmother had a taste in dresses. A dull green silk that brought out the russet glow of Jane's hair and the gold-brown of her eyes. Jane liked herself in it and was more anxious than ever to please grandmother with her recitation.

She was terribly worried the night before the concert. Wasn't she a little hoarse? Suppose it got worse? It did not . . . it was all gone the next day. But when Jane found herself on the concert platform facing an audience for the first time, a nasty little quiver ran down her spine. She had never supposed there would be so many people. For one dreadful moment she thought she was not going to be able to utter a word. Then she seemed to see Kenneth Howard's eyes, crinkling with laughter at her. "Never mind them. Do your stuff for *me*," he seemed to be saying. Jane got her mouth open.

The St. Agatha staff were quite amazed. Who could have supposed that shy, awkward Victoria Stuart could recite any poem so well, let alone a *habitant* one? Jane herself was feeling the delight of a certain *oneness* with her au-

dience . . . a realisation that she had captured them . . .
that she was delighting them . . . until she came to the last
verse. Then she saw mother and grandmother just in front
of her. Mother, in her lovely new blue fox furs, with the
little wine hat Jane loved tilted on one side of her head, was
looking more frightened than proud, and grandmother . . .
Jane had seen that expression too often to mistake it.
Grandmother was furious.

The last verse, which should have been the climax,
went rather flat. Jane felt like a candle-flame blown out,
though the applause was hearty and prolonged, and Miss
Semple behind the scenes whispered, "Excellent, Victoria,
excellent."

But there were no compliments on the road home. Not
a word was said . . . that was the dreadful part of it. Mother
seemed too frightened to speak and grandmother preserved
a stony silence. But when they got home she said,

"Who put you up to that, Victoria?"

"Put me up to what?" said Jane in honest bewilder-
ment.

"Please don't repeat my questions, Victoria. You know
perfectly well what I mean."

"Is it my recitation? No one. Miss Semple asked me to
recite, and I picked the recitation myself because I liked it,"
said Jane. It might even be said she retorted it. She was
hurt . . . angry . . . a little "pepped up" because of her success. "I thought it would please you. But you are never
pleased with anything I do."

"Don't be cheaply theatrical, please," said grandmother. "And in future, if you *have* to recite" . . . very
much as she might have said, "if you *have* to have smallpox"
. . . "please choose poems in decent English. *I* do not care
for *patois*."

Jane didn't know what *patois* was, but it was all too
evident that she had made a mess of things somehow.

"*Why* was grandmother so angry, mummy?" she asked
piteously, when mother came in to kiss her good-night,
cool, slim, and fragrant, in a dress of rose crêpe with little

wisps of lace over the shoulders. Mother's blue eyes seemed to mist a little.

"Some one she . . . did not like . . . used to be . . . very good at reading *habitant* poetry. Never mind, heart's delight. You did splendidly. I was proud of you."

She bent down and took Jane's face in her hands. Mother had such a dear way of doing that.

So, in spite of everything, Jane went very happily through the gates of sleep. After all, it does not take much to make a child happy.

9

THE letter was a bolt from the blue. It came one dull morning in early April . . . but such a bitter, peevish, unlovely April . . . more like March in its disposition than April. It was Saturday, so there would be no St. Agatha's, and when Jane wakened in her big black walnut bed she wondered just how she would put in the day, because mother was going to a bridge and Jody was sick with a cold.

Jane lay a little while, looking through the window, where she could see only dull grey sky and old tree tops having a fight with the wind. She knew that in the yard below the window on the north there was still a lingering bank of dirty grey snow. Jane thought dirty snow must be the dreariest thing in the world. She hated this shabby end of winter. And she hated the bedroom where she had to sleep alone. She wished she and mother could sleep together. They could have such lovely times talking to each other with no one else to hear, after they went to bed or early in the morning. And how lovely it would be when you woke up in the night to hear mother's soft breathing beside you and cuddle to her just a wee bit, carefully, so as not to disturb her.

But grandmother would not let mother sleep with her.

"It is unhealthy for two people to sleep in the same bed," grandmother had said with her chill, unsmiling smile. "Surely in a house of this size everybody can have a room to herself. There are many people in the world who would be grateful for such a privilege."

Jane thought she might have liked the room better if it had been smaller. She always felt lost in it. Nothing in it seemed to be related to her. It always seemed hostile, watchful, vindictive. And yet Jane always felt that if she were allowed to do things for it . . . sweep it, dust it, put flowers in it . . . she would begin to love it, huge as it was. Everything in it was huge . . . a huge black walnut wardrobe like a prison, a huge chest of drawers, a huge walnut bedstead, a huge mirror over the massive black marble mantelpiece . . . except a tiny cradle which was always kept in the alcove by the fireplace . . . a cradle that grandmother had been rocked in. Fancy grandmother a baby! Jane just couldn't.

Jane got out of bed and dressed herself under the stare of several old dead grands and greats hung on the walls. Below on the lawn robins were hopping about. Robins always made Jane laugh . . . they were so saucy, so sleek, so important, strutting over the grounds of 60 Gay just as if it were any common yard. Much they cared for grandmothers!

Jane slipped down the hall to mother's room at the far end. She was not supposed to do this. It was understood at 60 Gay that mother must not be disturbed in the mornings. But mother, for a wonder, had not been out the night before, and Jane knew she would be awake. Not only was she awake but Mary was just bringing in her breakfast tray. Jane would have loved to do this for mother but she was never allowed.

Mother was sitting up in bed wearing the daintiest breakfast jacket of tea-rose crêpe de chine edged with cobwebby beige lace. Her cheeks were just the colour of her jacket and her eyes were fresh and dewy. Mother, Jane reflected proudly, looked as lovely when she got up in the mornings as she did before she went to bed.

Mother had chilled melon balls in orange juice instead of cereal, and she shared them with Jane. She offered half of her toast too, but Jane knew she must save some appetite for her own breakfast and refused it. They had a lovely time, laughing and talking beautiful nonsense, very quietly, so as not to be overheard. Not that either of them ever put this into words; but both *knew*.

"I wish it could be like this every morning," thought Jane. But she did not say so. She had learned that whenever she said anything like that mother's eyes darkened with pain, and she would not hurt mother for the world. She could never forget the time she had heard mother crying in the night.

She had wakened up with toothache and had crept down to mother's room to see if mother had any toothache drops. And, as she opened the door ever so softly, she heard mother crying in a dreadful, smothered sort of way. Then grandmother had come along the hall with her candle.

"Victoria, what are you doing here?"

"I have toothache," said Jane.

"Come with me and I will get you some drops," said grandmother coldly.

Jane went . . . but she no longer minded the toothache. Why was mother crying? It couldn't be possible she was unhappy . . . pretty, laughing mother. The next morning at breakfast mother looked as if she had never shed a tear in her life. Sometimes Jane wondered if she had dreamed it.

Jane put the lemon verbena salts into the bath water for mother and got a pair of new stockings, thin as dew gossamers, out of the drawer for her. She loved to do things for mother and there was so little she could do.

She had breakfast alone with grandmother, Aunt Gertrude having had hers already. It is not pleasant to eat a meal alone with a person you do not like. And Mary had forgotten to put salt in the oatmeal.

"Your shoelace is untied, Victoria."

That was the only thing grandmother said during the meal. The house was dark. It was a sulky day that now and then brightened up a little and then turned sulkier than ever. The mail came at ten. Jane was not interested in it. There was never anything for her. Sometimes she thought it would be nice and exciting to get a letter from somebody. Mother always got no end of letters . . . invitations and advertisements. This morning Jane carried the mail into the library where grandmother and Aunt Gertrude and mother were sitting. Jane noticed among the letters one addressed to her mother in a black, spiky handwriting which Jane was sure she had never seen before. She hadn't the least idea that that letter was going to change her whole life.

Grandmother took the letters from her and looked them over as she always did.

"Did you close the vestibule door, Victoria?"

"Yes."

"Yes what?"

"Yes, grandmother."

"You left it open yesterday. Robin, here is a letter from Mrs. Kirby . . . likely about that bazaar. Remember it is my wish that you have nothing to do with it. I do not approve of Sarah Kirby. Gertrude, here is one for you from Cousin Mary in Winnipeg. If it is about that silver service she avers my mother left her, tell her I consider the matter closed. Robin, here is . . ."

Grandmother stopped abruptly. She had picked up the black-handed letter and was looking at it as if she had picked up a snake. Then she looked at her daughter.

"This is from . . . *him*," she said.

Mother dropped Mrs. Kirby's letter and turned so white that Jane involuntarily sprang toward her, but was barred by grandmother's outstretched arm.

"Do you wish me to read it for you, Robin?"

Mother trembled piteously but she said, "No . . . no . . . let me . . ."

Grandmother handed the letter over with an offended air and mother opened it with shaking hands. It did not seem as if her face could turn whiter than it was, but it did as she read it.

"Well?" said grandmother.

"He says," gasped mother, "that I must send Jane Victoria to him for the summer . . . that he has a right to her sometimes. . . ."

"Who says?" cried Jane.

"Do not interrupt, Victoria," said grandmother. "Let me see that letter, Robin."

They waited while grandmother read it. Aunt Gertrude stared unwinkingly ahead of her with her cold, grey eyes in her long, white face. Mother had dropped her head in her hands. It was only three minutes since Jane had brought the letters in, and in those three minutes the world had turned upside down. Jane felt as if a gulf had opened between her and all humankind. She knew now without being told who had written the letter.

"So!" said grandmother. She folded the letter up, put it in its envelope, laid it on her table and carefully wiped her hands with her fine lace handkerchief.

"You won't let her go, of course, Robin."

For the first time in her life Jane felt at one with grandmother. She looked imploringly at mother with a curious feeling of seeing her for the first time . . . not as a loving mother or affectionate daughter but as a woman . . . a woman in the grip of some terrible emotion. Jane's heart was torn by another pang in seeing mother suffer so.

"If I don't," she said, "he may take her from me altogether. He could, you know. He says . . ."

"I have read what he says," said grandmother, "and I still tell you to ignore that letter. He is doing this simply to annoy you. He cares nothing for her . . . he never cared for anything but his scribbling."

"I'm afraid . . ." began mother again.

"We'd better consult William," said Aunt Gertrude suddenly. "This needs a man's advice."

"A man!" snapped grandmother. Then she seemed to pull herself up. "You may be right, Gertrude. I shall lay the matter before William when he comes to supper tomorrow. In the meantime we shall not discuss it. We shall not allow it to disturb us in the least."

Jane felt as if she were in a nightmare the rest of the day. Surely it must be a dream . . . surely her father could not have written her mother that she must spend the summer with him, a thousand miles away in that horrible Prince Edward Island, which looked on the map to be a desolate little fragment in the jaws of Gaspé and Cape Breton. . . with a father who didn't love her and whom she didn't love.

She had no chance to say anything about it to mother . . . grandmother saw to that. They all went to Aunt Sylvia's luncheon . . . mother did not look as if she wanted to go anywhere . . . and Jane had lunch alone. She couldn't eat anything.

"Does your head ache, Miss Victoria?" Mary asked sympathetically.

Something was aching terribly but it did not seem to be her head. It ached all the afternoon and evening and far on into the night. It was still aching when Jane woke the next morning with a sickening rush of remembrance. Jane felt that it might help the ache a little if she could only have a talk with mother, but when she tried mother's door it was locked. Jane felt that mother didn't *want* to talk to her about this, and that hurt worse than anything else.

They all went to church . . . an old and big and gloomy church on a downtown street where the Kennedys had always gone. Jane was rather fond of going to church for the not very commendable reason that she had some peace there. She could be silent without someone asking her accusingly what she was thinking of. Grandmother had to let her alone in church. And if you couldn't be loved, the next best thing was to be let alone.

Apart from that Jane did not care for St. Barnabas'. The sermon was beyond her. She liked the music and some of the hymns. Occasionally there was a line that gave her a thrill. There was something fascinating about coral strands and icy mountains, tides that moving seemed asleep, islands that lifted their fronded palms in air, reapers that bore harvest treasures home and years like shadows on sunny hills that lie.

But nothing gave Jane any pleasure today. She hated the pale sunshine that sifted down between the chilly, grudging clouds. What business had the sun even to try to shine while her fate hung in the balance like this? The sermon seemed endless, the prayers dreary, there was not even a hymn line she liked. But Jane put up a desperate prayer on her own behalf.

"Please, dear God," she whispered, "make Uncle William say I needn't be sent to *him*."

Jane had to live in suspense as to what Uncle William would say until the Sunday supper was over. She ate little. She sat looking at Uncle William with fear in her eyes, wondering if God really could have much influence over him. They were all there . . . Uncle William and Aunt Minnie, Uncle David and Aunt Sylvia, and Phyllis; and after supper they all went to the library and sat in a stiff circle while Uncle William put on his glasses and read the letter. Jane thought every one must hear the beating of her heart.

Uncle William read the letter . . . turned back and read a certain paragraph twice . . . pursed his lips . . . folded up the letter and fitted it into its envelope . . . took off his glasses . . . put them into their case and laid *it* down . . . cleared his throat and reflected. Jane felt that she was going to scream.

"I suppose," said Uncle William at last, "that you had better let her go."

There was a good deal more said, though Jane said nothing. Grandmother was very angry.

But Uncle William said, "Andrew Stuart could take her altogether if he had a mind to. And, knowing him for what he is, I think he very likely would if you angered him. I agree with you, mother, that he is only doing this to annoy us, and when he sees that it has *not* annoyed us and that we are taking it quite calmly he will probably never bother about her again."

Jane went up to her room and stood alone in it. She saw with eyes of despair the great, big, unfriendly place.

She saw herself in the big mirror reflected in another dim, unfriendly room.

"God," said Jane distinctly and deliberately, "is no good."

10

"I THINK your father and mother might have got on if it hadn't been·for you," said Phyllis.

Jane winced. She hadn't known that Phyllis knew about her father. But it seemed that everybody had known except her. She did not want to talk about him, but Phyllis was bent on talking.

"I don't see," said Jane miserably, "why I made so much difference to them."

"Mother says your father was jealous because Aunt Robin loved you so much."

This, thought Jane, was a different yarn from the one Agnes Ripley had told. Agnes had said her mother hadn't wanted her. What *was* the truth? Perhaps neither Phyllis nor Agnes knew it. Anyhow, Jane liked Phyllis' version better than Agnes'. It was dreadful to think you ought never to have been born . . . that your mother wasn't glad to have you.

"Mother says," went on Phyllis, finding that Jane had nothing to say, "that if you lived in the States Aunt Robin could get a divorce easy as wink, but it's harder in Canada."

"What *is* a divorce?" asked Jane, remembering that Agnes Ripley had used the same word.

Phyllis laughed condescendingly.

"Victoria, don't you know *anything*? A divorce is when two people get unmarried."

"*Can* people get unmarried?" gasped Jane, to whom it was an entirely new idea.

"Of course they can, silly. Mother says your mother ought to go to the States and get a divorce, but father says it wouldn't be legal in Canada, and anyway the Kennedys don't believe in it. Father says grandmother wouldn't allow it either, for fear Aunt Robin would just go and marry somebody else."

"If . . . if mother got a divorce does that mean that *he* wouldn't be my father any more?" queried Jane hopefully.

Phyllis looked dubious.

"I shouldn't suppose it would make any difference that way. But whoever she married would be your stepfather."

Jane did not want a stepfather any more than she wanted a father. But she said nothing again and Phyllis was annoyed.

"How do you like the idea of going to P.E. Island, Victoria?"

Jane was not going to expose her soul to the patronising Phyllis.

"I don't know anything about it," she said shortly.

"I do," said Phyllis importantly. "We spent a summer there two years ago. We lived in a big hotel on the north shore. It's quite a pretty place. I daresay you'll like it for a change."

Jane knew she would hate it. She tried to turn the conversation but Phyllis meant to thrash the subject out.

"How do you suppose you'll get along with your father?"

"I don't know."

"He likes clever people, you know, and you're not *very* clever, are you, Victoria?"

Jane did not like being made to feel like a worm. Phyllis always made her feel like that . . . when she didn't make her feel like a shadow. And there was not a bit of use in getting mad with her. Phyllis never got mad. Phyllis, everybody said, was *such* a sweet child . . . had such a *lovely* disposition. She just went on condescending. Jane sometimes thought if they could have just one good fight she would like Phyllis better. Jane knew mother was a bit worried because she didn't make more friends among girls of her own age.

"You know," went on Phyllis, "that was one of the things . . . Aunt Robin thought she couldn't talk clever enough for him."

The worm turned.

"I am not going to talk any more about my mother , . . or *him*," said Jane distinctly.

Phyllis sulked a little and the afternoon was a failure. Jane was more thankful than usual when Frank came to take her home.

Little was being said at 60 Gay about Jane's going to the Island. How quickly the days flew by! Jane wished she could hold them back. Once, when she had been very small, she had said to mother, "Isn't there any way we can stop time, mummy?"

Jane remembered that mother had sighed and said, "We can never stop time, darling."

And now time just went stonily on . . . tick tock, tick tock . . .sunrise, sunset, ever and ever nearer to the day when she would be torn away from mother. It would be early in June . . . St. Agatha's closed earlier than the other schools. Grandmother took Jane to Marlborough's late in May and got some very nice clothes for her . . . much nicer than she had ever had before. Under ordinary circumstances Jane would have loved her blue coat and the smart little blue hat with its tiny scarlet bow . . . and a certain lovely frock of white, eyelet-embroidered in red, with a smart red leather belt. Phyllis had nothing nicer than that. But now she had no interest in them.

"I don't suppose she'll have much use for very fine clothes down there," mother had said.

"She shall go fitted out properly," said grandmother. "*He* shall not need to buy clothes for her, of that I shall make sure. And Irene Fraser shall have no chance to comment. I suppose he has some kind of a hovel to live in or he would not have sent for her. Did anyone ever tell you, Victoria, that it is not proper to butter your whole slice of bread at once? And do you think it would be possible, just for a change, to get through a meal without letting your napkin slip off your knee continually?"

Jane dreaded meal-times more than ever. Her preoccupation made her awkward and grandmother pounced on everything. She wished she need never come to the table, but, unluckily, one cannot live without eating a little. Jane ate very little. She had no appetite and grew noticeably thinner. She could not put any heart into her studies and she barely made the Senior Third, while Phyllis passed with honours.

"As was to be expected," said grandmother.

Jody tried to comfort her.

"After all, it won't be so long. Only three months, Jane."

Three months of absence from a beloved mother and three months' presence with a detested father seemed like an eternity to Jane.

"You'll write me, Jane? And I'll write you if I can get any postage stamps. I've got ten cents now . . . that Mr. Ransome gave me. That will pay for three stamps anyhow."

Then Jane told Jody a heart-breaking thing.

"I'll write you often, Jody. But I can write mother only once a month. And I'm never to mention *him*."

"Did your mother tell you that?"

"No, oh, no! It was grandmother. As if I'd want to mention *him*."

"I hunted up P. E. Island on the map," said Jody, her dark velvet-brown eyes full of sympathy. "There's such an awful lot of water round it. Ain't you afraid of falling over the edge?"

"I don't believe I'd mind if I did," said Jane dismally.

11

JANE was to go to the Island with Mr. and Mrs. Stanley, who were going down to visit a married daughter. Somehow Jane lived through the last days. She was determined she would not make any fuss because that would be hard on mother. There were no more good-night confidences and caressings . . . no more little tender, loving words spoken at special moments. But Jane, somehow, knew the two reasons for this. Mother could not bear it, for one thing, and, for another, grandmother was resolved not to permit it. But on Jane's last night at 60 Gay, mother did slip in when grandmother was occupied by callers below.

"Mother . . . mother!"

"Darling, be brave. After all, it is only three months and the Island *is* a lovely spot. You may . . . if I'd known . . . once I . . . oh, it doesn't matter now. Nothing matters. Darling, there's one thing I must ask you to promise. You are never to mention *me* to your father."

"I won't," choked Jane. It was an easy promise. She couldn't imagine herself talking to *him* about mother.

"He will like you better if . . . if . . . he thinks you don't love me too much," whispered mother. Down went her white lids over her blue eyes. But Jane had seen the look. She felt as if her heart was bursting.

The sky at sunrise was blood-red, but it soon darkened into sullen grey. At noon a drizzle set in. "I think the weather is sorry at your going away," said Jody. "Oh, Jane, I'll miss you so. And . . . I don't know if I'll be here when you come back. Miss West says she's going to put me in an orphanage, and I don't want to be put in an orphanage, Jane. Here's the pretty shell Miss Ames brought from the

West Indies for me. It's the only pretty thing I have. I want you to have it because if I go to the orphanage I s'pose they'll take it away from me."

The train left for Montreal at eleven that night and Frank took Jane and her mother to the station. She had kissed grandmother and Aunt Gertrude good-bye dutifully.

"If you meet your Aunt Irene Fraser down on the Island, remember me to her," said grandmother. There was an odd little tone of exultation in her voice. Jane felt that grandmother had got the better of Aunt Irene in some way, at some time, and wanted it rubbed in. It was as if she had said, "*She* will remember *me*." And who was Aunt Irene?

60 Gay seemed to scowl at her as they drove away. She had never liked it and it had never liked her, but she felt drearily as if some gate of life were shut behind her when the door closed. She and mother did not talk as they drove along over the elfish underground city that comes into view under the black street on a rainy night. She was determined she would not cry and she did not. Her eyes were wide with dismay but her voice was cool and quiet as she said good-bye. The last Robin Stuart saw of her was a gallant, indomitable little figure waving to her as Mrs. Stanley herded her into the door of the Pullman.

They reached Montreal in the morning and left at noon on the Maritime Express. The time was to come when the very name of Maritime Express was to thrill Jane with ecstasy, but now it meant exile. It rained all day. Mrs. Stanley pointed out the mountains but Jane was not having any mountains just then. Mrs. Stanley thought her very stiff and unresponsive and eventually left her alone . . . for which Jane would have thanked God, fasting, if she had ever heard of the phrase. Mountains! When every turn of the wheels was carrying her further away from mother!

The next day they went down through New Brunswick, lying in the grey light of a cheerless rain. It was raining when they got to Sackville and transferred to the little branch line that ran down to Cape Tormentine.

"We take the car ferry there across to the Island," Mrs. Stanley explained. Mrs. Stanley had given up trying to talk to her. She thought Jane quite the dumbest child she had ever encountered. She had not the slightest inkling that Jane's silence was her only bulwark against wild, rebellious tears. And Jane *would not* cry.

It was not actually raining when they reached the Cape. As they went on board the car ferry the sun was hanging, a flat red ball, in a rift of clouds to the west. But it soon darkened down again. There was a grey choppy strait under a grey sky with dirty rags of clouds around the edges. By the time they got on the train again it was pouring harder than ever. Jane had been seasick on the way across and was now terribly tired. So this was P. E. Island . . . this rain-drenched land where the trees cringed before the wind and the heavy clouds seemed almost to touch the fields. Jane had no eyes for blossoming orchard or green meadow or soft-bosomed hills with scarfs of dark spruce across their shoulders. They would be in Charlottetown in a couple of hours, so Mrs. Stanley said, and her father was to meet her there. Her father, who didn't love her, as mother said, and who lived in a hovel, as grandmother said. She knew nothing else about him. She wished she knew something . . . anything. What did he look like? Would he have pouchy eyes like Uncle David? A thin, sewed-up mouth like Uncle William? Would he wink at the end of every sentence like old Mr. Doran when he came to call on grandmother?

She was a thousand miles away from mother and felt as if it were a million. Terrible waves of loneliness went over her. The train was pulling into the station.

"Here we are, Victoria," said Mrs. Stanley in a tone of relief.

12

As Jane stepped from the train to the platform a lady pounced on her with a cry of "Is *this* Jane Victoria . . . can this be my *dear* little Jane Victoria?"

Jane did not like to be pounced on . . . and just then she was not feeling like anybody's Jane Victoria.

She drew herself away and took in the lady with one of her straight, deliberate glances. A very pretty lady of perhaps forty-five or fifty, with large, pale blue eyes and smooth ripples of auburn hair around her placid, creamy face. Was this Aunt Irene?

"Jane, if you please," she said politely and distinctly.

"For all the world like her grandmother Kennedy, Andrew," Aunt Irene told her brother the next morning.

Aunt Irene laughed . . . an amused little gurgle.

"You dear funny child! Of course it can be Jane. It can be just whatever you like. I am your Aunt Irene. But I suppose you've never heard of me?"

"Yes, I have." Jane kissed Aunt Irene's cheek obediently. "Grandmother told me to remember her to you."

"Oh!" Something a little hard crept into Aunt Irene's sweet voice. "That was very kind of her . . . *very* kind indeed. And now I suppose you're wondering why your father isn't here. He started . . . he lives out at Brookview, you know . . . but that dreadful old car of his broke down halfway. He phoned in to me that he couldn't possibly get in tonight but would be along early in the morning and would I meet you and keep you for the night. Oh, Mrs. Stanley, you're not going before I've thanked you for bringing our dear little girl safely down to us. We're so much obliged to you."

"Not at all. It's been a pleasure," said Mrs. Stanley,

politely and untruthfully. She hurried away, thankful to be relieved of the odd, silent child who had looked all the way down as if she were an early Christian martyr on her path to the lions.

Jane felt herself alone in the universe. Aunt Irene did not make a bit of difference. Jane did not like Aunt Irene. And she liked herself still less. What was the matter with her? Couldn't she like *anybody*? Other girls liked some of their uncles and aunts at least.

She followed Aunt Irene out to the waiting taxi.

"It's a terrible night, lovey . . . but the country needs rain . . . we've been *suffering* for weeks . . . you must have brought it with you. But we'll soon be home. I'm *so* glad to have you. I've been telling your father he ought to let you stay with me anyhow. It's really foolish of him to take you out to Brookview. He only boards there, you know . . . two rooms over Jim Meade's store. Of course, he comes to town in the winter. But . . . well, perhaps you don't know, Jane darling, how very determined your father can be when he makes up his mind."

"I don't know *anything* about him," said Jane desperately.

"I suppose not. I suppose your mother has never talked to you about him?"

"No," Jane answered reluctantly. Somehow, Aunt Irene's question seemed charged with hidden meaning. Jane was to learn that this was characteristic of Aunt Irene's questions. Aunt Irene squeezed Jane's hand . . . which she had held ever since she had helped her into the taxi . . . sympathetically.

"You poor child! I know exactly how you feel. And I couldn't feel it was the right thing for your father to send for you. I'm sure I don't know why he did it. I couldn't fathom his motive . . . although your father and I have always been very close to each other . . . *very* close, lovey. I am ten years older than he is and I've always been more like a mother to him than a sister. Here we are at home, lovey."

Home! The house into which Jane was ushered was cosy and sleek, just like Aunt Irene herself, but Jane felt

about as much at home as a sparrow alone on an alien
housetop. In the living room Aunt Irene took off her hat and
coat, patted her hair, and put her arm around Jane.

"Now let me look you over. I hadn't a chance in the
station. And I haven't seen you since you were three years
old."

Jane didn't want to be looked over and shrank back a
little stiffly. She felt that she was being appraised, and in
spite of Aunt Irene's kindness of voice and manner she
sensed that there was something in the appraisal not wholly
friendly.

"You are not at all like your mother. *She* was the prettiest thing I ever saw. You are like your father, darling. And
now we must have a bite of supper."

"Oh, no, *please* no," cried Jane impulsively. She knew
she couldn't swallow a mouthful . . . it was misery to think
of trying.

"*Just* a bite . . . just *one* little bite," said Aunt Irene
persuasively, as if coaxing a baby. "There's such a nice chocolate peppermint cake. I really made it for your father. He's
just like a boy in some ways, you know . . . *such* a sweet
tooth. And he has always thought my chocolate cakes just
about perfection. Your mother did try so hard to learn to
make them like mine . . . but . . . well, it's a *gift*. You have
it or you haven't. One really couldn't expect a lovely little
doll like her to be a cook . . . or a manager either, for that
matter, and I told your father that often enough. Men don't
always understand, do they? They expect *everything* in a
woman. Sit here, Janie."

Perhaps the "Janie" was the last straw. Jane was not
going to be "Janied."

"Thank you, Aunt Irene," she said very politely and
very resolutely, "but I can't eat anything and it wouldn't be
any use at all to try. Please may I go to bed?"

Aunt Irene patted her shoulder.

"Of course, you poor darling. You're all tired out and
everything so strange. *I* know how hard it is for you. I'll take
you right upstairs to your room."

The room was very pretty, with hangings of basketweave berosed cretonne and a silk-covered bed so smooth and sleek that it looked as if it had never been slept in. But Aunt Irene deftly removed the silk spread and turned down the sheets.

"I hope you'll have a good sleep, lovey. You don't know what it means to me to have you sleeping under my roof . . . Andrew's little girl . . . my only niece. And I was always so fond of your mother . . but . . . well, I don't quite think she ever really liked me. I always *felt* she didn't, but I never let it make any difference between us. She didn't like to see me and your father talking much together . . . I always realised that. She was so much younger than your father . . . a mere child . . . it was natural for him to turn to me for advice, as he'd always been used to do. He always talked things over with me first. She was a little jealous, I think . . . she could hardly help that, being Mrs. Robert Kennedy's daughter. *Never* let yourself be jealous, Janie. It wrecks more lives than anything else. Here's a puff, lovey, if you're chilly in the night. A wet night in P. E. Island is apt to be cool. Good night, lovey."

Jane stood alone in the room and looked about her. The bed lamp had a lamp-shade painted with roses with a bead fringe. For some reason, Jane couldn't endure that lamp-shade. It was too smooth and pretty, just like Aunt Irene. She went to it and put out the light. Then she went to the window. Beat, beat went the rain on the panes. Splash, splash went the rain on the roof of the veranda. Beyond it Jane could see nothing. Her heart swelled. This black, alien, starless land could never be home to her.

"If I only had mother," she whispered. But, though she felt that something had taken her life and torn it apart, she did not cry.

13

JANE was so tired after the preceding sleepless nights on the train that she went to sleep almost at once. But she wakened while it was still night. The rain had ceased. A bar of shining light·lay across her bed. She slipped out from between Aunt Irene's perfumed sheets and went to the window. The world had changed. The sky was cloudless and a few shining, distant stars looked down on the sleeping town. A tree not far away was all silvery bloom. Moonlight was spilling over everything from a full moon that hung like an enormous bubble over what must be a bay or harbour, and there was one splendid, sparkling trail across the water. So there was a moon in P. E. Island too. Jane hadn't really believed it before. And polished to the queen's taste. It was like seeing an old friend. That moon was looking down on Toronto as well as P. E. Island. Perhaps it was shining on Jody, asleep in her little attic room, or on mother coming home late from some gay affair. Suppose she were looking at it at this very moment! It no longer seemed a thousand miles to Toronto.

The door opened and Aunt Irene came in, in her night-dress.

"Lovey, what is the matter? I heard you moving about and was afraid you were ill."

"I just got up to look at the moon," said Jane.

"You *funny* childy! Haven't you seen moons before? You gave me a real fright. Now go back to bed like a darling. You want to look bright and fresh for father when he comes, you know."

Jane didn't want to look bright and fresh for anybody. Was she always to be spied upon? She got into bed silently

59

and was tucked in for the second time. But she could not sleep again.

Morning comes at last, be the night ever so long. The day that was to be such a marvellous day for Jane began like any other. The mackerel clouds . . . only Jane didn't know then they *were* mackerel clouds . . . in the eastern sky began to take fire. The sun rose without any unusual fuss. Jane was afraid to get up too early for fear of alarming Aunt Irene again, but at last she rose and opened the window. Jane did not know she was looking out on the loveliest thing on earth . . . a June morning in Prince Edward Island . . . but she knew it all seemed like a different world from last night. A wave of fragrance broke in her face from the lilac hedge between Aunt Irene's house and the next one. The poplars in a corner of the lawn were shaking in green laughter. An apple tree stretched out friendly arms. There was a faraway view of daisy-sprinkled fields across the harbour where white gulls were soaring and swooping. The air was moist and sweet after the rain. Aunt Irene's house was on the fringe of the town and a country road ran behind it . . . a road almost blood-red in its glistening wetness. Jane had never imagined a road coloured like that.

"Why . . . why . . . P. E. Island is a pretty place," thought Jane half grudgingly.

Breakfast was the first ordeal, and Jane was no hungrier than she had been the night before.

"I don't think I can eat anything, Aunt Irene."

"But you must, lovey. I'm going to love you but I'm not going to spoil you. I expect you've always had a little too much of your own way. Your father may be along almost any minute now. Sit right down here and eat your cereal."

Jane tried. Aunt Irene had certainly prepared a lovely breakfast for her. Orange juice . . . cereal with thick golden cream . . . dainty triangles of toast . . . a perfectly poached egg . . . apple jelly between amber and crimson. There was no doubt Aunt Irene was a good cook. But Jane had never had a harder time choking down a meal.

"Don't be so excited, lovey," said Aunt Irene with a smile, as to some very young child who needed soothing.

Jane did not think she was excited. She had merely a queer, dreadful, empty feeling which nothing, not even the egg, seemed able to fill up. And after breakfast there was an hour when Jane discovered that the hardest work in the world is waiting. But everything comes to an end, and when Aunt Irene said, "There's your father now," Jane felt that everything *had* come to an end.

Her hands were suddenly clammy but her mouth was dry. The ticking of the clock seemed unnaturally loud. There was a step on the path . . . the door opened . . . someone was standing on the threshold. Jane stood up but she could not raise her eyes . . . she could not.

"Here's your baby," said Aunt Irene. "Isn't she a little daughter to be proud of, 'Drew? A bit too tall for her age, perhaps, but . . ."

"A russet-haired jade," said a voice.

Only four words . . . but they changed life for Jane. Perhaps it was the voice more than the words . . . a voice that made everything seem like a wonderful secret just you two shared. Jane came to life at last and looked up.

Peaked eyebrows . . . thick reddish-brown hair springing back from his forehead . . . a mouth tucked in at the corners . . . squared cleft chin . . . stern hazel eyes with jolly-looking wrinkles around them. The face was as familiar to her as her own.

"Kenneth Howard," gasped Jane. She took a quite unconscious step towards him.

The next moment she was lifted in his arms and kissed. She kissed him back. She had no sense of strangerhood. She felt at once the call of that mysterious kinship of soul which has nothing to do with the relationships of flesh and blood. In that one moment Jane forgot that she had ever hated her father. She liked him . . . she liked everything about him from the nice tobaccoey smell of his heather-mixture tweed suit to the firm grip of his arms around her. She wanted to cry, but that was out of the question, so she laughed instead . . . rather wildly, perhaps, for Aunt Irene said tolerantly, "Poor child, no wonder she is a little hysterical."

Father set Jane down and looked at her. All the sternness of his eyes had crinkled into laughter.

"Are you hysterical, my Jane?" he said gravely.

How she loved to be called "my Jane" like that!

"No, father," she said with equal gravity. She never spoke of him or thought of him as "he" again.

"Leave her with me a month and I'll fatten her up," smiled Aunt Irene.

Jane felt a quake of dismay. Suppose father *did* leave her. Evidently father had no intention of doing anything of the sort. He pulled her down on the sofa beside him and kept his arm about her. All at once everything was all right.

"I don't believe I want her fattened up. I like her bones." He looked at Jane critically. Jane knew he was looking her over and didn't mind. She only hoped madly that he would like her. Would he be disappointed because she was not pretty? Would he think her mouth too big? "Do you know you have nice little bones, Janekin?"

"She's got her Grandfather Stuart's nose," said Aunt Irene. Aunt Irene evidently approved of Jane's nose, but Jane had a disagreeable feeling that she had robbed Grandfather Stuart of his nose. She liked it better when father said,

"I rather fancy the way your eyelashes are put on, Jane. By the way, do you like to be Jane? I've always called you Jane but that may be just pure cussedness. You've a right to whatever name you like. But I want to know which name is the real *you* and which the shadowy little ghost."

"Oh, I'm Jane," cried Jane. And was she glad to be Jane!

"That's setted then. And suppose you call me dad? I'm afraid I'd make a terribly awkward father, but I think I could be a tolerable dad. Sorry I couldn't get in last night, but my jovial, disreputable old car died right on the road. I managed to restore it to life this morning . . . at least long enough to hop into town like a toad . . . our mode of travelling added to the gaiety of P. E. Island . . . but I'm afraid it's got to go into a garage for a while. After dinner we'll drive across the Island, Jane, and get acquainted."

"We're acquainted now," said Jane simply. It was true. She felt that she had known dad for years. Yes, "dad" was nicer than "father." "Father" had unpleasant associations . . . she had hated father. But it was easy to love dad. Jane opened the most secret chamber of her heart and took him in . . . nay, found him there. For dad was Kenneth Howard and Jane had loved Kenneth Howard for a long, long time.

"This Jane person," dad remarked to the ceiling, "knows her onions."

14

JANE found that waiting for something pleasant was very different from waiting for something unpleasant. Mrs. Stanley would not have known her with the laughter and sparkle in her eyes. If the forenoon seemed long it was only because she was in such a hurry to be with dad again . . . and away from Aunt Irene. Aunt Irene was trying to pump her . . . about grandmother and mother and her life at 60 Gay. Jane was not going to be pumped, much to Aunt Irene's disappointment. Questioned she ever so cleverly, Jane had a disconcerting "yes" or "no" for every question and still more disconcerting silence for suggestive remarks that were disguised questions.

"So your grandmother Kennedy is good to you, Janie?"

"Very good," said Jane unflinchingly. Well, grandmother *was* good to her. There were St. Agatha's and the music lessons and the pretty clothes, the limousine and the balanced meals as evidence. Aunt Irene had looked carefully at all her clothes.

"She never had any use for your father, you know, Janie. I thought perhaps she might take her spite out on you. It was really she that made all the trouble between him and your mother."

Jane said nothing. She would not talk about that secret

bitterness to Aunt Irene. Aunt Irene gave up in disgust.

Dad came back at noon without his car but with a horse and buggy.

"It's going to take all day to fix it. I'm borrowing Jed Carson's rig and he'll take it back when he brings the car and Jane's trunk out tomorrow. Did you ever have a buggy ride, my Jane?"

"You're not going without your dinners," said Aunt Irene.

Jane enjoyed that dinner, having eaten next to nothing ever since she left Toronto. She hoped dad wouldn't think her appetite terrible. For all she knew he was poor . . . that car hadn't looked like wealth . . . and another mouth to fill might be inconvenient. But dad himself was evidently enjoying his dinner . . . especially that chocolate peppermint cake. Jane wished she knew how to make chocolate peppermint cake, but she made up her mind that she would never ask Aunt Irene how to make it.

Aunt Irene made a fuss over dad. She purred over him . . . actually purred. And dad liked her purring and her honey-sweet phrases just as well as he had liked her cake. Jane saw that clearly.

"It isn't really fair to the child to take her out to that Brookview boarding house of yours," said Aunt Irene.

"Who knows but I'll get a house of my own for the summer?" said dad. "Do you think you could keep house for me, Jane?"

"Yes," said Jane promptly. She *could*. She knew how a house should be kept even if she had never kept one. There are people who are born knowing things.

"Can you cook?" asked Aunt Irene, winking at dad, as if over some delicious joke. Jane was pleased to see that dad did not wink back. And he saved her the ordeal of replying.

"Any descendant of my mother's can cook," he said. "Come, my Jane, put on thy beautiful garments and let's be on our way."

As Jane came downstairs in her hat and coat she could not help hearing Aunt Irene in the dining room.

"She's got a secretive strain in her, Andrew, that I confess I don't like."

"Knows how to keep her own counsel, eh?" said dad.

"It's more than that, Andrew. She's deep . . . take my word for it, she's deep. Old Lady Kennedy will never be dead while she is alive. But she is a very dear little girl for all that, Andrew . . . we can't expect her to be faultless . . . and if there is anything I can do for her you have only to let me know. Be patient with her, Andrew. You know she's never been taught how to love you."

Jane fairly gritted her teeth. The idea of her having to be taught "how to love" dad! It was . . . why, it was funny! Jane's annoyance with Aunt Irene dissolved in a little chuckle, as low-pitched and impish as an owl's.

"*Do* be careful of poison ivy," Aunt Irene called after them as they drove away. "I'm told there is so much of it in Brookview. *Do* take good care of her, Andrew."

"You've got it wrong end foremost, Irene, like all women. Any one could see with half an eye that Jane is going to take care of *me*."

A blithe soul was Jane as they drove away. The glow at her heart went with her across the Island. She simply could not believe that only a few hours had elapsed since she had been the most miserable creature in the world. It was jolly to ride in a buggy, just behind a little red mare whose sleek hams Jane would have liked to bend forward and slap. She did not eat up the long, red miles as a car would have done, but Jane did not want them eaten up. The road was full of lovely surprises . . . a glimpse of far-off hills that seemed made of opal dust . . . a whiff of wind that had been blowing over a clover field . . . brooks that appeared from nowhere and ran off into green shadowy woods where long branches of spicy fir hung over the laced water . . . great white cloud mountains towering up in the blue sky . . . a hollow of tipsy buttercups . . . a tidal river unbelievably blue. Everywhere she looked there was something to delight her. Everything seemed just on the point of whispering a secret of happiness. And there was something else . . . the sea tang in the air. Jane sniffed it for the first time . . . sniffed again . . . drank it.

"Feel in my right-hand pocket," said dad.

Jane explored and found a bag of caramels. At 60 Gay she was not allowed to eat candy between meals . . . but 60 Gay was a thousand miles away.

"We're neither of us much for talking, it seems," said dad.

"No, but I think we entertain each other very well," said Jane, as distinctly as she could with her jaws stuck together with caramel.

Dad laughed. He had such a nice *understanding* laugh.

"I can talk a blue streak when the spirit moves me," he said. "When it doesn't, I like people to let me be. You're a girl after my own heart, Jane. I'm glad I was predestined to send for you. Irene argued against it. But I'm a stubborn dud, my Jane, when I take a notion into my noddle. It just occurred to me that I wanted to get acquainted with my daughter."

Dad did not ask about mother. Jane was thankful he did not . . . and yet she knew it was all wrong that he did not. It was all wrong that mother had asked her not to speak of her to him. Oh, there were too many things all wrong but one thing was indisputably and satisfyingly right. She was going to spend a whole summer with dad and they were here together, driving over a road which had a life of its own that seemed to be running through her veins like quicksilver. Jane knew that she had never been in any place or any company that suited her so well.

The most delightful drive must end.

"We'll soon be at Brookview," said dad. "I've been living at Brookview this past year. It is still one of the quiet places of the earth. I've a couple of rooms over Jim Meade's store. Mrs. Jim Meade gives me my meals and thinks I'm a harmless lunatic because I write."

"What do you write, dad?" asked Jane, thinking of *Peaceful Adjustments of International Difficulties*.

"A little of everything, Jane. Stories . . . poems . . .

essays . . . articles on all subjects. I even wrote a novel once. But I couldn't find a publisher. So I went back to my pot-boilers. Behold a mute inglorious Milton in your dad. To you, Jane, I will confide my dearest dream. It is to write an epic on the life of Methuselah. What a subject! Here we are."

"Here" was a corner where two roads crossed and in the corner was a building which was a store at one end and a dwelling place at the other. The store end was open to the road but the house end was fenced off with a paling and a spruce hedge. Jane learned at once and forever the art of getting out of a buggy and they went through a little white gate, with a black wooden decoy duck on one of its posts, and up a red walk edged with ribbon grass and big quahaug shells.

"Woof, woof," went a friendly little brown and white dog sitting on the steps. A nice gingery smell of hot cookies floated out of the door as an elderly woman came out . . . a trim body wearing a white apron edged with six-inch deep crochet lace and with the reddest cheeks Jane had ever seen on anybody in her life.

"Mrs. Meade, this is Jane," said dad, "and you see now why I shall have to shave every morning after this."

"Dear child," said Mrs. Meade and kissed her. Jane liked her kiss better than Aunt Irene's.

Mrs. Meade at once gave Jane a slice of bread and butter and strawberry jam, to "stay her stomach" till supper. It was wild-strawberry jam, and Jane had never tasted wild-strawberry jam in her life before. The supper table was spread in a spotless kitchen where all the big windows were filled with flowering geraniums and begonias with silver-spotted leaves.

"I like kitchens," thought Jane.

Through another door that opened into a garden was a faraway view of green pastures to the south. The table in the centre of the room was covered with a gay red and white checkered cloth. There was a fat, squat little beanpot full of golden-brown beans before Mr. Meade, who gave Jane a liberal helping, besides a big square of fluffy cornmeal cake. Mr. Meade looked very much like a cabbage in spectacles and flying jibs, but Jane liked him.

Nobody found fault with Jane for things done or left undone. Nobody made her feel silly and crude and always in the wrong. When she finished her johnny-cake, Mr. Meade put another slice on her plate without even asking her if she wanted it.

"Eat all you like, but pocket nothing," he told her solemnly.

The brown and white dog sat beside her, looking up with hungry, hopeful eyes. Nobody took any notice when Jane fed him bits of johnny-cake.

Mr. and Mrs. Meade did the most of the talking. It was all about people Jane had never heard of, but somehow she liked to listen to it. When Mrs. Meade said in a solemn tone that poor George Baldwin was very ill with an ulster in his stomach, Jane's eyes and dad's laughed to each other, though their faces remained as solemn as Mrs. Meade's. Jane felt warm and pleasant all over. It was jolly to have someone to share a joke with. Fancy laughing with your eyes at any one in 60 Gay! She and mother exchanged glimmers but they never dared laugh.

The east was paling to moonrise when Jane went to bed in Mrs. Meade's spare room. The bureau and the washstand were very cheap, the bed an iron one enamelled in white, the floor painted brown. But there was a gorgeous hooked rug of roses and ferns and autumn leaves on it, the prim, starched lace curtains were as white as snow, the wallpaper was so pretty . . . silver daisy clusters on a creamy ground with circles of pale blue ribbon round them . . . and there was a huge scarlet geranium with scented, velvety leaves on a stand before one of the windows.

There was something friendly about the room. Jane slept like a top and was up and down in the morning when Mrs. Meade was lighting the kitchen fire. Mrs. Meade gave Jane a big fat doughnut to stay her stomach till breakfast and sent her out into the garden to wait till dad came down. It lay in the silence of the dewy morning. The wind was full of wholesome country smells. The little flower-beds were edged with blue forget-me-nots, and in one corner was a big, clump of early, dark red peonies. Violets and plots of red and white daisies grew under the parlor windows. In a near field cows were cropping gold-green grass and a dozen little fluffy chicks were running about. A tiny yellow bird was tilting on a spirea spray. The brown and white dog came out and followed Jane about. A funny, two-wheeled cart, such as Jane had never seen before, went by on the road, and the driver, a lank youth in overalls, waved to her as to an old friend. Jane promptly waved back with what was left of her doughnut.

How blue and high the sky was! Jane liked the country sky. "P. E. Island is a lovely place," thought Jane, not at all grudgingly. She picked a pink cabbage rose and shook the dew from it all over her face. Fancy washing your face with a rose! And then she remembered how she had prayed that she might not come here.

"I think," said Jane decidedly, "that I should apologise to God."

15

"WE must go and buy us a house soon, duck," said dad, jumping right into the middle of the subject, as Jane was to find was his habit.

Jane turned it over in her mind.

"Is 'soon' today?" she asked.

Dad laughed.

"Might as well be. This happens to be one of the days when I like myself reasonably well. We'll start as soon as Jed brings our car."

Jed did not bring the car till noon so they had dinner before they set out, and Mrs. Meade gave Jane a bag of butter cookies to stay their stomachs till supper-time.

"I like Mrs. Meade," Jane told dad, a pleasant warmth filling her soul as she realised that here was somebody she did like.

"She's the salt of the earth," agreed dad, "even if she does think the violet ray is a girl."

The violet ray might have been a girl for anything Jane knew to the contrary . . . or cared. It was enough to know that dad and she were off in a car that would have given Frank a conniption at sight, bouncing along red roads that were at once friendly and secretive, through woods that were so gay and bridal with wild cherry trees sprinkled through them and over hills where violet cloud-shadows rolled until they seemed to vanish in little hollows filled with blue. There were houses on every side in that pleasant land and they were going to buy one . . ."Let's buy a house, Jane" . . . just like that, as one might have said, "Let's buy a basket." Delightful!

"As soon as I knew you were coming I began inquiring about possible houses. I've heard of several. We'll take a look at them all before we decide. What kind of a house would you like, Jane?"

"What kind of a house can you afford?" said Jane gravely. Dad chuckled.

"She's got some of the little common sense still left in the world," he told the sky. "We can't pay a fancy price, Jane. I'm not a plutocrat. On the other hand, neither am I on relief. I sold quite a lot of stuff last winter."

"*Peaceful Adjustments of International Difficulties,*" murmured Jane.

"What's that?"

Jane told him. She told him how she had liked Kenneth Howard's picture and cut it out. But she did not tell him that grandmother had torn it, nor about the look in mother's eyes.

"*Saturday Evening* is a good customer of mine. But let us return to our muttons. Subject to the fluctuations of the market, what kind of a house would you like, my Jane?"

"Not a big one," said Jane, thinking of the enormous 60

Gay. "A little house . . . with some trees around it . . . *young* trees."

"White birches?" said dad. "I rather fancy a white birch or two. And a few dark green spruces for contrast. And the house must be green and white to match the trees. I've always wanted a green and white house."

"Couldn't we paint it?" asked Jane.

"We could. Clever of you to think of that, Jane. I might have turned down our predestined house just because it was mud colour. And we must have at least one window where we can see the gulf."

"Will it be near the gulf?"

"It must be. We're going up to the Queen's Shore district. All the houses I've heard about are up there."

"I'd like it to be on a hill," said Jane wistfully.

"Let's sum up . . . a little house, white and green or to be made so . . . with trees, preferably birch and spruce . . . a window looking seaward . . . on a hill. That sounds very possible . . . but there is one other requirement. There must be magic about it, Jane . . . lashings of magic . . . and magic houses are scarce, even on the Island. Have you any idea at all what I mean, Jane?"

Jane reflected.

"You want to feel that the house is *yours* before you buy it," she said.

"Jane," said dad, "you are too good to be true."

He was looking at her closely as they went up a hill after crossing a river so blue that Jane had exclaimed in rapture over it . . . a river that ran into a bluer harbour. And when they reached the top of the hill, there before them lay something greater and bluer still than Jane knew must be the gulf.

"Oh!" she said. And again, "Oh!"

"This is where the sea begins. Like it, Jane?"

Jane nodded. She could not speak. She had seen Lake Ontario, pale blue and shimmering, but this . . . this? She continued to look at it as if she could never have enough of it.

"I never thought anything could be so blue," she whispered.

"You've seen it before," said dad softly. "You may not know it, but it's in your blood. You were born beside it, one sweet, haunted April night . . . you lived by it for three years. Once I took you down and dipped you in it, to the horror of . . . of several people. You were properly baptised before that in the Anglican church in Charlottetown . . . but that was your real baptism. You are the sea's child and you have come home."

"But you didn't like me," said Jane, before she thought.

"Not like you! Who told you that?"

"Grandmother." She had not been forbidden to mention grandmother's name to him.

"The old . . ." dad checked himself. A mask seemed to fall over his face.

"Let us not forget we are house-hunting, Jane," he said coolly.

For a little while Jane felt no interest in house-hunting. She didn't know what to believe or whom to believe. She thought dad liked her now . . . but did he? Perhaps he was just pretending. Then she remembered how he had kissed her.

"He *does* like me *now*," she thought. "Perhaps he didn't like me when I was born but I know he does now." And she was happy again.

16

HOUSE-HUNTING, Jane decided, was jolly. Perhaps it was really more the pleasure of the driving and talking and being silent with dad that was jolly, for most of the houses on dad's list were not interesting. The first house they looked at was too big; the second was too small.

"After all, we must have room to swing the cat," said dad.

"Have you a cat?" demanded Jane.

"No. But we can get one if you like. I hear the kitten crop is tops this year. Do you like cats?"

"Yes."

"Then we'll have a bushel of them."

"No," said Jane, "two."

"And a dog. I don't know how you feel about dogs, Jane, but if you're going to have a cat, I must have a dog. I haven't had a dog since . . ."

He stopped short again, and again Jane had the feeling that he had been just on the point of saying something she wanted very much to hear.

The third house looked attractive. It was just at the turn of a wooded road dappled with sunshine through the trees. But on inspection it proved hopeless. The floors were cut and warped and slanted in all directions. The doors didn't hang right. The windows wouldn't open. There was no pantry.

There was too much gingerbread about the fourth house, dad said, and neither of them looked twice at the fifth . . . a dingy, square, unpainted building with a litter of rusty cans, old pails, fruit baskets, rags, and rubbish all over its yard.

"The next on my list is the old Jones house," said dad.

It was not so easy to find the old Jones house. The new Jones house fronted the road boldly, but you had to go past it and away down a deep-rutted, neglected lane to find the old one. You could see the gulf from the kitchen window. But it was too big, and both dad and Jane felt that the view of the back of the Jones barns and pig-sty was not inspiring. So they bounced up the lane again, feeling a little dashed.

The sixth house seemed to be all a house should be. It was a small bungalow, new and white, with a red roof and dormer windows. The yard was trim, though treeless; there was a pantry and a nice cellar and good floors. And it had a wonderful view of the gulf.

Dad looked at Jane.

"Do you sense any magic about this, my Jane?"

"Do *you*?" challenged Jane.

Dad shook his head.

"Absolutely none. And, as magic is indispensable, no can do."

They drove away, leaving the man who owned the house wondering who them two lunatics were. What on earth was magic? He must see the carpenter who had built the house and find out why he hadn't put any in it.

Two more houses were impossible.

"I suppose we're a pair of fools, Jane. We've looked at all the houses I've heard of that are for sale . . . and what's to be done now? Go back and eat our words and buy the bungalow?"

"Let's ask this man who is coming along the road if he knows of any house we haven't seen," said Jane composedly.

"The Jimmy Johns have one, I hear," said the man. "Over on Lantern Hill. The house their Aunt Matilda Jollie lived in. There's some of her furniture in it too, I hear. You'd likely git it reasonable if you jewed him down a bit. It's two miles to Lantern Hill and you go by Queen's Shore."

The Jimmy Johns and a Lantern Hill and an Aunt Matilda Jollie! Jane's thumbs pricked. Magic was in the offing.

Jane saw the house first . . . at least she saw the upstairs window in its gable end winking at her over the top of a hill. But they had to drive around the hill and up a winding lane between two dykes, with little ferns growing out of the stones and young spruces starting up along them at intervals.

And then, right before them, was the house . . . *their* house!

"Dear, don't let your eyes pop quite out of your head," warned dad.

It squatted right against a little steep hill whose toes were lost in bracken. It was small . . . you could have put half a dozen of it inside of 60 Gay. It had a garden, with a stone dyke at the lower end of it to keep it from sliding down the hill, a paling and a gate, with two tall white birches leaning over it, and a flat-stone walk up to the only door, which had eight small panes of glass in its upper half. The door was locked but they could see in at the windows. There was a good-sized room on one side of the door, stairs going up right in front of it, and two small rooms on the other side whose windows looked right into the side of the hill where ferns grew as high as your waist, and there were stones lying about covered with velvet green moss.

There was a bandy-legged old cook-stove in the kitchen, a table, and some chairs. And a dear little glass-paned cupboard in the corner fastened with a wooden button.

On one side of the house was a clover field and on the other a maple grove, sprinkled with firs and spruces, and separated from the house lot by an old, lichen-covered board fence. There was an apple tree in the corner of the yard, with pink petals falling softly, and a clump of old spruces outside of the garden gate.

"I like the pattern of this place," said Jane.

"Do you suppose it's possible that the view goes with the house?" said dad.

Jane had been so taken up with her house that she had not looked at the view at all. Now she turned her eyes on it and lost her breath over it. Never, never had she seen . . . had she dreamed anything so wonderful.

Lantern Hill was at the apex of a triangle of land which had the gulf for its base and Queen's Harbour for one of its sides. There were silver and lilac sand-dunes between them and the sea, extending into a bar across the harbour where great, splendid, blue and white waves were racing to the long sun-washed shore. Across the channel a white lighthouse stood up against the sky and on the other side of the harbour were the shadowy crests of purple hills that dreamed with their arms around each other. And over it all the indefinable charm of a Prince Edward Island landscape.

Just below Lantern Hill, skirted by spruce barrens on the harbour side and a pasture field on the other, was a little pond . . . absolutely the bluest thing that Jane had ever seen.

"Now, that is my idea of a pond," said dad.

Jane said nothing at first. She could only look. She had never been there before but it seemed as if she had known it all her life. The song the sea-wind was singing was music native to her ears. She had always wanted to "belong" somewhere and she belonged here. At last she had a feeling of home.

"Well, what about it?" said dad.

Jane was so sure the house was listening that she shook her finger at him.

"Sh . . . sh," she said.

"Let's go down to the shore and talk it over," said dad.

It was about fifteen minutes' walk to the outside shore. They sat down on the bone-white body of an old tree that had drifted from heaven knew where. The snapping salty breeze whipped their faces; the surf creamed along the shore; the wee sand-peeps flitted fearlessly past them. "How *clean* salt air is!" thought Jane.

"Jane, I have a suspicion that the roof leaks."

"You can put some shingles on it."

"There's a lot of burdocks in the yard."

"We can root them out."

"The house may have once been white, but . . ."

"It can be white again."

"The paint on the front door is blistered."

"Paint doesn't cost very much, does it?"

"The shutters are broken."

"Let's fix them."

"The plaster is cracked."

"We can paper over it."

"Who knows if there's a pantry, Jane?"

"There are shelves in one of the little rooms on the right. I can use that for a pantry. The other little room would do you for a study. You'd have to have some place to write, wouldn't you?"

"She's got it all planned out," dad told the Atlantic. But added,

"That big maple wood is a likely place for owls."

"Who's afraid of owls?"

"And what about magic, my Jane?"

Magic! Why, the place was simply jammed with magic. You were falling over magic. Dad knew that. He was only talking for the sake of talking. When they went back Jane sat down on the big red sandstone slab which served as a doorstep, while dad went through the maple wood by a little twisted path the cows had made to see Jimmy John . . . otherwise Mr. J. J. Garland. The Garland house could be seen peeping around the corner of the maples . . . a snug, butter-coloured farmhouse decently dressed in trees.

Jimmy John came back with dad, a little fat man with twinkling grey eyes. He hadn't been able to find the key, but they had seen the ground floor and he told them there were three rooms upstairs with a spool bed in one of them and a closet in each of them.

"And a boot-shelf under the stairs."

They stood on the stone walk and looked at the house.

"What are you going to do with me?" said the house as plainly as ever a house spoke.

"What is your price?" said dad.

"Four hundred with the furniture thrown in for good measure," said Jimmy John, winking at Jane. Jane winked rakishly back. After all, grandmother was a thousand miles away.

"Bang goes saxpence," said dad. He did not try to "jew" Jimmy John down. That he could buy all this loveliness for four hundred dollars was enough luck.

Dad handed over fifty dollars and said the rest would be paid next day.

"The house is yours," said Jimmy John with an air of making them a present of it. But Jane knew the house had always been theirs.

"The house . . . and the pond . . . and the harbour . . . and the gulf! A good buy," said dad. "And half an acre of land. All my life I've wanted to own a bit of land . . . just enough to stand on and say, 'This is mine.' And now, Jane, it's brillig."

"Four o'clock in the afternoon." Jane knew her *Alice* too well to be caught tripping on that.

Just as they were leaving, a pocket edition of Jimmy

John, with a little impudent face, came tearing through the maple grove with the key, which had turned up in his absence. Jimmy John handed it to Jane with a bow. Jane clutched it tightly all the way back to Brookview. She loved it. Think what it would open for her!

They discovered they were hungry, having forgotten all about dinner, so they fished out Mrs. Meade's butter cookies and ate them.

"You'll let me do the cooking, dad?"

"Why, you'll have to. *I* can't."

Jane glowed.

"I wish we could move in tomorrow, dad."

"Why not? I can get some bedding and some food. We can go on from there."

"I just can't bear to have this day go," said Jane. "It doesn't seem as if there could ever be another so happy."

"We've got tomorrow, Jane . . . let me see . . . we've got about ninety-five tomorrows."

"Ninety-five," gloated Jane.

"And we'll do just as we want to, inside of decency. We'll be clean but not too clean. We'll be lazy but not too lazy . . . just do enough to keep three jumps ahead of the wolf. And we'll never have in our house that devilish thing known as an intermittent alarm clock."

"But we must have some kind of a clock," said Jane.

"Timothy Salt down at the harbour mouth has an old ship's clock. I'll get him to lend it to us. It only goes when it feels like it, but what matter? Can you darn my socks, Jane?"

"Yes," said Jane, who had never darned a sock in her life.

"Jane, we're sitting on the top of the world. It was a piece of amazing luck, your asking that man, Jane."

"It wasn't luck. I *knew* he'd know," said Jane. "And oh, dad, can we keep the house a secret till we've moved in?"

"Of course," agreed dad. "From every one except Aunt Irene. We'll have to tell her, of course."

Jane said nothing. She had not known till dad spoke

that it was really from Aunt Irene she wished to keep it secret.

Jane didn't believe she would sleep that night. How could one go to sleep with so many wonderful things to think of? And some that were very puzzling. How *could* two people like mother and dad hate each other? It didn't make sense. They were both so lovely in different ways. They must have loved each other once. What had changed them? If she, Jane, only knew the whole truth, perhaps she could do something about it.

But as she drifted off into dreams of spruce-shadowed red roads that all led to dear little houses, her last conscious thought was "I wonder if we can get our milk at the Jimmy Johns'."

17

THEY "moved in" the next afternoon. Dad and Jane went to town in the forenoon and got a load of canned stuff and some bedding. Jane also got some gingham dresses and aprons. She knew none of the clothes grandmother had bought for her would be of any use at Lantern Hill. And she slipped into a bookstore unbeknown to dad and bought a *Cookery for Beginners*. Mother had given her a dollar when she left, and she was not going to take any chances.

They called to see Aunt Irene but Aunt Irene was out. Jane had her own reasons for being pleased about this but she kept them to herself. After dinner they tied Jane's trunk and suitcase on the running-boards and bounced off to Lantern Hill. Mrs. Meade gave them a box of doughnuts, three loaves of bread, a round pat of butter with a pattern of clover leaves on it, a jar of cream, a raisin pie, and three dried codfish.

"Put one in soak tonight and broil it for your breakfast in the morning," she told Jane.

The house was still there. Jane had been half afraid it would be stolen in the night. It seemed so entirely desirable to her that she couldn't imagine anyone else not wanting it. She felt so sorry for Aunt Matilda Jollie who had had to die and leave it. It was hard to believe that, even in the golden mansions, Aunt Matilda Jollie wouldn't miss the house on Lantern Hill.

"Let me unlock the door, please, dad." She was trembling with delight as she stepped over the threshold.

"This . . . this is home," said Jane. Home . . . something she had never known before. She was nearer crying then than she had ever been in her life.

They ran over the house like a couple of children. There were three rooms upstairs . . . a quite large one to the north, which Jane decided at once must be father's.

"Wouldn't you like it yourself, blithe spirit? The window looks over the gulf."

"No, I want this dear little one at the back. I want a *little* room, dad. And the other one will do nicely for a guest room."

"Do we need a guest room, Jane? Let me remind you that the measure of anyone's freedom is what he can do without."

"Oh, but of course we need a guest room, dad." Jane was quite tickled over the thought. "We'll have company sometimes, won't we?"

"There isn't a bed in it."

"Oh, we'll get one somewhere. Dad, the house is *glad* to see us . . . glad to be lived in again. The chairs just *want* someone to sit on them!"

"Little sentimentalist!" jeered dad. But there was understanding laughter behind his eyes.

The house was surprisingly clean. Jane was to learn later that as soon as they knew Aunt Matilda Jollie's house was sold, Mrs. Jimmy John and Miranda Jimmy John had come over, got in at one of the kitchen windows and given the whole place a Dutch cleaning from top to bottom. Jane was almost sorry the house was clean. She would have liked to clean it. She wanted to do everything for it.

"I am as bad as Aunt Gertrude," she thought. And a little glimmer of understanding of Aunt Gertrude came to her.

There was nothing to do just now but put the mattresses and clothes on the beds, the cans in the kitchen cupboard, and the butter and cream in the cellar. Dad hung Mrs. Meade's codfish on the nails behind the kitchen stove.

"We'll have sausages for supper," Jane was saying.

"Janekin," said dad, clutching his hair in dismay, "I forgot to buy a frying pan."

"Oh, there's an iron frying pan in the bottom of the cupboard," said Jane serenely. "And a three-legged cooking pot," she added in triumph.

There was nothing about the house that Jane did not know by this time. Dad had kindled a fire in the stove and fed it with some of Aunt Matilda Jollie's wood, Jane keeping a watchful eye on him as he did it. She had never seen a fire made in a stove before, but she meant to know how to do it herself next time. The stove was a bit wobbly on one of its feet, but Jane found a piece of flat stone in the yard which fitted nicely under it and everything was shipshape. Dad went over to the Jimmy Johns' to borrow a pail of water . . . the well had to be cleaned out before they could use it . . . and Jane set the table with a red and white cloth like Mrs. Meade's and the dishes dad had got at the five-and-ten. She went out to the neglected garden and picked a bouquet of bleeding-heart and June lilies for the centre. There was nothing to hold them, but Jane found a rusty old tin can somewhere, swathed it in a green silk scarf she had dug out of her trunk . . . it was an expensive silk scarf Aunt Minnie had given her . . . and arranged her flowers in it. She cut and buttered bread, she made tea and fried the sausages. She had never done anything of the kind before but she had not watched Mary for nothing.

"It's good to get my legs under my own table again," said dad, as they sat down to supper.

"I suppose," thought Jane wickedly, "if grandmother

could see me eating in the kitchen . . . and liking it . . . she would say it was just my low tastes."

Aloud all she said was . . . but she nearly burst with pride as she said it . . . "How do you take your tea, dad?"

There was a tangle of sunbeams on the bare white floor. They could see the maple wood through the east window, the gulf and the pond and the dunes through the north, the harbour through the west. Winds of the salt seas were blowing in. Swallows were swooping through the evening air. Everything she looked at belonged to dad and her. She was mistress of this house . . . her right there was none to dispute. She could do just as she wanted to without making excuses for anything. The memory of that first meal together with dad in Aunt Matilda Jollie's house was to be "a thing of beauty and a joy forever." Dad was so jolly. He talked to her just as if she were grown up. Jane felt sorry for anyone who didn't have her father.

Dad wanted to help her wash the dishes but Jane would have none of it. Wasn't she to be the housekeeper? She knew how Mary washed dishes. She had always wanted to wash dishes . . . it must be such fun to make dirty plates clean. Dad had bought a dishpan that day, but neither of them had thought about a dishcloth or dish towels. Jane got two new undervests out of her trunk and slit them open.

At sunset Jane and dad went down to the outside shore . . . as they were to do almost every night of that enchanted summer. All along the silvery curving sand ran a silvery curving wave. A dim, white-sailed vessel drifted past the bar of the shadowy dunes. The revolving light across the channel was winking at them. A great headland of gold and purple ran out behind it. At sunset that cape became a place of mystery to Jane. What lay behind it? "Magic seas in fairylands forlorn?" Jane couldn't remember where she had heard or read that phrase but it suddenly came alive for her.

Dad smoked a pipe . . . which he called his "Old Contemptible" . . . and said nothing. Jane sat beside him in the shadow of the bones of an old vessel and said nothing. There was no need to say anything.

When they went back to the house they discovered that though dad had gotten three lamps, he had forgotten to get any coal-oil for them or any gasoline for his study lamp.

"Well, I suppose we can go to bed in the dark for once."

No need of that. Indefatigable Jane remembered she had seen a piece of an old tallow candle in the cupboard drawer. She cut it in two, stuck the pieces in the necks of two old glass bottles, likewise salvaged from the cupboard, and what would you ask more?

Jane looked about her tiny room, her heart swelling with satisfaction. There was as yet only the spool bed and a little table in it; the ceiling was stained with old leaks and the floor was slightly uneven. But this was the first room to be her very own, where she need never feel that someone was peeping at her through the keyhole. She undressed, blew out her candle, and looked out of the window, from which she could almost have touched the top of the steep little hill. The moon was up and had already worked its magic with the landscape. A mile away the lights of the little village at Lantern Corners shone. To the right of the window a young birch tree seemed a-tiptoe trying to peer over the hill. Soft, velvety shadows moved among the bracken.

"I am going to pretend this is a magic window," thought Jane, "and sometime when I look out of it I shall see a wonderful sight. I shall see mother coming up that road, looking for the lights of Lantern Hill."

Dad had picked a good mattress, and Jane was bone-tired after her strenuous day. But how lovely it was to lie in this comfortable little "spool" bed . . . neither Jane nor the Jimmy Johns knew that Aunt Matilda Jollie had been offered fifty dollars by a collector for that bed . . . and watch the moonlight patterning the walls with birch leaves and know that dad was just across the little "landing" from you, and that outside were free hills and wide, open fields where you could run wherever you liked, none daring to make you afraid, spruce barrens and shadowy sand dunes, instead of an iron fence and locked gates. And how quiet it all was . . . no honking, no glaring lights. Jane had pushed the window open and the scent of fern came in. Also a strange, soft faraway sound . . . the moaning call of the sea. The night seemed to be filled with it. Jane heard it and something deep down in her responded to it with a thrill that was between anguish and rapture. Why was the sea calling? What was its secret sorrow?

Jane was just dropping off to sleep when a terrible remembrance tore through her mind. She had forgotten to put the codfish to soak.

Two minutes later the codfish was soaking.

18

JANE, to her horror, slept in next morning, and when she rushed downstairs she saw an extraordinary sight . . . dad coming over from the Jimmy Johns' with a rocking chair on his head. He also had a gridiron in his hand.

"Had to borrow one to broil the codfish on, Jane. And Mrs. Jimmy John made me take the chair. She said it belonged to Aunt Matilda Jollie and they had more rocking chairs than they had time to sit in. I made the porridge and it's up to you to broil the codfish."

Jane broiled it and her face as well, and it was delicious. The porridge was a bit lumpy.

"Dad isn't a very good cook, I guess," thought Jane affectionately. But she did not say so and she heroically swallowed all the lumps. Dad didn't; he ranged them along the edge of his plate and looked at her quizzically.

"I can write, my Jane, but I can't make porridgeable porridge."

"You won't have to make it after this. I'll never sleep in again," said Jane.

There is no pleasure in life like the joy of achievement. Jane realised that in the weeks that followed, if she did not put it in just those words. Old Uncle Tombstone, the general handy man of the Queen's Shore district, whose name was really Tunstone and who hadn't a niece or nephew in the world, papered all the rooms for them, patched the roof and mended the shutters, painted the house white with green trim and taught Jane how, when, and where to dig for clams. He had a nice old rosy face with a fringe of white whisker under his chin.

Jane, bubbling over with energy, worked like a beaver, cleaning up after Uncle Tombstone, arranging the bits of furniture as dad brought them home, and getting curtains up all over the house.

"That girl can be in three places at once," said dad. "I don't know how she manages it. . . . I suppose there really is such a thing as witchcraft."

Jane was very capable and could do almost anything she tried to do. It was nice to live where you could show how capable you were. This was her own world and she was a person of importance in it. There was joy in her heart the clock round. Life here was one endless adventure.

When Jane was not cleaning up she was getting the meals. She studied her *Cookery for Beginners* every spare moment and went about muttering, "All measurements are level," and things like that. Because she had watched Mary and because it was born in her to be a cook, she got on amazingly well. From the very first her biscuits were never soggy or her roast underdone. But one day she flew too high and produced for dessert something that a charitable person might have called a plum pudding. Uncle Tombstone ate some of it and had to have the doctor that night . . . or so he said. He brought his own dinner the next day . . . cold bacon and cold pancakes tied up in a red handkerchief, and told Jane he was on a diet.

"That pudding of yours yesterday, miss, it was a mite too rich. My stomach ain't used to Toronto cookery. Them there vitamins now . . . I reckon you have to be brought up on them for them to agree with you."

To his cronies he averred that that pudding would have given the rats indigestion. But he liked Jane.

"Your daughter is a very superior person," he told dad. "Most of the girls nowadays are all tops and no taters. But she's superior—yes, sir, she's superior." How dad and Jane laughed over that. Dad called her "Superior Jane" in a tone of mock awe till the joke wore out.

Jane liked Uncle Tombstone too. In fact, nothing in her new life amazed her more than the ease with which she liked people. It seemed as if everyone she met was sealed of her tribe. She thought it must be that the P. E. Islanders were nicer, or at least more neighbourly, than the Toronto people. She did not realise that the change was in herself. She was no longer rebuffed, frightened, awkward because she was frightened. Her foot was on her native heath and her name was Jane. She felt friendly towards all the world and all the world responded. She could love all she wanted to . . . everybody she wanted to . . . without being accused of low tastes. Probably grandmother would not have recognised Uncle Tombstone socially; but the standards of 60 Gay were not the standards of Lantern Hill.

As for the Jimmy Johns, Jane felt as if she must have known them all her life. They were so called, she discovered, because Mr. James John Garland had a James Garland to the northeast of him and a John Garland to the southwest of him, and so had to be distinguished in some way. Her first forenoon at Lantern Hill all the Jimmy Johns came galloping over in a body. At least, the young fry galloped with the three dogs . . . a brindled bull-terrier, a golden collie and a long brown dog who was just a dog. Mrs. Jimmy John, who was as tall and thin as her Jimmy John was short and fat, with very wise, gentle grey eyes, walked briskly, carrying in her arms a baby as fat as a sausage. Miranda Jimmy John, who was sixteen, was tall as her mother and as fat as her father. She had had a double chin at ten and nobody would ever believe that she was secretly overflowing with romance. Polly Jimmy John was Jane's age but looked younger because she was short and thin. "Punch" Jimmy John, who had brought the key, was thirteen. There were the eight-year-old twins . . . the George twin and the

Ella twin . . . their bare chubby legs all spotted with mosquito bites. And every one of them had a pleasant smile.

"Jane Victoria Stuart?" said Mrs. Jimmy John with a questioning smile.

"Jane!" said Jane, with such an intonation of triumph that the Jimmy Johns all stared at her.

"Jane, of course," smiled Mrs. Jimmy John. Jane knew she was going to like Mrs. Jimmy John.

Everybody except the baby had brought a present for Jane. Mrs. Jimmy John gave her a lamb skin dyed red for a bedside rug. Miranda brought her a little fat white jug with pink roses on its sides, Punch brought her some early radishes, Polly brought her a rooted geranium slip and the twins brought a toad apiece "for her garden."

"You have to have toads in your garden for luck," explained Punch.

Jane felt it would never do to let her first callers go home without something to eat, especially when they had come bearing gifts.

"Mrs. Meade's pie will go round if I don't take a piece," she thought. "The baby won't want any."

The baby *did* want some, but Mrs. Jimmy John shared hers with him. They sat around in the kitchen on the chairs and on the sandstone doorstep and ate the pie while Jane radiated hospitality.

"Come over whenever you can, dear," Mrs. Jimmy John told her. Mrs. Jimmy John thought Jane pretty young to be keeping house for anybody. "If there's any way we can help you, we'll be glad to."

"Will you teach me how to make bread?" said Jane coolly. "We can get it at the Corners, of course, but dad likes home-made bread. And what kind of cake flour would you recommend?"

Jane got acquainted with the Snowbeams also that week. The Solomon Snowbeams were a rather neglected rapscallion family who lived in a ramshackle house where the spruce barrens ran down to a curve of the harbour shore known as Hungry Cove. Nobody knew how Solomon Snowbeam contrived to feed his family . . . he fished a little and "worked out" a little and shot a little. Mrs. Snowbeam was a big, pink, overblown woman, and Caraway Snowbeam, "Shingle" Snowbeam, Penny Snowbeam, and "Young John" Snowbeam were impudent, friendly little creatures who certainly did not look starved. Millicent Mary Snowbeam, aged six, was neither impudent nor friendly. Millicent Mary was, so Polly Garland told Jane, not all there. She had blank, velvety nut-brown eyes . . . all the Snowbeams had beautiful eyes . . . reddish-golden hair and a dazzling complexion. She could sit for hours without speaking . . . perhaps that was why the chattering Jimmy Johns thought her not all there . . . with her fat arms clasped around her fat knees. She seemed to be possessed of a dumb admiration for Jane and haunted Lantern Hill all that summer, gazing at her. Jane did not mind her.

If Millicent Mary did not talk, the rest of the Snowbeams made up for it. At first they were inclined to resent Jane a bit, thinking she must know everything because she came from Toronto and would be putting on airs about it. But when they discovered she hardly knew anything . . . except the little Uncle Tombstone had taught her about clams . . . they became very friendly. That is to say, they asked innumerable questions. There was no false delicacy about any of the Snowbeams.

"Does your pa put live people in his stories?" asked Penny.

"No," said Jane.

"Everybody round here says he does. Everybody's scared he'll put them in. He'd better not put *us* in if he doesn't want his snoot busted. I'm the toughest boy in Lantern Hill."

"Do you think you are interesting enough to put in a story?" said Jane.

Penny was a little scared of her after that.

"We've been wanting to see what you looked like," said Shingle, who wore overalls and looked like a boy but wasn't, "because your pa and ma are divorced, ain't they?"

"No," said Jane.

"Is your pa a widow then?" persisted Shingle.

"No."

"Does your ma live in Toronto?"

"Yes."

"Why doesn't she live here with your pa?"

"If you ask me any more questions about my parents," said Jane, "I'll get dad to put you into one of his stories . . . every one of you."

Shingle was cowed but Caraway took up the tale.

"Do you look like your mother?"

"No. My mother is the most beautiful woman in Toronto," said Jane proudly.

"Do you live in a white marble house at home?"

"No."

"Ding-dong Bell said you did," said Caraway in disgust. "Ain't he the awful liar? And I s'pose you don't have satin bedspreads either?"

"We have silk ones," said Jane.

"Ding-dong *said* you had satin."

"I see the butcher bringing your dinner up the lane," said Young John. "What are you having?"

"Steak."

"My stars! We never have steak . . . nothing but bread and molasses and fried salt pork. Dad says he can't look a pig in the face 'thout grunting and mam says let him bring her home something else and she'll be mighty glad to cook it. Is that a cake you're making? Say, will you let me lick out the pan?"

"Yes, but stand back from the table. Your shirt is all over chaff," ordered Jane.

"Ain't you the bossy snip?" said Young John.

"Foxy-head," said Penny.

They all went home mad because Jane Stuart had insulted Young John. But they all came back next day and forgivingly helped her weed and clean up her garden. It was hard work and it was a hot day, so that their brows were wet with honest sweat long before they had done it to Jane's taste. If anybody had made them work as hard as that they would have howled to high heaven; but when it was for fun . . . why, it *was* fun.

Jane gave them the last of Mrs. Meade's cookies. She meant to try a batch of her own next day anyhow.

Jane had already decided that there was never a garden in the world like hers. She was crazy about it. An early, old-fashioned yellow rose bush was already in bloom. Shadows of poppies danced here and there. The stone dyke was smothered in wild rose bushes starred with crimson bud-sheaths. Pale lemon lilies and creamy June lilies grew in the corners. There were ribbon-grass and mint, bleeding-heart, prince's feather, southernwood, peonies, sweet balm, Sweet May, Sweet William, all with sated velvet bees humming over them. Aunt Matilda Jollie had been content with old-fashioned perennials and Jane loved them too, but she made up her mind that by hook or crook she would have some annuals next summer. Jane, at the beginning of this summer, was already planning for next.

In a very short time she was to be full of garden lore and was always trying to extract information about fertilisers from anybody who knew. Mr. Jimmy John gravely advised well-rotted cow manure, and Jane dragged basketfuls of it home from his barnyard. She loved to water the flowers . . . especially when the earth was a little dry and they drooped pleadingly. The garden rewarded her . . . she was one of those people at whose touch things grow. No weed was ever allowed to show its face. Jane got up early every morning to weed. It was wonderful to wake as the sun came over the sea.

The mornings at Lantern Hill seemed different from the mornings anywhere else . . . more morningish. Jane's heart sang as she weeded and raked and hoed and pruned and thinned out.

"Who taught you these things, woman?" asked dad.

"I think I've always known them," said Jane dreamily.

The Snowbeams told Jane their cat had kittens and she could have one. Jane went down to choose. There were four, and the poor, lean, old mother cat was so proud and happy.

Jane picked a black one with a pansy face . . . a really pansy
face, so dark and velvety, with round golden eyes. She
named it Peter on the spot. Then the Jimmy Johns, not to
be outdone, brought over a kitten also. But this kitten was
already named Peter and the Ella twin wept frantically over
the idea of anybody changing it. So dad suggested calling
them First Peter and Second Peter . . . which Mrs. Snowbeam thought was sacrilegious. Second Peter was a dainty
thing in black and silver, with a soft white breast. Both Peters slept at the foot of Jane's bed and swarmed over dad the
minute he sat down.

"What is home without a dog?" said dad, and got one
from old Timothy Salt at the harbour mouth. They named
him Happy. He was a slim white dog with a round brown
spot at the root of his tail, a brown collar and brown ears. He
kept the Peters in their place and Jane loved him so much it
hurt her.

"I like *living* things around me, dad."

Dad brought home the ship clock with the dog. Jane
found it useful to time meals by, but as far as anything else
was concerned there was really no such thing as time at
Lantern Hill.

By the end of a week Jane knew the geography and
people of Lantern Hill and Lantern Corners perfectly.
Every hill seemed to belong to somebody . . . Big Donald's
hill . . . Little Donald's hill . . . Old Man Cooper's hill. She
could pick out Big Donald Martin's farm and little Donald
Martin's farm. Every household light she could see from the
hill-top had its own special significance. She knew just
where to look to see Min's ma's light sparkle out every night
from the little white house in a misty fold of the hills. Min
herself, an owl-eyed gypsy scrap, full of ginger, was already
a bosom friend of Jane's. Jane knew that Min's colourless ma
was entirely unimportant except as a background for Min.
Min never would wear shoes or stockings in summer and
her bare feet twinkled over the red roads to Lantern Hill
every day. Sometimes Elmer Bell, better known as Ding-
dong, came with her. Ding-dong was freckled and his ears
stuck out, but he was popular, though pursued through life

by some scandalous tale of having sat in his porridge when he was an infant. When Young John wanted to be especially annoying he yelled at Ding-dong, "Sot in your porridge, you did . . . sot in your porridge!"

Elmer and Min and Polly Garland and Shingle and Jane were all children of the same year and they all liked each other and snubbed each other and offended each other and stood up for each other against the older and younger fry. Jane gave up trying to believe she hadn't always been friends with them. She remembered the woman who had called Gay Street dead. Well, Aunt Matilda Jollie's house wasn't dead. It was alive, every inch of it. Jane's friends swarmed all over it.

"You're so nice you ought to have been born in P. E. Island," Ding-dong told her.

"I was," said Jane triumphantly.

19

ONE day a blue two-wheeled cart lumbered up the lane and left a big packing-box in the yard.

"A lot of my mother's china and silver are in that, Jane," said dad. "I thought you might like to have them. You were named after her. They've been packed up ever since . . ."

Dad suddenly stopped, and the frown that Jane always wanted to smooth out came over his brow.

"They've been packed up for years."

Jane knew perfectly well that he had started to say, "ever since your mother went away," or words to that effect. She had a sudden realisation of the fact that this was not the first time dad had helped fix up a home . . . not the first time he had been nicely excited over choosing wallpaper and curtains and rugs. He must have had it all before with mother. Perhaps they had had just as much fun over it as dad and she were having now . . . more. Mother must have been sweet over fixing up her own home. She never had anything to say over the arrangements at 60 Gay. Jane wondered where the house dad and mother had lived in was . . . the house where she had been born. There were so many things she would have liked to ask dad if she had dared. But he was so nice. How could mother ever have left him?

It was great fun unpacking Grandmother Stuart's box. There was lovely bits of glass and china in it . . . Grandmother Stuart's dinner set of white and gold . . . slender-stemmed glass goblets . . . quaint pretty dishes of all kinds. And silver! A tea-set, forks, spoons—"Apostle spoons"—salt-cellars.

"That silver does need cleaning," said Jane in rapture. What fun she would have cleaning it and washing up all those dainty and delicate dishes! Polishing up the moon was nothing to this. In fact, the moon life had lost its old charm. Jane had enough to do keeping her house spotless without going on moon sprees. Anyhow, the Island moons never seemed to need polishing.

There were other things in the box . . . pictures and a delightful old framed motto worked in blue and crimson wool. "May the peace of God abide in this house." Jane thought this was lovely. She and dad had endless palavers as to where the pictures should go, but eventually they were all hung and made such a difference.

"As soon as you hang a picture on a wall," said dad, "the wall becomes your friend. A blank wall is hostile."

They hung the motto in Jane's room and every night when she went to bed and every morning when she got up Jane read it over like a prayer.

The beds blossomed out in wonderful patchwork quilts after that box came home. There were three of them that Grandmother Stuart had pieced . . . an Irish Chain, a Blazing Star, and a Wild Goose. Jane put the Wild Goose on dad's bed, the blue Irish Chain on her own, and the scarlet Blazing Star on the boot-shelf against the day when they would have a bed for the spare room.

They found a bronze soldier on horseback in the box and a shiny brass dog. The soldier went up on the clock-shelf but dad said the dog must go on his desk to keep his china cat in order. Dad's desk had been brought from Mr. Meade's and was set up in the "study" . . . an old shining mahogany desk with sliding shelves and secret drawers and pigeonholes. The cat sat on one corner . . . a white, green-spotted cat with a long snaky neck and gleaming diamond eyes. For some reason Jane could not fathom, dad seemed to prize the thing. He had carried it all the way from Brookview to Lantern Hill in his hand so that it shouldn't get broken.

Jane's own particular booty was a blue plate with a white bird flying across it. She would eat every meal off it after this. And the old hour-glass, with its golden sands, on its walnut base was charming.

"Early eighteenth century," said dad. "My great-grand-father was a U.E. Loyalist and this hour-glass was about all he had when he came to Canada . . . that and an old copper kettle. I wonder . . . yes, here it is. More polishing for you, Jane. And here's an old bowl of blue and white striped china. Mother mixed her salads in it."

"I'll mix mine in it," said Jane.

There was a little box at the very bottom of the big box. Jane pounced on it.

"Dad, what's this?"

Dad took it from her. There was a strange look on his face.

"That? Oh, that's nothing."

"Dad, it's a Distinguished Service Medal! Miss Colwin had one in her room at St. Agatha's . . . her brother won it in the Great War. Oh, dad, you . . . you . . ."

Jane was breathless with pride over her discovery.

Dad shrugged his shoulders.

"You can never deceive your faithful Jane, says she. I won it at Paschendale. Once I was proud of it. It seemed to mean something when . . . throw it out."

Dad's voice was oddly savage but Jane was not afraid of it . . . any more than she was afraid of his quick brief spurts of temper. Just a flash and a snap, like lightning from a summer cloud, then sunshine again. He had never been angry with her, but he and Uncle Tombstone had had a spat or two.

"I won't throw it out. I'm going to keep it, dad."

Dad shrugged.

"Well; don't let me see it then."

Jane put it on her bureau and gloated over it every day. But she was so excited over the contents of the box that she put icing sugar instead of salt in the Irish stew she made for dinner and her humiliation robbed her for a time of her high delight in life. Happy liked the stew, though.

20

"LET'S entertain, my Jane. A very old friend of mine, Dr. Arnett, is in Charlottetown. I'd like to invite him out for supper and a night. Can we manage it?"

"Of course. But we must get a bed for the guest room. We've got the chest of drawers and the looking-glass and the wash-stand, but no bed. You know we heard Little Donald's had a bed to sell."

"I'll see to all that. But about the supper, Jane? Shall we be extravagant? Shall we buy a chicken . . . two chickens . . . from Mrs. Jimmy John? If we do, can you cook them?"

"Of course. Oh, let me plan it, dad! We'll have cold chicken and potato salad. I know exactly how Mary made potato salad . . . I've often helped her peel the potatoes . . . and hot biscuits . . . you must get me a can of Flewell's Baking Powder at the Corners, dad . . . Flewell's, mind . . . it's the only one you can rely on" . . . already Jane was an authority on baking powders . . . "and wild strawberries and cream. Min and I found a bed of wild strawberries down the hill yesterday. We ate a lot but we left plenty."

Unluckily, Aunt Irene came the very afternoon they were expecting Dr. Arnett. She passed them in her car as Jane and her father were carrying an iron bedstead up the lane. Dad had bought it from Little Donald and Little Donald had left it at the end of the lane because he was in too much of a hurry to bring it all the way. It was a windy day, and Jane had her head tied up in an old shawl of Aunt Matilda Jollie's because she had had a slight toothache the night before. Aunt Irene looked quite horrified but kissed them both as they came into the yard.

"So you've bought old Tillie Jollie's house, 'Drew? What a funny little place! Well, I think you might have spoken to me about it first."

"Jane wanted it kept a secret . . . Jane loves secrets," dad explained lightly.

"Oh, Jane's secretive enough," said Aunt Irene, shaking a finger tenderly at Jane. "I hope it's only 'secretive' . . . but I do think you're a little inclined to be sly."

Aunt Irene was smiling, but there was an edge to her voice. Jane thought she would almost prefer grandmother's venom. You didn't have to look as if you liked that.

"If I had known I would have advised against it strongly, Andrew. I hear you paid four hundred for it. Jimmy John simply cheated you. Four hundred for a little old shack like this! Three would have been enough."

"But the view, Irene . . . the view. The extra hundred was for the view."

"You're so impractical, Andrew," shaking a laughing finger at him in his turn. At least, you felt the finger laughed. "Jane, you'll have to hold the purse-strings. If you don't, your father will be penniless by the fall."

"Oh, I think we'll be able to make both ends meet, Irene. If not, we'll pull them as close together as possible. Jane's a famous little manager. She looketh well to the ways of her household and eateth not the bread of idleness."

"Oh, Jane!" Aunt Irene was kindly amused over Jane. "If you had to have a house, 'Drew, why didn't you get one

near town? There's a lovely bungalow out at Keppoch . . .
you could have rented it for the summer. I could have been
near you then to help . . . and advise. . . ."

"We like the north shore best. Jane and I are both owls
of the desert and pelicans of the wilderness. But we both
like onions so we hit it off together. Why, we've even hung
the pictures without quarrelling. That's phenomenal, you
know."

"It isn't any joking matter, Andrew." Aunt Irene was
almost plaintive. "How about your food supplies?"

"Jane digs clams," said dad solemnly.

"Clams! Do you expect to live on clams!"

"Why, Aunt Irene, the fishman calls every week and
the butcher from the Corners comes twice a week," said
Jane indignantly.

"Darrrling!" Aunt Irene became patronising in an in-
stant. She patronised everything . . . the guest room and
the ruffled curtains of yellow net Jane was so proud of . . . "a
dear little closet," she called it sweetly. . . . She patronised
the garden . . . "such a darling old-fashioned spot, isn't it,
Jane?" . . . She patronised the boot-shelf. . . . "Really, Aunt
Matilda Jollie had all the conveniences, hadn't she, lovey?"

The only thing she didn't patronise was the Apostle
spoons. There was something acid in her sweetness when
she spoke of them.

"I always think mother intended *I* should have them,
'Drew."

"She gave them to Robin," said 'Drew quietly.

Jane felt a tingle go over her. This was the first time she
had heard dad mention mother's name.

"But when she left . . ."

"We won't discuss it, Irene, if you please."

"Of course not, dear one. *I* understand. Forgive me.
And now, Jane lovey, I'll borrow an apron and help you get
ready for Dr. Arnett. Bless her little heart, trying to get
ready for company all by herself."

Aunt Irene was *amused* at her . . . Aunt Irene was
laughing at her. Jane was furious and helpless. Aunt Irene
took smiling charge. The chickens were already cooked and

the salad was already made but she insisted on making the biscuits and slicing the chickens and she would not hear to Jane going for wild strawberries.

"Luckily I brought a pie with me. I knew Andrew would like it. Men like something substantial, you know, lovey."

This maddened Jane. She vowed in her heart that she would learn pie-making in a week's time. Meanwhile she could only submit. When Dr. Arnett came, Aunt Irene, a smiling and gracious hostess, made him welcome. Aunt Irene, still more smiling and gracious, sat at the head of the table and poured the tea and was charmed because Dr. Arnett took a second helping of potato salad. Both men enjoyed the pie. Dad told Aunt Irene she was the best pie-maker in Canada.

"Eating is not such bad fun after all," said dad, with a faint air of surprise, as if he had just discovered the fact, thanks to the pie. Bitterness overflowed the heart of Jane. At that moment she could cheerfully have torn everybody in pieces.

Aunt Irene helped Jane wash the dishes before she went away. Jane thanked her stars that she and Min had walked to Lantern Corners three days before and bought towels. What would Aunt Irene have said if she had had to wipe dishes with an undervest?

"I have to go now, lovey . . . I want to get home before dark. I do wish you were nearer me . . . but I'll come out as often as I can. I don't know what your mother would have done without me many a time, poor child. 'Drew and Dr. Arnett are off to the shore . . . I daresay they'll argue and shout at each other there most of the night. Andrew shouldn't leave you here alone like this. But men are like that . . . so thoughtless."

And Jane adored being left alone. It was so lovely to have a chance to talk to yourself.

"I don't mind it, Aunt Irene. And I *love* Lantern Hill."

"You're easily pleased" . . . as if she were a dear little fool to be so easily pleased. Somehow Aunt Irene had the most extraordinary knack of making you feel that what you liked or thought or did was of small account. And how Jane did resent her airs of authority in dad's house! Had she acted that way when mother was with dad? If she had . . .

"I've brought you a cushion for your living room, lovey. . . ."

"It's a kitchen," said Jane.

. . . "And I'll bring my old chintz chair the next time I come—for the spare room."

Jane, remembering the "dear little closet," permitted herself one satisfaction.

"I think there'll hardly be room for it," she said.

She eyed the cushion malevolently when Aunt Irene had gone. It was so new and gorgeous it made everything look faded and countrified.

"I think I'll stow it away on the boot-shelf," said Jane with a relish.

21

IT was a sultry night and Jane went out and up and sat on the hill . . . "to get back into herself," as she expressed it. She had really been out of herself ever since the morning, more or less, because she had burned the toast for breakfast and walked in the humiliation of it all day. Cooking the chickens had been a bit of a strain . . . the wood-stove oven was not like that of Mary's electric range . . . and making up the guest-room bed under Aunt Irene's amused eyes . . . "fancy this baby having a spare-room," they seemed to say . . . had been worse. But now she was blessedly alone again and there was nothing to prevent her sitting on the hill in the cool velvet night as long as she wanted to. The wind was blowing from the southwest and brought with it the scent of Big Donald's clover field. All the Jimmy Johns' dogs were barking together. The great dune that they called the Watch Tower was scalloping up against the empty north sky. Beyond it sounded the long, low thunder of the surf. A silver moth of dusk flew by, almost brushing her face. Happy had gone with dad and Dr. Arnett but the Peters came skittering up the hill and played about her. She held their purring silken flanks against her face and let them bite her cheeks delicately. It was all like a fairy-tale come true.

When she went back into the house Jane was her own woman again. Who cared for smooth, smiling Aunt Irene? She, Jane Stuart, was mistress at Lantern Hill; and she would learn to make pie crust, that she would, by the three wise monkeys, as dad was so fond of saying.

Since dad was out, Jane sat down at his desk and wrote a page or two of her letter to mother. At first she hadn't known how she could live if she could write to mother only once a month. Then it occurred to her that though she could mail a letter only once a month, she could write a little of it every day.

"We had company for supper," wrote Jane. Being forbidden to mention dad she got around it by adopting the style royal. "Dr. Arnett and Aunt Irene. Did you like Aunt Irene, mummy? Did she make you feel stupid? I cooked the chickens but Aunt Irene thought pie was better than strawberries. Don't you think wild strawberries would be more *elegant* than pie, mummy? I never tasted wild strawberries before. They are delicious. Min and I know where there is a bed of them. I'm going to get up early tomorrow morning and pick some for breakfast. Min's ma says if I can pick enough of them she will show me how to make them up into jam. I like Min's ma. Min likes her too. Min only weighed three and a half pounds when she was born. Nobody thought she'd live. Min's ma has a pig she is feeding for their winter pork. She let me feed it yesterday. I like feeding things, mummy. It makes you *important* to feed things. Pigs have great appetites. So have I. There's something in the Island air, I guess.

"Miranda Jimmy John can't bear to be joked about being fat. Miranda milks four of the cows every night. The

Jimmy Johns have fifteen cows. I haven't got acquainted with them yet. I don't know whether I'll like cows or not. I think they have an unfriendly look.

"The Jimmy Johns have big hooks in the kitchen rafters to hang hams on.

"The Jimmy John baby is so funny and solemn. It has neve laughed yet although it is nine months old. They are worried about it. It has long, curly, black eyelashes. I didn't know babies were so sweet, mummy.

"Shingle Snowbeam and I have found a robin's nest in one of the little spruce trees behind the house. There are four blue eggs in it. Shingle says we must keep it a secret from Penny and Young John or they would blow the eggs. Some secrets are nice things.

"I like Shingle now. Her real name is Marilyn Florence Isabel. Mrs. Snowbeam says the only thing she could give her children was real fancy names.

"Shingle's hair is almost white but her eyes are just the right kind of blue, something like yours, mummy. But nobody could have quite such nice eyes as you.

"Shingle is ambishus. She is the only one of the Snowbeams that has any ambishun. She says she is going to make a lady of herself or die in the attempt. I told her if she wanted to be a lady she must never ask personal questions and she is not going to do it anymore. But Caraway isn't particular whether she is a lady or not so she asks them and Shingle hears the answers. I don't like Young John Snowbeam much. He makes snoots. But he can pick up sticks with his toes.

"I like the sound of the wind here at night, mummy. I like to lie awake just to listen to it.

"I made a plum pudding one day last week. It would have been very successful if it had succeeded. Mrs. Jimmy John says I should have steamed it, not boiled it. I don't mind Mrs. Johnny John knowing about my mistakes. She has such sweet eyes.

"It's such fun to boil potatoes in a three-legged iron pot, mummy.

"The Jimmy Johns have four dogs. Three who go everywhere with them and one who stays home. We have one dog. Dogs are very nice, mummy.

"Step-a-yard is the name of the Jimmy Johns' hired man. Not his real name of course. Miranda says he has been in love all his life with Miss Justina Titus and knows it's quite hopeless because Miss Justina is faithful to the memory of Alec Jacks who was killed in the Great War. She still wears her hair pompadore, Miranda says, because that is how she wore it when she said good-bye to Alec. I think that is touching, mummy.

"Mummy darling, I love to think you'll read this letter and hold it in your hands."

It did not give Jane so much pleasure to reflect that grandmother would read it too. Jane could just see grandmother's thin-lipped smile over parts of it. "Well, like takes to like, you know, Robin. Your daughter has always had the knack of making friends with the wrong people. Snoots!"

"How nice it would be," thought Jane, as she took a flying leap into bed for the fun of it, "if mummy was down there with dad instead of Dr. Arnett and they would be coming back to me soon. It *must* have been that way once."

It was in the wee sma's that Andrew Stuart showed his guest to the neat guest room where Jane had set Grandmother Stuart's blue and white bowl full of crimson peonies on the little table. Then he tiptoed into Jane's room. Jane was sound asleep. He bent over her with such love radiating from him that Jane felt it and smiled in her sleep. He touched one tumbled lock of russet-brown hair.

"It is well with the child," said Andrew Stuart.

22

WITH the help of *Cookery for Beginners*, Mrs. Jimmy John's advice, and her own "gumption," Jane learned to make pie crust surprisingly soon and surprisingly well. She did not mind asking Mrs. Jimmy John for advice, whereas she would have died before she would have asked Aunt Irene. Mrs. Jimmy John was a wise, serene creature, with a face full of kindliness and wisdom. She had the reputation in Lantern Hill of never getting upset over anything, even church suppers. She did not laugh when Jane came over, white with despair, because a cake had fallen or a lemon filling had run all over the plate and dad had quirked a humorous eyebrow over it. In truth, Jane, for all her natural flair for cooking, would have made a good many muddles if it had not been for Mrs. Jimmy John.

"*I'd* use a heaping tablespoon of cornstarch instead of a level one, Jane."

"It *says* all measurements are level," said Jane doubtfully.

"You can't always go by what the books say," said Step-a-yard, who was as much interested in Jane's progress as anyone. "Just use gumption. Cooks are born, not made, I've always said, and you're a born one or I miss my guess. Them codfish balls you made the other day were the owl's whiskers."

The day Jane achieved unaided a dinner of roast lamb with dressing, creamed peas, and a plum pudding that even Uncle Tombstone could have eaten was the proudest day of her life. What bliss to have dad pass his plate with "A little more of the same, Jane. What matter the planetesimal hypothesis or the quantum theory compared to such a dinner? Come, Jane, don't tell me you're ignorant of the quantum theory. A woman may get by without knowing about the planetesimal hypothesis, but the quantum theory, Jane, is a necessity in any well-regulated household."

Jane didn't mind when dad ragged her. If she didn't know what the quantum theory was, she did know the plum pudding was good. She had got the recipe from Mrs. Big Donald. Jane was a great forager for recipes, and counted that day lost whose low-descending sun didn't see her copying a new one on the blank leaves at the back of *Cookery for Beginners*. Even Mrs. Snowbeam contributed one for rice pudding.

"Only kind we ever get," said Young John. "It's cheap."

Young John always came in for "the scrapings." He had some sixth sense whereby he always knew when Jane was going to make a cake. The Snowbeams thought it was great fun when Jane named all her cooking utensils. The teakettle that always danced on the stove when it was coming to a boil was Tipsy, the frying pan was Mr. Muffet, the dishpan was Polly, the stew pan was Timothy, the double boiler was Bootles, the rolling pin was Tillie Tid.

But Jane met her waterloo when she tried to make doughnuts. It sounded so easy . . . but even the Snowbeams couldn't eat the result. Jane, determined not to be defeated, tried again and again. Everybody took an interest in her tribulations over the doughnuts. Mrs. Jimmy John suggested and Min's ma gave hints. The store keeper at the Corners sent her a new brand of lard. Jane had begun by frying them in Timothy, then she tried Mr. Muffet. No use. The perverse doughnuts soaked fat every time. Jane woke up in the lone of the night and worried about it.

"This won't do, my adored Jane," said dad. "Don't you know that worry killed the widow's cat? Besides, people are telling me that you are old for your years. Just turn yourself into a wind-song, my Jane, and think no more on doughnuts."

In fact, Jane never did learn to make really good doughnuts . . . which kept her humble and prevented her showing off when Aunt Irene came. Aunt Irene came quite often. Sometimes she stayed all night. Jane hated to put her in the beloved guest room. Aunt Irene was always so delicately amused over Jane's having a guest room. And Aunt Irene thought it just too funny to find Jane splitting kindling."

"Dad mostly does it but he's been busy writing all day and I wouldn't disturb him," said Jane. "Besides, I *like* to split kindling."

"What a little philosopher it is!" said Aunt Irene, trying to kiss her.

Jane went crimson to the ears.

"Please, Aunt Irene, I don't like to be kissed."

"A nice thing to say to your own aunt, lovey" . . . speaking volumes by an amused lift of her fair eyebrows. Smooth, smiling Aunt Irene would never get angry. Jane thought she might have liked her better after a good fight with her. She knew dad was a little annoyed with her because she and Aunt Irene didn't click better and that he thought it must be her fault. Perhaps it was. Perhaps it was very naughty of her not to like Aunt Irene. "Trying to patronise us," Jane thought indignantly. It was not so much what she said as the way she said it . . . as if you were just *playing* at being a housekeeper for dad.

Sometimes they went to town and had dinner with Aunt Irene . . . gorgeous dinners, certainly. At first Jane writhed over them. But as the weeks went on, she began to feel she could hold her own even with Aunt Irene when it came to getting up a meal.

"You're wonderful, lovey, but you have too much responsibility. I keep telling your father that."

"I like responsibility," said Jane huffily.

"Don't be so sensitive, lovey" . . . as if it were a crime.

If Jane couldn't learn to make doughnuts she had no trouble learning to make jam.

"I *love* making jam," she said, when dad asked her why she bothered. Just to go into the pantry and look at shelf after shelf of ruby and amber jams and jellies gave her the deep satisfaction of a job well done. Morning after morning she got up early to go raspberrying with Min or the Snowbeams. Later on, Lantern Hill reeked with the spicy smells of pickles. When Jennie Lister at the Corners was given a jam and pickle shower before her wedding, Jane went proudly with the others and took a basket full of jellies and pickles. She had great fun at the shower, for by this time she knew everybody and everybody knew her. A walk to the village was a joy . . . she could stop to chat now with everyone she met and every dog would pass the time of day with her. Jane thought almost everybody was nice in a way. There were so many different kinds of niceness.

She found no difficulty in talking to anybody on any subject. She liked to play with the young fry but she liked to talk to the older people. She could hold the most enthralling discussions with Step-a-yard on green feed and the price of pork and what made cows chew wood. She walked round Jimmy John's farm with him every Sunday morning and judged the crops. Uncle Tombstone taught her how to drive a horse and buggy.

"She could cramp a wheel after one showing," he told the Jimmy Johns.

Step-a-yard, not to be outdone, let her drive a load of hay into Jimmy John's big barn one day.

"Couldn't 'a' done it better myself. You've got a feeling for horses, Jane."

But Jane's favourite boy friend was old Timothy Salt who lived down near the harbour's mouth in a low-eaved house under dark spruces. He had the jolliest, shrewdest old face of wrinkled leather that Jane had ever seen, with deep-sunk eyes that were like wells of laughter. Jane would sit with him for hours while he opened quahaugs and told her tales of old disaster on the sea, fading old legends of dune and headland, old romances of the North Shore that were like misty wraiths. Sometimes other old fishermen and sailors were there swapping yarns. Jane sat and listened and shooed Timothy's tame pig away when it came too near. The salt winds blew around her. The little waves on the harbour would run so fleetly from the sunset and later on the fishing boats would be bobbing to the moon. Sometimes a ghostly white fog would come creeping up from the dunes, the hills across the harbour would be phantom hills in the mist, and even ugly things would be lovely and mysterious.

"How's life with ye?" Timothy would say gravely, and Jane would tell him just as gravely that life was very well with her.

Timothy gave her a glass box full of corals and seashells from the West and the East Indies. He helped her drag up flat stones from the shore to make paths in her garden. He taught her to saw and hammer in nails and swim. Jane swallowed most of the Atlantic Ocean learning to swim, or thought she did, but she learned, and ran home, a wet, delighted creature, to brag to dad. And she made a hammock out of barrel staves that was the talk of Lantern Hill.

"That child will stick at nothing," said Mrs. Snowbeam.

Timothy swung it between two of the spruces for her . . . dad wasn't much good at doing things like that, though he told her he would do it if she would get him a rhyme for silver.

Timothy taught her to discern the signs of the sky. Jane had never felt acquainted with the sky before. To stand on Lantern Hill and see the whole sky around you was wonderful. Jane could sit for hours at the roots of the spruces gazing at sky and sea, or in some happy golden hollow among the dunes. She learned that a mackerel sky was a sign of fine weather and mare's tails meant wind. She learned that red sky at morning foretokened rain, as did the dark firs on Little Donald's hill when they looked so near and clear. Jane welcomed rain at Lantern Hill. She had never liked rain in the city, but here by the sea she loved it. She loved to listen to it coming down in the night on the ferns outside her window; she liked the sound and the scent and the freshness of it. She loved to get out in it . . . get sopping wet in it. She liked the showers that sometimes fell across the harbour, misty and purple, when it was quite fine on the Lantern Hill side. She even liked thunderstorms, when they passed out to sea beyond the bar of the shadowy dunes, and didn't come too close. But one night there was a terrible one. Blue swords of lightning stabbed the darkness . . . thunder crackled all about Lantern Hill. Jane was crouching in bed, her head buried in a pillow, when she felt dad's arm go around her. He lifted her up and held her close to him, displacing an indignant pair of Peters.

"Frightened, my Jane?"

"No-o-o," lied Jane valiantly. "Only . . . it isn't *decent*."

Dad shouted with laughter.

"You've got the word. Thunder like that is an insult to decency. But it will soon pass . . . it is passing now. 'The pillars of heaven tremble and are astonished at His reproof.' Do you know where that is found, Jane?"

"It sounds like the Bible," said Jane, as soon as she got

her breath after a crash that must have split the hill in two. "I don't like the Bible."

"Not like the Bible? Jane, Jane, this will never do. If anyone doesn't like the Bible there's something wrong either with him or with the way he was introduced to it. We must do something about it. The Bible is a wonderful book, my Jane. Full of corking good stories and the greatest poetry in the world. Full of the most amazingly human 'human nature.' Full of incredible, ageless wisdom and truth and beauty and common sense. Yes, yes, we'll see about it. I think the worst of the storm is over . . . and tomorrow morning we'll hear the little waves whispering to each other again in the sunlight . . . and there'll be a magic of silver wings over the bar when the gulls go out. I shall begin the second canto of my epic on Methuselah's life and Jane will swither in delightful anguish trying to decide whether to have breakfast indoors or out. And all the hills will be joyful together . . . more of the Bible, Jane. You'll love it."

Perhaps so . . . though Jane thought it would really need a miracle. Anyhow, she loved dad. Mother still shone on her life, like a memory of the evening star. But dad was . . . dad!

Jane dropped asleep again and had a terrible dream that she couldn't find the onions and dad's socks with the blue toes that needed mending.

23

AFTER all Jane found it did not require a miracle to make her like the Bible. She and dad went to the shore every Sunday afternoon and he read to her from it. Jane loved those Sunday afternoons. They took their suppers with

them and ate them squatted on the sand. She had an inborn
love of the sea and all pertaining to it. She loved the dunes
. . . she loved the music of the winds that whistled along
the silvery solitude of the sand-shore . . . she loved the far
dim shores that would be jewelled with home-lights on fine
blue evenings. And she loved dad's voice reading the Bible
to her. He had a voice that would make anything sound
beautiful. Jane thought if dad had had no other good quality
at all, she must have loved him for his voice. And she loved
the little comments he made as he read . . . things that
made the verses come alive for her. She had never thought
that there was anything like that in the Bible. But then, dad
did not read about knops and taches.

"*When all the morning stars sang together*' . . . the
essence of creation's joy is in that, Jane. Can't you hear that
immortal music of the spheres? '*Sun, stand thou still upon
Gibeon and thou, moon, in the vale of Ajalon.*' Such sub-
lime arrogance, Jane . . . Mussolini himself couldn't rival
that. '*Here shall thy proud waves be stayed*' . . . look at
them rolling in there, Jane . . . 'so far and no further' . . .
the majestic law to which they yield obedience never falters
or fails. '*Give me neither poverty nor riches*' . . . the prayer
of Agar, son of Jakeh. A sensible man was Agar, my Jane.
Didn't I tell you the Bible was full of common sense? '*A fool
uttereth all his mind.*' *Proverbs* is harder on the fool than on
anybody else, Jane . . . and rightly. It's the fools that make
all the trouble in the world, not the wicked. '*Whither thou
goest I will go; and where thou lodgest I will lodge; thy
people shall be my people and thy God my God; where thou
diest will I die and there will I be buried; the Lord do so to
me and more also if aught but death part thee and me.*' The
high-water mark of the expression of emotion in any language that I'm acquainted with, Jane . . . Ruth to Naomi
. . . and all such simple words. Hardly any of more than one
syllable . . . the writer of that verse knew how to marry
words as no one else has ever done. And he knew enough
not to use too many of them. Jane, the most awful as well as
the most beautiful things in the world can be said in three
words or less . . . *I love you* . . . *he is gone* . . . *he is come*

109

. . . *she is dead . . . too late . . .* and life is illumined or ruined. *'All the daughters of music shall be brought low'* . . . aren't you a little sorry for them, Jane . . . those foolish, light-footed daughters of music? Do you think they quite deserved such a humiliation? *'They have taken away my lord and I know not where they have laid him'* . . . that supreme cry of desolation! *'Ask for the old paths and walk therein and ye shall find rest.'* Ah, Jane, the feet of some of us have strayed far from the old paths . . . we can't find our way back to them, much as we may long to. *'As cold water to a thirsty soul so is good news from a far country.'* Were you ever thirsty, Jane . . . really thirsty . . . burning with fever . . . thinking of heaven in terms of cold water? I was, more than once. *'A thousand years in thy sight is but as yesterday when it is past and as a watch in the night.'* Think of a Being like that, Jane, when the little moments torture you. *'Ye shall know the truth and the truth shall make you free.'* The most terrible and tremendous saying in the world, Jane . . . because we are all afraid of truth and afraid of freedom . . . that's why we murdered Jesus."

Jane did not understand all dad said, but she put it all away in her mind to grow up to. All her life she was to have recurring flashes of insight when she recalled something dad had said. Not only of the Bible but of all the poetry he read to her that summer. He taught her the loveliness of words . . . dad read words as if he *tasted* them.

"*'Glimpses of the moon . . .'* one of the immortal phrases of literature, Jane. There are phrases with sheer magic in them. . . ."

"I know," said Jane. "*'On the road to Mandalay'* . . . I read that in one of Miss Colwin's books . . . and *'horns of elfland faintly blowing.'* That gives me a beautiful ache."

"You have the root of the matter in you, Jane. But, oh, my Jane, why . . . *why* . . . did Shakespeare leave his wife his second best bed?"

"Perhaps because she liked it best," said Jane practically.

"*'Out of the mouths of babes and sucklings'* . . . to be sure. I wonder if that eminently sane suggestion has ever occurred to the commentators who have agonised over it. Can you guess who the dark lady was, Jane? You know when a poet praises a woman she is immortal . . . witness Beatrice . . . Laura . . . Lucasta . . . Highland Mary. All talked about hundreds of years after they are dead because great poèts loved them. The weeds are growing over Troy but we remember Helen."

"I suppose she didn't have a big mouth," said Jane wistfully.

Dad kept a straight face.

"Not too small a one, Jane. You couldn't imagine goddess Helen with a rosebud mouth, could you?"

"*Is* my mouth too big, dad?" implored Jane. "The girls at St. Agatha's said it was."

"Not too big, Jane. A generous mouth . . . the mouth of a giver, not a taker . . . a frank, friendly mouth . . . with very well cut corners, Jane. No weakness about them . . . *you* wouldn't have eloped with Paris, Jane, and made all that unholy mess. You would have been true to your vows, Jane . . . in spirit as well as in letter, even in this upside-down world."

Jane had the oddest feeling that dad was thinking of mother, not of Argive Helen. But she was comforted by what he said about her mouth.

Dad did not always read from the masters. One day he took to the shore a thin little volume of poems by Bernard Freeman Trotter.

"I knew him overseas . . . he was killed . . . listen to his song about the poplars, Jane.

"'And so I sing the poplars and when I come to die
I will not look for jasper walls but cast about my eye
For a row of wind-blown poplars against an English sky.'

"What will you want to see when you get to heaven, Jane?"

"Lantern Hill," said Jane.

Dad laughed. It was so delightful to make dad laugh . . . and so easy. Though a good many times Jane didn't know exactly what he was laughing at. Jane didn't mind that a bit . . . but sometimes she wondered if mother had minded it.

One evening after dad had been spouting poetry until he was tired, Jane said timidly, "Would you like to hear *me* recite, dad?"

She recited *The Little Baby of Mathieu*. It was easy . . . dad made such a good audience.

"You can do it, Jane. That was *good*. I must give you a bit of training along that line too. I used to be rather good at interpreting the *habitant* myself."

"Some one she did not like used to be rather good at reading *habitant* poetry" . . . Jane remembered who had said that. She understood another thing now.

Dad had rolled over to where he could see their house in a gap in the twilit dunes.

"I see the Jimmy Johns' light . . . and the Snowbeam light at Hungry Cove. . . but our house is dark. Let's go home and light it up, Jane. And is there any of that apple-sauce you made for supper left?"

So they went home together and dad lighted his gas-oline lamp and sat down at his desk to work on his epic of Methuselah . . . or something else. . . and Jane got a can-dle to light her to bed. She liked a candle better than a lamp. It went out so graciously . . . the thin trail of smoke. . . the smouldering wick, giving one wild little wink at you before it left you in the dark.

When dad had converted Jane to the Bible, he set about making history and geography come alive for her. She had told him she always found those subjects hard. But soon history no longer seemed a clutter of dates and names in some dim, cold antiquity but became a storied road of time when dad told her old tales of wonder and the pride of kings. When he told the simplest incident with the sound of the sea in his voice, it seemed to take on such a colouring of romance and mystery that Jane knew she could never forget it. Thebes . . . Babylon . . . Tyre . . . Athens . . . Galilee . . . were places where real folks lived . . . folks she *knew*. And, knowing them, it was easy to be interested in everything pertaining to them. Geography, which had once meant merely a map of the world, was just as fascinating.

"Let's go to India," dad would say . . . and they went . . . though Jane would sew buttons on dad's shirts all the way. Min's ma was hard on buttons. Soon Jane knew all the fair lands far, far away as she knew Lantern Hill . . . or so it seemed to her after she had journeyed through them with father.

"Some day, Jane, you and I will really go and see them. The Land of the Midnight Sun . . . doesn't that phrase fascinate you, Jane? . . . far Cathay . . . Damascus . . . Samarkand . . . Japan in cherry-blossom time . . . Euphrates among its dead empires . . . moonrise over Karnak . . . lotus vales in Kashmir . . . castles on the banks of the Rhine. There's a villa in the Apennines . . . 'the cloudy Apennines' . . . I want you to see, my Jane. Meanwhile, let's draw a chart of Lost Atlantis."

"Next year I'll be beginning French," said Jane. "I think I'll like that."

"You will. You'll wake up to the fascination of languages. Think of them as doors opening into a stately palace for you. You'll even like Latin, dead and all as it is. Isn't a dead language rather a sad thing, Janet? Once it lived and burned and glowed. People said loving things in it . . . bitter things . . . wise and silly things in it. I wonder who was the very last person to utter a sentence in living Latin. Jane, how many boots would a centipede need if a centipede needed boots?"

That was dad all over. Tender . . . serious . . . dreamy . . . and then a tag of some delightful nonsense. But Jane knew just how grandmother would have liked that.

Sundays were interesting at Lantern Hill not only because of the Bible readings with dad but because she went to the Queen's Shore church with the Jimmy Johns in the mornings. Jane liked it tremendously. She put on the little green linen jumper dress grandmother had bought her and carried a hymn-book proudly. They went across the fields by a path that wound around the edge of Big Donald's woods, through a cool back pasture where sheep grazed, down the road past Min's ma's house, where Min joined them, and finally along a grassy lane to what was called "the little south church" . . . a small white building set in a grove of beech and spruce where lovable winds seemed always purring. Anything less like St. Barnabas' could hardly be imagined, but Jane liked it. The windows were plain glass and you could see out of them right into the woods and past the big wild cherry tree that grew close up to the church. Jane wished she could have seen it in blossom time. All the people had what Step-a-yard called their Sunday faces on and Elder Tommy Perkins looked so solemn and otherworldly that Jane found it almost impossible to believe that he was the same man as the jolly Tommy Perkins of weekdays. Mrs. Little Donald always passed her a peppermint over the top of the pew, and though Jane didn't like peppermints, she seemed to like that one. There was, she reflected, something so nice and religious about its flavour.

For the first time Jane could join in the singing of the hymns and she did it lustily. Nobody at 60 Gay had ever supposed Jane could sing; but she found that she could at least follow a tune and was duly thankful therefor, as otherwise she would have felt like an outsider at the Jimmy Johns' "sing-songs" in their old orchard on Sunday evenings. In a way Jane thought the sing-songs the best part of Sunday. All the Jimmy Johns sang like linnets and everybody could have his or her favourite hymn in turn. They sang what Step-a-yard, who carried a tremendous bass, called "giddier hymns" than were sung in church, out of little dog-eared, limp-covered hymn-books. Sometimes the stay-at-home dog tried to sing too. Beyond them was the beauty of a moonlit sea.

They always ended up with *God Save the King* and Jane went home, escorted to the door of Lantern Hill by all the Jimmy Johns and the three dogs who didn't stay at home. Once dad was sitting in the garden, on the stone seat Timothy Salt had built for her, smoking his Old Contemptible and "enjoying the beauty of the darkness," as he said. Jane sat down beside him and he put his arm around her. First Peter prowled darkly around them. It was so still

they could hear the cows grazing in Jimmy John's field and
so cool that Jane was glad of the warmth of father's tweed
arm across her shoulders. Still and cool and sweet . . . and
in Toronto at that moment every one was gasping in a sti-
fling heat wave, so the Charlottetown paper had said yesterday. But mother was with friends in Muskoka. It was poor
Jody who would be smothering in that hot little attic room.
If only Jody were here!

"Jane," dad was saying, "should I have sent for you last
spring?"

"Of course," said Jane.

"But *should* I? Did it hurt . . . anybody?"

Jane's heart beat more quickly. It was the first time dad
had ever come so near to mentioning mother.

"Not very much . . . because I would be home in September."

"Ah, yes. Yes, you will go back in September."

Jane waited for something more but it did not come.

24

"Do you ever see anything of Jody?" wrote Jane to mother.
"I wonder if she is getting enough to eat. She never says she
isn't in her letters . . . I've had three . . . but sometimes
they sound *hungry* to me. I still love her best of all my
friends but Shingle Snowbeam and Polly Garland and Min
are very nice. Shingle is making *great* progress. She always
washes behind her ears now and keeps her nails clean. And
she *never* throws spit balls, though she thinks it was great
fun. Young John throws them. Young John is collecting bottle caps and wears them on his shirt. We are all saving bottle
caps for him.

"Miranda and I decorate the church every Saturday

night with flowers. We have a good many of our own and we get some from the Titus ladies. We go over on Ding-dong's brother's truck to get them. They live at a place called Brook Valley. Isn't that a nice name? Miss Justina is the oldest and Miss Violet the youngest. They are both tall and thin and very ladylike. They have a lovely garden, and if you want to stand in well with them, Miranda says you must compliment them on their garden. Then they will do anything for you. They have a cherry walk which is wonderful in spring, Miranda says. They are both pillows in the church and every one respects them highly, but Miss Justina has never forgiven Mr. Snowbeam because he once called her 'Mrs.' when he was absent-minded. He said he would have thought she'd be pleased.

"Miss Violet is going to teach me hemstitching. She says every lady ought to know how to sew. Her face is old but her eyes are young. I am very fond of them both.

"Sometimes they quarrel. They have had a bad time this summer over a rubber plant that was their mother's who died last year. They both think it ugly but sacred and would never dream of throwing it away, but Miss Violet thinks that now their mother is gone they could keep it in the back hall, but Miss Justina said, no, it must stay in the parlour. Sometimes they would not speak to each other on account of it. I told them I thought they might keep it in the parlour one week and in the back hall one week, turn about. They were very much struck with the idea and adopted it and now everything is smooth at Brook Valley.

"Miranda sang *Abide with Me* in church last Sunday night. (They have preaching at night once a month.) She says she loves to sing because she always feels thin when she sings. She is so fat she is afraid she will never have any beaus but Step-a-yard says no fear, the men like a good armful. Was that coarse, mummy? Mrs. Snowbeam says it was.

"We sing every Sunday night in the Jimmy Johns' orchard . . . all sacred songs of course. I like the Jimmy Johns' orchard. The grass is so nice and long there and the trees grow just as they like. The Jimmy Johns have such fun together. I think a big family is splendid.

"Punch Jimmy John is teaching me how to run across a stubble-field on bare feet so it won't hurt. I go barefoot sometimes here. The Jimmy Johns and Snowbeams all do. It's so nice to run through the cool wet grass and wriggle your toes in the sand and feel wet mud squashing up between them. You don't mind, do you, mother?

"Min's ma does our washing for us. I'm sure I could do it but I am not allowed to. Min's ma does washing for all the summer boarders at the Harbour Head too. Min's ma's pig was very sick but Uncle Tombstone doctored it up and cured it. I'm so glad it got well, for if it had died I don't know what Min and her ma would have to live on next winter. Min's ma is noted for her clam chowder. She is teaching me how to make it. Shingle and I dig the clams.

"I made a cake yesterday and ants got in the icing. I was so mortyfied because we had company for supper. I wish I knew how to keep ants in their place. But Uncle Tombstone says I can make soup that *is* soup. We are going to have chicken for dinner tomorow. I've promised to save the neck for Young John and a drumstick for Shingle. And oh, mother, the pond is full of trout. We catch them and eat them. Just fancy catching fish in your own pond and frying them for supper.

"Step-a-yard has false teeth. He always takes them out and puts them in his pocket when he eats. When he is out of an evening and they give him lunch, he always says, 'Thanks, I'll call again,' but if they don't, he never goes back. He says he has to be self-respecting.

"Timothy Salt lets me look through his spy-glass. It's such fun looking at things through the wrong end. They seem so small and far away as if you were in another world.

"Polly and I found a bed of sweet grass on the sandhills yesterday. I've picked a bunch to take back for you, mother. It's nice to put among handkerchiefs, Miss Violet Titus says.

"We named the Jimmy Johns' calves today. We called the pretty ones after people we like and the ugly ones after people we don't like.

"Shingle and Polly and I are to sell candy at the ice-cream social in the Corners hall next week.

"We all made a fire of driftwood on the shore the other night and danced about it.

"Penny Snowbeam and Punch Jimmy John are very busy now bugging potatoes. I don't like potato bugs. When Punch Jimmy John said I was a brave girl because I wasn't afraid of mice, Penny said, 'Oh ho, put a bug on her and see how brave she'll be.' I am glad Punch did not put me to the test because I am afraid I could not have stood it.

"The front door had got sticky so I borrowed Step-a-yard's plane and fixed it. I also patched Young John's trousers. Mrs. Snowbeam said she'd run out of patches and his little bottom was almost bare.

"Mrs. Little Donald is going to show me how to make marmalade. She puts hers up in such dinky little stone jars her aunt left her, but I'll have to put mine in sealers.

"Uncle Tombstone got me to write a letter to his wife who is visiting in Halifax. I started it 'My dear wife' but he said he never called her that and it might give her a turn and I'd better put 'Dear Ma.' He says he can write himself but it is the spelling sticks him.

"Mummy, I love you, love you, love you."

Jane laid her head down on the letter and swallowed a lump in her throat. If only mother were here . . . with her and daddy . . . going swimming with them . . . lying on the sand with them . . . eating fresh trout out of the pond with them . . . laughing with them over the little household jokes that were always coming up . . . running with them under the moon . . . how beautiful everything would be!

25

LITTLE Aunt Em had sent word to Lantern Hill that Jane
Stuart was to come and see her.

"You must go," said dad. "Little Aunt Em's invitations
are like those of royalty in this neck of the woods."

"Who is little Aunt Em?"

"Blest if I know exactly. She's either Mrs. Bob Barker
or Mrs. Jim Gregory. I never can remember which of them
was her last husband. Anyway, it doesn't matter . . . everybody calls her Little Aunt Em. She's about as high as my
knee and so thin she once blew over the harbour and back.
But she's a wise old goblin. She lives on that little side-road
you were asking about the other day and does weaving and
spinning and dyeing rug rags. Dyes them in the good old-
fashioned way with herbs and barks and lichens. What Little Aunt Em doesn't know about the colours you can get
that way isn't worth knowing. They never fade. Better go
this evening, Jane. I've got to get the third canto of my
Methuselah epic done this evening. I've only got the young
chap along as far as his first three hundred years."

At first Jane had believed with a touching faith in that
epic of Methuselah. But now it was just a standing joke at
Lantern Hill. When dad said he must knock off another
canto, Jane knew he had to write some profound treatise for
Saturday Evening and must not be disturbed. He did not
mind having her around when he wrote poetry . . . love
lyrics, idylls, golden sonnets . . . but poetry did not pay
very well and *Saturday Evening* did.

Jane set out after supper for Little Aunt Em's. The
Snowbeams, who had already missed one excitement that
afternoon, wanted to go with her in a body, but Jane refused

their company. Then they were all mad and . . . with the exception of Shingle who decided it wasn't ladylike to push yourself in where you weren't wanted and went home to Hungry Cove . . . persisted in accompanying Jane for quite a distance, walking close to the fence in exaggerated awe and calling out taunts as she marched disdainfully down the middle of the road.

"Ain't it a pity her ears stick out?" said Penny.

Jane knew her ears didn't stick out so this didn't worry her. But the next thing did.

"S'posen you meet a crocodile on the side-road?" called Caraway. "That'd be worse than a cow."

Jane winced. How in the world did the Snowbeams know she was afraid of cows? She thought she had hidden that very cleverly.

The Snowbeams had got their tongues loosened up now and peppered Jane with a perfect barrage of insults.

"Did you ever see such a high-and-lofty, stuck-up minx?"

"Proud as a cat driving a buggy, ain't you?"

"Too grand for the likes of us."

"I always said you'd a proud mouth."

"Do you think Little Aunt Em will give you any lunch?"

"If she does I know what it will be," yelled Penny. "Raspberry vinegar and two cookies and a sliver of cheese. Yah! Who'd eat that? Yah!"

"I'll bet you're afraid of the dark."

Jane, who was not in the least afraid of the dark, still preserved a withering silence.

"You're a foreigner," said Penny.

Nothing else they had said mattered. Jane knew her Snowbeams. But this infuriated her. She . . . a foreigner! In her own darling Island where she had been born! She stopped short at Penny.

"Just you wait," she said with concentrated venom, "till the next time any of you want to scrape a bowl."

The Snowbeams all stopped short. They had not thought of this. Better not rile Jane Stuart any more.

"Aw, we didn't mean to hurt your feelings . . . honest," protested Caraway. They promptly started homeward, but the irrepressible Young John yelled, "Good-bye, Collarbones," as he turned.

Jane, after she had shrugged off the Snowbeams, had a good time with herself on that walk. That she could go where she liked over the countryside, unhindered, uncriticised, was one of the most delightful things about her life at Lantern Hill. She was glad of an excuse to explore the side-road where Little Aunt Em lived. She had often wondered where it went to . . . that timid little red road, laced with firs and spruces, that tried to hide itself by twisting and turning. The air was full of the scent of sun-warmed grasses gone to seed, the trees talked all about her in some lost sweet language of elder days, rabbits hopped out of the ferns and into them. In a little hollow she saw a faded sign by the side of the road . . . straggling black letters on a white board, put up years agone by and old man, long since dead. "Ho, every one that thirsteth, come ye to the waters." Jane followed the pointing finger down a fairy path between the trees and found a deep, clear spring, rimmed in by mossy stones. She stooped and drank, cupping the water in her brown palm. A squirrel was impudent to her from an old beech and Jane sassed him back. She would have liked to linger there but the western sky above the tree-tops was already filled with golden rays, and she must hasten. When she passed up out of the brook hollow, she saw Little Aunt Em's house curled up like a cat on the hillside. A long lane led up to it, edged with clumps of white and gold life-everlasting. When Jane reached the house she found Little Aunt Em spinning on a little wheel set before her kitchen door, with a fascinating pile of silvery wool rolls lying on the bench beside her. She stood up when Jane opened the gate . . . she was really a little higher than dad's knee but she was not so tall as Jane. She wore an old felt hat that had belonged to one of her husbands on her rough, curly grey head, and her little black eyes twinkled in a friendly fashion in spite of her blunt question.

"Who are you?"

"I'm Jane Stuart."

"I knew it," said Aunt Em in a tone of triumph. "I knew it the minute I saw you walking up the lane. You can always tell a Stuart anywhere you see him by his walk."

Jane had her own way of walking . . . quickly but not jerkily, lightly but firmly. The Snowbeams said she strutted but Jane did not strut. She felt very glad that Little Aunt Em thought she walked like the Stuarts. And she liked Little Aunt Em at first sight.

"You might come and sit down a spell if you've a mind to," said Little Aunt Em, offering a wrinkled brown hand. "I've finished this lick of work I was doing for Mrs. Big Donald. Ah, I'm not up to much now but I was a smart woman in my day, Jane Stuart."

Not a floor in Aunt Em's house was level. Each one sloped in a different direction. It was not notoriously tidy but there was a certain hominess about it that Jane liked. The old chair she sat down in was a friend.

"Now we can have a talk," said Little Aunt Em. "I'm in the humour for it today. When I'm not, nobody can get a word out of me. Let me get my knitting. I neither tat, sew, embroider nor crochet, but the hull Maritimes can't beat me knitting. I've been wanting to see you for some time . . . everybody's talking about you. I'm hearing you're smart. Mrs. Big Donald says you can cook like a blue streak. Where did you learn it?"

"Oh, I guess I've always known how," said Jane airily. Not under torture would she have revealed to Little Aunt Em that she had never done any cooking before she came to the Island. That might reflect on mother.

"I didn't know you and your dad was at Lantern Hill till Mrs. Big Donald told me last week at Mary Howe's funeral. I don't get anywhere much now 'cept to funerals. I always make out to get to them. You see everybody and hear all the news. Soon as Mrs. Big Donald told me I made up my mind I'd see you. What thick hair you've got! And what nice little ears! You have a mole on your neck . . . that's money by the peck. You don't look like your ma, Jane Stuart. I knew her well."

Jane's spine felt tickly.

"Oh, did you?" breathlessly.

"I did. They lived in a house at the Harbour Head, and I was living there too, on a bit of a farm, beyant the barrens. It was just after I'd married my second, worse luck. The way the men get round you! I used to take butter and eggs to your ma and I was in the house the night you were born . . . a wonderful fine night it was. How is your ma? Pretty and silly as ever?"

Jane tried to resent mother being called silly but couldn't manage it. Somehow, you couldn't resent anything Little Aunt Em said. She twinkled at you so. Jane suddenly felt that she could talk to Little Aunt Em about mother . . . ask her things she had never been able to ask any one.

"Mother is well . . . oh, Aunt Em, can you tell me . . . I *must* find out . . . why didn't father and mother go on living together?"

"Now you're asking, Jane Stuart!" Aunt Em scratched her head with a knitting needle. "Nobody ever knew rightly. Every one had a different guess."

"Did they . . . were they . . . did they really love each other to begin with, Aunt Em?"

"They did. Make no mistake about that, Jane Stuart. They hadn't a lick of sense between them but they were crazy about each other. Will you have an apple?"

"And why didn't it last? Was it me? They didn't want me?"

"Who said so? I know your ma was wild with joy when you was born. Wasn't I there? And I always thought your pa uncommon fond of you, though he had his own way of showing it."

"Then why . . . why . . ."

"Lots of people thought your Grandmother Kennedy was at the bottom of it. She was dead against them marrying, you know. They were staying at the big hotel on the South Shore that summer after the war. Your dad was just home. It was love at first sight with him. I dunno's I blamed him. Your ma was the prettiest thing I ever did see . . . like a little gold butterfly she was. That little head of hers sorter shone like."

Oh, didn't Jane know it! She was seeing that wonderful knot of pale luminous gold at the nape of mother's white neck.

"And her laugh . . . it was a little tinkling, sparkling, *young* laugh. Does she laugh like that yet, Jane Stuart?"

Jane didn't know what to say. Mother laughed a great deal . . . very tinkly . . . very sparkly . . . but was it *young*?

"Mother laughs a good deal," she said carefully.

"She was spoiled, of course. She'd always had everything she wanted. And when she wanted your pa . . . well, she had to have him too. For the first time in her life, I'm guessing, she wanted something her mother wouldn't get for her. The old madam was dead against it. Your ma couldn't stand up to her but she ran away with your pa. Old Mrs. Kennedy went back to Toronto in a towering rage. But she kept writing to your ma and sending her presents and coaxing her to go for visits. Your pa's folks weren't any more in favour of the match that your ma's. He could have had any Island girl he liked. One in particular . . . Lillian Morrow. She was yaller and spindling then, but she's grown into a handsome woman. Never married. Your Aunt Irene favoured her. I've always said it was that two-faced Irene made more trouble than your grandmother. She's poison, that woman, just sweet poison. Even when she was a girl she could say the most p'isonous things in the sweetest way. But she had your pa roped and tied . . . she'd always petted and pampered him . . . men are like that, Jane Stuart, every one of them, clever or stupid. He thought Irene was perfection and he'd never believe she was a mischief-maker. Your pa and ma had their ups and downs, of course, but it was Irene put the sting into them, wagging that smooth tongue of hers . . . 'She's only a child, 'Drew' . . . when your dad was wanting to believe he'd married a woman, not a child . . . 'You're so young, lovey' . . . when your ma was feeling scared she'd never be old and wise enough for your pa. And patronising her . . . she'd patronise God, that one . . . running her house for her . . . not that your ma knew much about it . . . that was one of her troubles, I guess . . . she'd never been taught how to manage or connive . . . but a woman don't like another woman sailing in, putting things to rights. I'd have sent her off with a flea in her ear . . . but your ma had darn too little spunk . . . she couldn't stand up to Irene."

Of course, mother couldn't stand up to Aunt Irene . . . mother couldn't stand up to any one. Jane bit deep into a juicy apple rather savagely.

"I wonder," she said, as if more to herself than to Little Aunt Em, "if father and mother would have been happier if they had married other people."

"No, they wouldn't," said Aunt Em sharply. "They was meant for each other, whatever spoiled it. Don't you go thinking different, Jane Stuart. 'Course they fought. Who don't? The times I've had with my first and second! If they'd been let alone they'd likely have worked it out sooner or later. At the last, when you was rising three, your ma went to Toronto to visit the old madam and never come back. That's all anybody knows about it, Jane Stuart. Your pa sold the house and went for a trip round the world. Leastwise, that's what they said, but I ain't believing the world is round. If it was, when it turned round all the water would fall out of the pond, wouldn't it? Now, I'm going to get you a bite to eat. I've got some cold ham and pickled beets and there's red currants in the garden."

They ate the ham and beets and then went out to the garden for the currants. The garden was an untidy little place, sloping to the south, which somehow contrived to be pleasant. There was honeysuckle over the paling . . . "to bring the hummingbirds," said Little Aunt Em . . . and white and red hollyhocks against the dark green of a fir coppice and rampant tiger lilies along the walk. And one corner was rich in pinks.

"Nice out here, ain't it?" said Little Aunt Em. "It's a fine, marvellous world . . . oh, it's a very fine, marvellous world. Don't you like life, Jane Stuart?"

"Yes," agreed Jane heartily.

"I do. I smack my lips over life. I'd like to go on living forever and hearing the news. Always a tang to the news. Some of these days I'm going to scrape up enough spunk to go in a car. I've never done it yet, but I will. Mrs. Big Donald says it's the dream of her life to go up in an airyplane but I draw the line at sky-hooting. What if the engine stopped going while you was up there? How are you going to get down? Well, I'm glad you come, Jane Stuart. We're both wove out of the same yarn."

Little Aunt Em gave Jane a bunch of pansies and a handful of geranium slips when she went away.

"It's the right time of the moon to plant them," she said. "Good-bye, Jane Stuart. May you never drink out of an empty cup."

Jane walked home slowly, thinking over several things. She loved beng out alone at night. She liked the great white clouds that occasionally sailed over the stars. She felt, as she always felt when alone with the night, that she shared some lovely secret with the darkness.

Then the moon rose . . . a great, honey-hued moon. The fields all about were touched with her light. The grove of pointed firs on an eastern hill was like a magic town of slender steeples. Jane tripped along gaily, singing to herself, while her black shadow ran before her on the moonlit road. And then, just around a turn, she saw cows before her. One of them, a big black one with a strange white face, was standing squarely in the middle of the road.

Jane came out in gooseflesh. She could not try to pass those cows . . . she could not. The only thing to do was to execute a flanking movement by climbing the fence into Big Donald's pasture and going through it until she was past the cows. Ingloriously, Jane did so. But half-way along the field she suddenly stopped.

"How can I blame mother for not standing up to grandmother when I can't stand up to a few cows?" she thought.

She turned and went back. She climbed the fence into the road. The cows were still there. The white-faced one had not moved. Jane set her teeth and walked on with steady, gallant eyes. The cow did not budge. Jane went past it, head in air. When she was beyond the last cow, she turned and looked back. Not a cow of them had paid her the slightest attention.

"To think I was afraid of you," said Jane contemptuously.

And there was Lantern Hill and the silver laughter of the harbour underneath the moon. Jimmy John's little red heifer was in the yard and Jane drove it out fearlessly.

Dad was scribbling furiously when she peeped into the study. Ordinarily Jane would not have interrupted him, but she remembered that there was something she ought to tell him.

"Dad, I forgot to tell you the house caught fire this afternoon."

Dad dropped his pen and stared at her.

"Caught fire?"

"Yes, from a spark that fell on the roof. But I went up with a pail of water and put it out. It only burned a little hole. Uncle Tombstone will soon fix it. The Snowbeams were awful mad they missed it."

Dad shook his head helplessly.

"What a Jane!" he said.

Jane, having discharged her conscience and being hungry again after her walk, made a meal off a cold fried trout and went to bed.

26

"I LIKE a patch of excitement about once a week," dad would say and then they would get into the old car, taking Happy with them and leaving milk for the Peters, travelling east, west and sideways, as the road took them. Monday was generally the day for these gaddings. Every day meant something at Lantern Hill. Tuesday Jane mended, Wednesday she polished the silver, Thursday she swept and dusted downstairs, Friday upstairs, Saturday she scrubbed the floor and did extra baking for Sunday. On Monday, as dad said, they just did fool things.

They explored most of the Island that way, eating their meals by the side of the road whenever they felt hungry. "For all the world like a pair of gypsies," condescended Aunt Irene smilingly. Jane knew Aunt Irene held her responsible for the vagabondish ways dad was getting into now. But Jane was beginning to fence herself against Aunt Irene by a sturdy little philosophy of her own. Aunt Irene felt it, though she couldn't put it into words. If she could have, she would have said that Jane looked at her and then, quietly and politely, shut some door of her soul in her face.

"I can't get *near* to her, Andrew," she complained.

Dad laughed.

"Jane likes a clear space round her . . . as I do."

They did not often include Charlottetown in their Mondays, but one day in late August they pacified Aunt Irene by having supper with her. Another lady was there . . . a Miss Morrow to whom Jane took no great fancy . . . perhaps because when she smiled at Jane she looked too much like a toothpaste advertisement. Perhaps because dad seemed to like her. He and she laughed and chaffed a great deal. She was tall and dark and handsome, with rather prominent brown eyes. And she tried so hard to be nice to Jane that it was almost painful.

"Your father and I have always been great friends. So we should be friends too."

"An old sweetheart of your father's, lovey," Aunt Irene whispered to Jane when Miss Morrow had gone, attended to the gate by father. "If your mother hadn't come along . . . who knows? Even yet . . . but I don't know if a United States divorce would be legal in P. E. Island."

They stayed in to see a picture and it was late when they left for home. Not that that mattered. The Peters wouldn't care.

"We'll take the Mercer road home," said dad. "It's a base-line road and not many houses along it, but I'm told it's simply lousy with leprechauns. Perhaps we'll manage to see one, skipping madly out of reach of the car lights. Keep your eyes peeled, Jane."

Leprechauns or no leprechauns, the Mercer road was not a very good place to be cast away in. As they were rocking joyously down a dark narrow hill, shadowy with tall firs and spruces, the car stopped short, never to go again . . . at least, not until something decisive had been done to its innards. So dad decided after much fruitless poking and probing.

"We're ten miles from a garage and one from the nearest house where everyone will be asleep, Jane. It's after twelve. What shall we do?"

"Sleep in the car," said Jane coolly.

"I know a better plan. See that old barn over there? It's Jake Mallory's back barn and full of hay. I've a yen for sleeping in a hay loft, Jane."

"I think that will be fun," agreed Jane.

The barn was in a pasture field that had "gone spruce." Tiny trees were feathering up all over it . . . at least, they looked like trees in the soft darkness. Maybe they were really leprechauns, squatting there. There was a loft filled with clover hay and they lay down on it before the open window where they could watch the stars blazing down. Happy lay cuddled up to Jane and was soon dreaming blissfully of rabbits.

Jane thought father had gone to sleep too. Somehow, she couldn't sleep; she didn't especially want to. She was at one and the same time very happy and a little miserable. Happy because she was there with dad under the spell of the moonless night. Jane rather liked a night with no moon. You got closer to the secret moods of the fields then; and there were such beautiful mysterious sounds on a dark night. They were too far inland to hear the haunting rhythm of the sea, but there were whispers and rustles in the poplars behind the barn . . . "there's magic in the poplars when the wind goes through," remembered Jane . . . and sounds like fairy footsteps pattering by. Who knew but that the elves were really out in the fern? And each far wooded

hill with a star for its friend seemed listening . . . listening
. . . couldn't you hear it too, if you listened? Jane had never,
before she came to the Island, known how beautiful night
could be.

But along with all this she was thinking of what Aunt
Irene had said about Miss Morrow and a United States divorce. Jane felt that she was haunted by those mysterious
United States divorces. Hadn't Phyllis talked of them? Jane
wished peevishly that the United States would keep their
divorces at home.

Little Aunt Em had told her father could have had lots
of girls. Jane rather liked to speculate on those girls father
might have had, secure in the knowledge that he could
never have them now. But Miss Morrow made them seem
disagreeably real. *Had* dad held her hand a shade too long
when he said good-bye? Somehow, life was all snarled up.

Jane suppressed several sighs and then allowed one to
escape her. Instantly dad turned over and a lean, strong
hand touched hers.

"It seems impossible to avoid the conclusion that something is bothering my superior Jane. Tell Happy about it
and I'll listen in."

Jane lay very still and silent. Oh, if she could only tell
him everything—find out everything she wanted so much
to know! But she couldn't. There was a barrier between
them.

"Did your mother teach you to hate me, Jane?"

Jane's heart gave a bound that almost choked her. She
had promised mother that *she* wouldn't mention her name
to dad and she had kept that promise. It was dad who had
done the mentioning. Would it be wrong to allow him?

Jane decided then and there to take a chance on it.

"No, oh, no, dad. I didn't even know you were alive
until about a year and a half ago."

"You didn't! Ah, that would be your grandmother's
doings. And who told you then that I was?"

"A girl in school. And I thought you couldn't have been
good to mother or she wouldn't have . . . left . . . you and I
did hate you then for that. But nobody ever told me to hate

you . . . only grandmother said you had sent for me just to annoy mother. You didn't . . . did you, dad?"

"No. I may be selfish, Jane, no doubt I am . . . I was told so more than once . . . but I'm not so selfish as that. I thought you were being brought up to hate me and I didn't think that fair. I thought you ought to have a chance to like me if you could. That was why I sent for you. Your mother and I made a failure of our marriage, Jane, as many other young fools have done. That is the bare bones of it."

"But why . . . why . . . mother is so sweet. . . ."

"You don't need to tell me how sweet she is, Jane. When I first saw her, I was just out of the mud and stench and obscenity of the trenches and I thought that she was a creature from another star. I had never been able to understand the Trojan war before that. Then I realised that Helen of Troy might have been worth fighting for if she were like my Robin of the golden hair. And her eyes. All blue eyes are not beautiful, but hers were so lovely that they made you feel that no eyes other than blue were worth looking at. Her lashes did things to me you wouldn't believe. She wore a green dress the first time I saw her . . . well, if any other girl had worn the dress, it would have been a green dress and nothing more. On Robin it was magic . . . mystery . . . the robe of Titania. I would have kissed the hem of it."

"And did she fall in love with you, dad?"

"Something like that. Yes, she must have loved me for a while. We ran away, you know . . . her mother had no use for me. I don't think she'd have liked any man who took Robin from her . . . but I was poor and a nobody so I was quite impossible.

"I asked Robin one moonlight night to come away with me. The old moonlight enchantment did not fail. Never trust yourself in moonlight, Superior Jane. If I'd my way I'd lock everybody up on moonlight nights. We went to live at the Harbour Head and we were happy . . . why, I found a new word for sweetheart every day . . . I discovered I was a poet . . . I babbled of pools and grots, Jane . . . yes, we were happy that first year. I've always got that . . . the gods themselves can't take *that* from me."

Dad's voice was almost savage.

"And then," said Jane bitterly, "I came . . . and neither of you wanted me . . . and you were never happy again."

"Never let anyone tell you that, Jane. I admit I didn't want you terribly . . . I was so happy I didn't want any third party around. But I remember when I saw your big round eyes brighten the first time you picked me out in a roomful of other men. *Then* I knew how much I wanted you. Perhaps your mother wanted you too much . . . at any rate she didn't seem to want anyone else to love you. You wouldn't have thought I had any rights in you at all. She was so wrapped up in you that she hadn't any time or love left for me. If you sneezed she was sure you were taking pneumonia and thought me heartless because I wouldn't go off the deep end about it. She seemed afraid even to let me hold you for fear I'd drop you. Oh well, it wasn't all you. I suppose by that time she had found she had married some mythical John Doe of her imagination and that he had turned out to be no dashing hero but just a very ordinary Richard Roe. There were so many things . . . I was poor and we had to live by my budget . . . I wasn't going to have my wife live on money her mother sent her . . . I made her send it back. I *will* say she was quite willing to. But we began quarrelling over trifles . . . oh, you know I've a temper, Jane. I remember once I told her to shut her head . . . but every normal husband says that to his wife at least once in his life, Jane. I don't wonder that hurt her . . . but she was hurt by so many things I never thought would hurt her. Perhaps I don't understand women, Jane."

"No, you don't," agreed Jane.

"Eh! What!" Dad seemed a bit startled and only half pleased over Jane's candid agreement with him. "Well, upon my word . . . well, we won't argue it. But Robin didn't understand me either. She was jealous of my work . . . she thought I put it before her. . . . I know she was secretly glad when my book was rejected."

Jane remembered that mother had thought dad was jealous too.

"Don't you think Aunt Irene had something to do with it, dad?"

"Irene? Nonsense! Irene was her best friend. And your mother was jealous of my love for Irene. Your mother couldn't help being a little jealous . . . *her* mother was the most jealous creature that ever breathed. It was a disease with her. In the end Robin went back to Toronto for a visit . . . and when she got there, she wrote me that she was not coming back."

"Oh, dad!"

"Well, I suppose her mother got round her. But she had stopped loving me. I knew that. And I didn't want to see hate growing in the eyes where I had seen love. That is a terrible thing, Jane. So I didn't answer the letter."

"Oh, dad . . . if you had . . . if you had asked her . . ."

"I agree with Emerson that the highest price you can pay for a thing is to ask for it. Too high sometimes. A year later I weakened . . . I *did* write and ask her to come back. I knew it had been as much my fault as hers . . . I'd teased her . . . once I said you had a face like a monkey . . . well, you *had*, Jane, at that time . . . I'll swear you had. I never got any answer. So I knew it was no use."

A question came into Jane's head. *Had mother ever seen that letter?*

"It's all best as it is, Jane. We weren't suited to each other . . . I was ten years her senior and the war had made me twenty. I couldn't give her the luxuries and good times she craved. She was very . . . wise . . . to discard me. Let's not discuss it further, Jane. I merely wanted you to know the rights of it. And you must not mention anything I've said to your mother. Promise me that, Jane."

Jane promised dismally. There were so many things she wanted to say and she couldn't say them. It mightn't be fair to mother.

But she had to falter, "Perhaps . . . it isn't too late yet, dad."

"Don't get any foolish notions like that into your russet head, my Jane. It *is* too late. I shall never again ask Mrs.

133

Robert Kennedy's daughter to come back to me. We must make the best of things as they are. You and I love each other . . . I am to be congratulated on that."

For a moment Jane was perfectly happy. Dad loved her . . . she was sure of it at last.

"Oh, dad, can't I come back next summer . . . every summer?" she burst out eagerly.

"Do you really want to, Jane?"

"Yes," said Jane eloquently.

"Then we'll have it so. After all, if Robin has you in the winter, I should have you in the summer. She needn't grudge me that. And you're a good little egg, Jane. In fact, I think we're both rather nice."

"Dad" . . . Jane had to ask the question . . . she had to go right to the root of the matter . . . "do you . . . love . . . mother still?"

There was a moment of silence during which Jane quaked. Then she heard dad shrug his shoulders in the hay.

"'The rose that once has blown forever dies,'" he said.

Jane did not think that was an answer at all but she knew it was all she was going to get.

She turned things over in her mind before she went to sleep. So dad hadn't sent for her just to annoy mother. But he didn't understand mother. That habit of his . . . ragging you . . . she, Jane, liked it but perhaps mother hadn't understood. And father hadn't liked it because he thought mother neglected him for her baby. And he *couldn't* see through Aunt Irene. And was this what mother had cried about that night in the darkness? Jane couldn't bear to think of mother crying in the dark.

Between Little Aunt Em and dad she now knew a good deal she had not known before but . . .

"I'd like to hear mummy's side of it," was Jane's last thought as she finally fell asleep.

There was a pearllike radiance of dawn over the eastern hills when she awoke . . . awoke knowing something she had not known when she went to sleep. Dad still loved mother. There was no further question in Jane's mind about that.

Dad was still asleep but she and Happy slipped down the ladder and out. Surely there had never before been a day that dawned so beautifully. The old pasture around the barn was the quietest place Jane had ever seen, and on the grass between the little spruces . . . spruces by day all right whatever they were by night . . . were gossamers woven on who knew what fairy loom. Jane was washing her face in morning dew when dad appeared.

"It is the essence of adventure to see the break of a new day, Jane. What may it not be ushering in? An empire may fall today . . . a baby may be born who will discover a cure for cancer . . . a wonderful poem may be written. . . ."

"Our car will have to be fixed," reminded Jane.

They walked a mile to a house and telephoned a garage. Some time before noon the car was on its legs again.

"Watch our smoke," said dad.

Home . . . and the Peters welcoming them back . . . the gulf singing . . . Millicent Mary toddling adoringly in at the gate. It was a lovely August day but the Jimmy John wheat-field was tawny gold and September was waiting behind the hills . . . and September meant Toronto and grandmother and St. Agatha's again where she would be on the edge of things instead of hunting with the pack as here. The ninety-five tomorrows had shrunk to only a few. Jane sighed . . . then shook herself. What was the matter with her? She loved mother . . . she longed to see her . . . but . . .

"I want to stay with dad," said Jane.

27

AUGUST slipped into September. Jimmy John began to summer fallow the big pasture field below the pond. Jane liked the look of the fresh red furrows. And she liked Mrs. Jimmy John's flock of white geese swimming about the pond. There had been a time when Jane had kept a flock of white swans on a purple lake in the moon, but now she preferred the geese. Day by day the wheat- and oat-fields became more golden. Then Step-a-yard mowed the Jimmy John wheat. The Peters grew so fat catching evicted field-mice that dad told Jane she would really have to put them on a slimming diet.

Summer was ended. A big storm marked the ending, preceded by a week of curiously still weather. Step-a-yard shook his head and didn't like it. Something uncommon was brewing, he said.

The weather all summer had behaved itself well . . . days of sun and days of friendly rain. Jane had heard of the North Shore storms and wanted to see one. She got her wish with a vengeance.

One day the gulf changed sulkily from blue to grey. The hills were clear and sharp, foretelling rain. The sky to the northeast was black, the clouds were dark with bitter wind.

"Lots of int'resting weather coming . . . don't hold me responsible for it," warned Step-a-yard when Jane started home from the Jimmy Johns'. She literally blew along the path and felt that if Lantern Hill hadn't stood in the way she might have emulated Little Aunt Em's reputed exploit of blowing over the harbour. There was a wild, strange, hostile look all over the world. The very trees seemed strangers in the oncoming storm.

"Shut the doors and windows tight, Jane," said dad. "Our house will just laugh at the east wind."

The storm broke presently and lasted for two days. The wind that night didn't sound like wind at all . . . it sounded like the roar of a wild beast. For two days you could see nothing but a swirl of grey rain over a greyer sea . . . hear nothing but the tremendous music of huge breakers booming against the stubborn rocks of lower Queen's Shore. Jane liked it all after she got used to it. Something in her thrilled to it. And they were very cosy, sitting before their fire of white birchwood those wild nights, while the rain poured against the window and the wind roared and the gulf thundered.

"This is something like, Jane," said dad puffing at the Old Contemptible with a Peter on either shoulder. "Mankind must have its hearth-fire after all. It's a cold life warming yourself before other people's stoves."

And then he told Jane that he had decided to keep on living at Lantern Hill.

Jane gave a gasp of joy and relief. At first it had been vaguely understood that when Jane went, dad would shut up Lantern Hill and go to town for the winter; and Jane had consequently been cumbered with certain worries.

What would become of her windowful of geraniums? The Jimmy Johns had enough of their own to look after. Dad would take Happy with him but what about the Peters? And the house itself . . . the thought of its unlighted windows was unbearable. It would be so lonely . . . so deserted.

"Oh, dad, I'm so glad . . . I couldn't bear to think of it missing us. But won't you . . . how about your meals?"

"Oh, I can get up a bite for myself, I daresay."

"I'm going to teach you to fry a steak and boil potatoes before I go," said Jane resolutely. "You can't starve then."

"Jane, you'll beat your husband . . . I know you will. It is no use trying to teach me to cook. Remember our first porridge. I daresay the Jimmy Johns won't see me starve. I'll arrange for one good meal a day there. Yes, I'm staying on here, Jane. I'll keep the heart of Lantern Hill beating for you. I'll water the geraniums and see that the Peters don't get rheumatism in their legs. But I can't imagine what the place will be like without you. . . ."

"You *will* miss me a little, won't you, dad?"

"A little! My Jane is trying to be humorous. But one consolation is that I'll likely get a little real work done on my Methuselah epic. I won't have so many interruptions. And I'll be able to growl without getting dirty looks."

"You may just have one growl a day," grinned Jane. "Oh, I'm so glad I made lots of jam. The pantry is full of it."

It was the next night dad showed her the letters. He

was at his desk with Second Peter snoozing at his feet when Jane went in after washing the supper dishes. He was leaning his head on his hand and Jane thought with a sudden pang that he looked old and tired. The cat with the green spots and the diamond eyes was winking at him.

"Where did you get that cat, dad?"

"Your mother gave it to me . . . for a joke . . . before we were married. We saw it in a shop-window and were taken by the weirdness of it. And here . . . here are some letters I wrote her, Jane . . . one week she and her mother went over to Halifax. I found them tonight when I was cleaning out a drawer. I've been laughing at myself . . . the bitterest kind of laughter in the world. You'll laugh, too, Jane. Listen . . . *'To-day I tried to write a poem to you, Robin, but it is not finished because I could not find words fine enough, as a lover could not find raiment dainty enough for his bride. The old words that other men have used in singing to their loves seemed too worn and common for you. I wanted new words, crystal clear or coloured only by the iris of light. Not words that have been stamped and stained with all the hues of other men's thoughts' . . .* wasn't I a sentimental fool, Jane? *'I watched the new moon tonight, Robin. You told me you always watched the new moon set. It has been a bond between us ever since'* . . . *'Oh, how dear and human and girlish and queenly you are . . . half saint and half very womanly woman'. . . 'It is so sweet to do something for one we love, even if it be only opening a door for her to pass through or handing her a book' . . , 'you are like a rose, my Robin . . . like a white tea-rose by moonlight. . . .'"*

"I wonder if anyone will ever compare me to a rose," thought Jane. It didn't seem likely. She couldn't think of any flower she resembled.

"She didn't care enough about those letters to take them with her, Jane. After she went away I found them in the drawer of the little desk I had given her."

"But she didn't know she wasn't coming back then, dad."

Second Peter snarled as if he had been pushed aside by a foot.

"Didn't she? I think she did."

"I'm sure she didn't." Jane was sure, though she couldn't have given any reason for her sureness. "Let me take them back to her."

"No!" Dad brought his hand down so heavily on his desk that he hurt himself and winced. "I'm going to burn them."

"Oh, no, no." Somehow Jane couldn't bear to think of those letters being burned. "Give them to me, dad. I won't take them to Toronto . . . I'll leave them in my table drawer . . . but please don't burn them."

"Well!" Dad pushed the letters over to her and picked up a pen, as if dismissing the subject of the letters and her at the same time. Jane went out slowly, looking back at him. How she loved him . . . she loved even his shadow on the wall . . . his lovely clear-cut shadow. How could mother ever have left him?

The storm spent itself that night with a wild red sunset and a still wilder northwest wind . . . the wind of fine weather. The beach was still a maelstrom of foam the next day and the shadows of wild black clouds kept tearing over the sands, but the rain had ceased and the sun shone between the clouds. The harvest fields were drenched and tangled, the ground in the Jimmy John orchard was covered with apples . . . and the summer was ended. There was an undefinable change over everything that meant autumn.

28

THOSE last few days were compounded of happiness and
misery for Jane. She did so many things she loved to do and
would not do again until next summer . . . and next summer seemed a hundred years away. It was funny. . . . She
hadn't wanted to come and now she didn't want to go. She
cleaned everything up and washed every dish in the house
and polished all the silver and scoured Mr. Muffet and
Company till their faces shone. She felt lonely and left out
when she heard the Jimmy Johns and the Snowbeams talking about the cranberrying in October, and when dad said,
"I wish you could see those maples over yonder against that
spruce hill in two weeks' time," and she realised that in two
weeks' time there would be a thousand miles between them
. . . well, it seemed to her that she just couldn't bear it.

Aunt Irene came out one day when Jane was house-
cleaning furiously.

"Aren't you tired of playing at housekeeping yet,
lovey?"

But that true Aunt Irenian touch could not disturb Jane.

"I'm coming back next summer," said Jane triumphantly.

Aunt Irene sighed.

"I suppose that would be nice . . . in some ways. But
so many things may happen before then. It's a whim of your
father's to live here now, but we don't know when he'll take
another. Still, we can always hope for the best, can't we,
lovey?"

The last day came. Jane packed her trunk, not forget-
ting a jar of very special wild-strawberry jam she was taking
home to mother and two dozen russet apples Polly Snow-

beam had given her for her own and Jody's consumption. Polly knew all about Jody and sent her her love.

They had a chicken dinner—the Ella twin and the George twin had brought the birds over with Miranda's compliments, and Jane wondered when she would have a slice off the breast again. In the afternoon she went down alone to say good-bye to the shore. She could hardly bear the loneliness of the waves lapping on the beach. The sound and the tang and the sweep of the sea would not let her go. She knew the fields and the windy golden shore were a part of her. She and her Island understood each other.

"I belong here," said Jane.

"Come back soon. P. E. Island needs you," said Timothy Salt, offering her the quarter of an apple on the point of his knife. "You will," he added. "The Island's got into your blood. It does that to some folks."

Jane and dad had expected a last quiet evening together but instead there was a surprise party. All Jane's particular friends, old and young, came, even Mary Millicent who sat in a corner all the evening, staring at Jane and never spoke a word. Step-a-yard came and Timothy Salt and Min and Min's ma and Ding-dong Bell and the Big Donalds and the Little Donalds and people from the Corners that Jane didn't know knew her.

Every one brought her a farewell gift. The Snowbeams clubbed together and brought her a white plaster of Paris plaque to hang on her bedroom wall. It cost twenty-five cents and had a picture of Moses and Aaron on it in blue turbans and red gowns . . . and Jane saw grandmother looking at it! Little Aunt Em could not come but she sent word to Jane Stuart that she would save some holly-hock seeds for her. They had a very gay evening, although all the girls cried after they had sung, "For she's a jolly good fellow." Shingle Snowbeam cried so much into the tea towel with which she was helping Polly dry the dishes that Jane had to get a dry one out.

Jane did not cry but she was thinking, "It's the last good time I'll have for ages. And everybody has been so lovely to me."

"You don't know how much I'm feeling this, Jane, right here in my heart," said Step-a-yard, patting his stomach.

Dad and Jane sat up a little while after the folks had gone.

"They love you here, Jane."

"Polly and Shingle and Min are going to write to me every week," said Jane.

"You'll get the news of the Hill and the Corners then," said dad gently. "You know I can't write to you, Jane . . . not while you're living in that house."

"And grandmother won't let me write to you," said Jane sadly.

"But as long as you know there's a dad and I know there's a Jane, it won't matter too much, will it? I'll keep a diary, Jane, and you can read it when you come next summer. It will be like getting a bundle of letters all at once. And while we'll think of each other in general quite often, let's arrange one particular time for it. Seven o'clock in the evening here is six in Toronto. At seven o'clock every Saturday night I'll think of you and at six you think of me."

It was like dad to plan something like that.

"And, dad, will you sow some flower seeds for me next spring? I won't be here in time to do it. Nasturtiums and cosmos and phlox and marigolds . . . oh, Mrs. Jimmy John will tell you what to get, and I'd like a little patch of vegetables, too."

"Consider it done, Queen Jane."

"And can I have a few hens next summer, dad?"

"Those hens are hatched already," said dad.

He squeezed her hand.

"We've had a good time, haven't we, Jane?"

"We've *laughed* so much together," said Jane, thinking of 60 Gay where there was no laughter. "You won't forget to send for me next spring, will you, dad?"

"No," was all dad said. No is sometimes a horrible word, but there are times when it is beautiful.

They had to get up early the next morning because dad was going to drive Jane to town to catch the boat train and meet a certain Mrs. Wesley who was going to Toronto. Jane thought she could travel very well by herself, but for once dad was adamant.

The morning sky was red with trees growing black against it. The old moon was visible, like a new moon turned the wrong way, above the birches on Big Donald's hill. It was still misty in the hollows. Jane bade every room farewell and just before they left dad stopped the clock.

"We'll start it again when you come back, Janekin. My watch will do me for the winter."

The purring Peters had to be said good-bye to, but Happy went to town with them. Aunt Irene was at the station and so was Lilian Morrow, the latter all perfume and waved hair. Dad seemed glad to see her; he walked up and down the platform with her. She called him "'Drew." You could hear the apostrophe before it like a coo or a kiss. Jane could have done very well without Miss Morrow to see her off.

Aunt Irene kissed her twice and cried.

"Remember you always have a friend in *me*, lovey" . . . as if she thought Jane had no other.

"Don't look so woebegone, dear," smiled Lilian Morrow. "Remember you're going home."

Home! "Home is where the heart is." Jane had heard or read that. And she knew she was leaving her heart on the Island with dad, to whom she presently said good-bye with all the anguish of all the good-byes that have ever been said in her voice.

Jane watched the red shores of the Island from the boat until they were only a dim blue line against the sky. And now to be Victoria again!

When Jane went through the gates of the Toronto station, she heard a laugh she would have known anywhere. There was only one such laugh in the world. And there was mother, in a lovely new crimson velvet wrap with a white fur collar and underneath a dress of white chiffon embroidered with brilliants. Jane knew this meant that mother was going out to dinner . . . and she knew grandmother had not allowed mother to break her engagement for the sake of spending Jane's first evening home with her. But mother, smelling of violets, was holding her tight, laughing and crying.

"My dearest . . . my very own little girl. You're home again. Oh, darling, I've missed you so . . . I've missed you so."

Jane hugged mother fiercely . . . mother as beautiful as ever, her eyes as blue as ever, though . . . as Jane saw instantly . . . a little thinner than she had been in June.

"Are you glad to be back, darling?"

"*So* glad to be with you again, mummy," and Jane.

"You've grown . . . why, darling, you're up to my shoulder . . . and such a lovely tan. But I can never let you go away again . . . never."

Jane kept her own counsel about that. She felt curiously changed and grown-uppish as she went through the big lighted station with mother. Frank was waiting with the limousine and they went home through the busy, crowded streets to 60 Gay. 60 Gay was neither busy nor crowded. The clang of the iron gates behind her seemed a knell of doom. She was reentering prison. The great, cold, still house struck a chill to her spirit. Mother had gone on to the dinner and grandmother and Aunt Gertrude were meeting her. She kissed Aunt Gertrude's narrow, white face and grandmother's soft, wrinkled one.

"You've grown, Victoria," said grandmother icily. She did not like Jane looking into her eyes on the level. And grandmother saw at a glance that Jane had somehow learned what to do with her arms and legs and was looking entirely too much mistress of herself. "Don't smile with your lips closed, if you please. I've never really been able to see the charm of *La Gioconda*."

They had dinner. It was six o'clock. Down home it would be seven. Dad would be . . . Jane felt she coud not swallow a mouthful.

"Will you be good enough to pay attention when I am speaking to you, Victoria?"

"I beg your pardon, grandmother."

"I am asking you what you wore this summer. I have

looked into your trunk and the clothes you took with you don't seem to have been worn at all."

"Only the green linen jumper suit," said Jane. "I wore it to church and the ice-cream social. I had gingham dresses to wear at home. I kept house for father, you know."

Grandmother wiped her lips daintily with her napkin. It seemed as if she were wiping some disagreeable flavour off them.

"I am not enquiring about your rural activities" . . . Jane saw grandmother looking at her hands . . . "It will be wise for you to forget them. . . ."

"But I'm going back next summer, grandmother. . . ."

"Be kind enough not to interrupt me, Victoria. And as you must be tired after your journey, I would advise you to go to bed at once. Mary has prepared a bath for you. I suppose you will be rather glad to get into a real bathtub once more."

When she had had the whole gulf for a bathtub all summer!

"I must run over and see Jody first," said Jane . . . and went. She could not forget her new freedom so quickly. Grandmother watched her go with tightening lips. Perhaps she realised that never again would Jane be quite the meek, overawed Victoria of the old days. She had grown in mind as well as in body.

Jane and Jody had a rapturous reunion. Jody had grown too. She was thinner and taller and her eyes were sadder then ever.

"Oh, Jane, I'm so glad you're back. It's been so long."

"I'm so glad you're still here, Jody. I was afraid Miss West might have sent you to the orphanage."

"She's always saying she will . . . I guess she will yet. Did you really like the Island so much, Jane?"

"I just loved it," said Jane, glad that here was at least one person to whom she could talk freely about her Island and her father.

Jane was horribly homesick as she climbed the soft-carpeted stairway to bed. If she were only skipping up the bare, painted steps at Lantern Hill! Her old room had not grown any friendlier. She ran to the window, opened it, and gazed out . . . but not on starry hills and the moon shining on woodland fields. The clamour of Bloor Street assailed her ears. The huge old trees about 60 Gay were sufficient unto themselves . . . they were not her friendly birches and spruces. A wind was trying to blow . . . Jane felt sorry for it . . . checked here, thwarted there. But it was blowing from the west. Would it blow right down to the Island . . . to the velvety black night starred with harbour lights beyond Lantern Hill? Jane leaned out of the window and sent a kiss to dad on it.

"And now," remarked Jane to Victoria, "there will be only nine months to put in."

29

"She will soon forget everything about Lantern Hill," said grandmother.

Mother wasn't so sure. She felt the change in Jane, as did everybody. Uncle David's family thought Jane "much improved." Aunt Sylvia said Victoria had actually become able to get through a room without danger to the furniture. And Phyllis was a shade less patronising, though with plenty of room for improvement yet.

"I heard you went barefoot down there," she said curiously.

"Of course," said Jane. "All the children do in summer."

"Victoria has gone quite P. E. Island," said grandmother with her bitter little smile, much as if she had said, "Victoria has gone quite savage." Grandmother had already learned a new way to get under Jane's skin. It was to say little biting things about the Island. Grandmother employed it quite mercilessly. She felt that Jane, in so many respects, had somehow slipped beyond her power to hurt. All the colour still went out of Jane in grandmother's presence but she was not thereby reduced to the old flabbiness. Jane had not been chatelaine of Lantern Hill and the companion of a keen, mature intellect all summer for nothing. A new spirit looked out of her hazel eyes . . . something that was free and aloof . . . something that was almost beyond grandmother's power to tame or hurt. All the venom of her stings seemed unable to touch this new Jane . . . except when she sneered at the Island.

Because in a very real sense Jane was still living on the Island. This helped to take the edge off her first two weeks of unbearable homesickness. While she was practicing her scales she was listening for the thunder of the breakers on Queen's Shore; while she ate her meals she was waiting for dad to come in from one of his long hikes with Happy trotting at his heels; when she was alone in the big gloomy house she was companioned by the Peters . . . who could have imagined that a couple of cats a thousand miles away could be such comforts? . . . when she lay awake at night she was hearing all the sounds of her Island home. And while she was reading the Bible chapter to grandmother and Aunt Gertrude in that terrible, unchanged drawing-room, she was reading it to dad on the old Watch Tower.

"I should prefer a little more *reverence* in reading the Bible, Victoria," said grandmother. Jane had been reading an old Hebrew war tale as father would have read it, with a trumpet clang of victory in her voice. Grandmother looked at her vindictively. It was plain that reading the Bible was no longer a penance to Jane. She seemed positively to enjoy it. And what could grandmother do about it?

Jane had made a list of the months that must pass before her return to the Island on the back of her arithmetic notebook and smiled when she ticked off September.

She had felt very reluctant to go back to St. Agatha's. But in a short time she found herself saying one day in amazement, "I *like* going to school."

She had always felt vaguely left out . . . excluded . . . at St. Agatha's. Now, for some reason unknown to her, she no longer felt so. It was as if she had become a comrade and a leader overnight. The girls of her class looked up to her. The teachers began to wonder why they had never before suspected what a remarkable child Victoria Stuart was. Why, she was simply full of executive ability.

And her studies were no longer a tribulation. They had become a pleasure. She *wanted* to study as hard as she could, to catch up with dad. Dim ghosts of history . . . exquisite, unhappy queens . . . grim old tyrants . . . had become real . . . marked poems in the reader she and dad had read together were full of meaning for her . . . the ancient lands where they had roamed in fancy were places she knew and loved. It was so easy to learn about them. Jane brought home no more bad reports. Mother was delighted but grandmother did not seem overly pleased. She picked up a letter one day which Jane was writing to Polly Jimmy John, glanced over it, dropped it with disdain.

"Phlox is not spelled f-l-o-x, Victoria. But I suppose it does not matter to your haphazard friends how you spell."

Jane blushed. She knew perfectly well how to spell phlox but there was so much to tell Polly . . . to ask Polly . . . so many messages to send to the people in that far, dear Island by the sea . . . she just scribbled away furiously without thinking.

"Polly Garland is the best speller at Lantern Corners school," said Jane.

"Oh, I have no doubt . . . no doubt whatever . . . that she has all the backwoods virtues," said grandmother

Grandmother's sneers could not poison Jane's delight in the letters she got from the Island. They came as thick as autumn leaves in Vallambroso. Somebody at Lantern Hill or Hungry Cove or the Corners was always writing to Jane. The Snowbeams sent composite letters, dreadfully spelled and blotted, written paragraph about. They possessed the knack of writing the most amusing things, illustrated along the edges with surprisingly well-done thumbnail sketches by Shingle. Jane always wanted to shriek with laughter over the Snowbeam letters.

Elder Tommy had the mumps . . . fancy Elder Tommy with the mumps . . . Shingle had fancied it in a few side-splitting curves. . . . The tail-board of Big Donald's cart had come out when he was going up Little Donald's hill and all his turnips had rolled out and down the hill and was he mad! The pigs had got into the Corners graveyard; Min's ma was making a silk quilt . . . Jane immediately began saving patches for Min's ma's quilt . . . Ding-dong's dog had torn the whole seat out of Andy Pearson's second best trousers, the frost had killed all the dahlias, Step-a-yard was having boils, there had been a lovely lot of funerals this fall, old Mrs. Dougald MacKay had died and people who were at the funeral said she looked perfectly gorgeous, the Jimmy John's baby had laughed at last, the big tree on Big Donald's hill had blown down . . . Jane was sorry for that, she had loved that tree . . . "we miss you just awful, Jane" . . . "Oh Jane, we wish you could be here for Hallowe'en night."

Jane wished it too. If one could but fly in the darkness over rivers and mountains and forests to the Island for just that one night! What fun they would have running round putting turnip and pumpkin Jack-o'-lanterns on gateposts and perhaps helping to carry off somebody's gate.

"What are you laughing at, darling?" asked mother.

"A letter from home," said Jane thoughtlessly.

"Oh, Jane Victoria, isn't this your home?" cried mother piteously.

Jane was sorry she had spoken. But she had to be honest. Home! A little house looking seaward . . . a white gull . . . ships going up and down . . . spruce woods . . . misty barrens . . . salt air cold from leagues of gulf . . . quiet . . . silence. *That* was home . . . the only home she knew. But she hated to hurt mother. Jane had begun to feel curiously protective about mother . . . as if, somehow, she must be shielded and guarded. Oh, if she could only talk things over with her mother . . . tell her everything about dad . . . find out everything. What fun it would be to read those letters to mother! She did read them to Jody. Jody was as much interested in the Lantern Hill folks as Jane herself. She began sending messages to Polly and Shingle and Min.

The elms around 60 Gay turned a rusty yellow. Far away the red leaves would be falling from the maples . . . the autumn mists would be coming in from the sea. Jane opened her notebook and ticked off October.

November was a dark, dry, windy month. Jane scored a secret triumph over grandmother one week of it.

"Let me make the croquettes for lunch, Mary," she begged one day. Mary consented very sceptically, remembering that there was plenty of chicken salad in the refrigerator if the croquettes were ruined. They were not. They were everything croquettes should be. Nobody knew who had made them, but Jane had the fun of watching folks eat them. Grandmother took a second helping.

"Mary seems to have learned how to make croquettes properly at last," she said.

Jane wore a poppy on Armistice Day because dad was a D.S. She was hungry to hear about him but she would not ask her Island correspondents. They must not know she and dad did not exchange letters. But sometimes there was a bit about him in some of the letters . . . perhaps only a sentence or two. She lived for and by them. She got up in the night to reread the letters they were in. And every Saturday afternoon she shut herself up in her room and wrote him a letter which she sealed up and asked Mary to hide in her trunk. She would take them all to dad next summer and let him read them while she read his diary. She made a little ritual of dressing up to write to dad. It was delightful to be writing to him, while the wind howled outside, to father so far away and yet so near, telling him everything you had done that week, all the little intimate things you loved.

The first snow came one afternoon as she wrote, in flakes as large as butterflies. Would it be snowing on the Island? Jane hunted up the morning paper and looked to see what the weather report in the Maritimes was. Yes . . . cold, with showers of snow . . . clearing and cold at night. Jane shut her eyes and saw it. Great soft flakes falling over the grey landscape against the dark spruces . . . her little garden a thing of fairy beauty . . . egg flakes in the empty robin's nest she and Shingle knew of . . . the dark sea around the white land. "Clearing and cold at night." Frosty stars gleaming out in still frostier evening blue over quiet fields thinly white with snow. Would dad remember to let the Peters in?

Jane ticked off November.

30

CHRISTMAS had never meant a great deal to Jane. They always did the same things in the same way. There were neither tree nor stockings at 60 Gay and no morning celebration because grandmother so decreed. She said she liked a quiet forenoon and she always went to the service at St. Barnabas', though, for some queer reason of her own, she always wanted to go alone that day. Then they all went for lunch to Uncle William's or Uncle David's and there was a big family dinner at night at 60 Gay, with the presents on display. Jane always got a good many things she didn't want especially and one or two she did. Mother always seemed even a little gayer on Christmas than on any other day . . . too gay, as if, Jane in her new wisdom felt, she were afraid of remembering something if she stopped being gay for a moment.

But the Christmas season this year had a subtle meaning for Jane it had never possessed before. There was the concert at St. Agatha's for one thing, in which Jane was one of the star performers. She recited another *habitant* poem and did it capitally . . . because she was reciting to an audience of one a thousand miles away and didn't care a hoot for grandmother's scornful face and compressed lips. The last number was a tableau in which four girls represented the spirits of the four seasons kneeling around the Christmas spirit. Jane was the spirit of autumn, with maple leaves in her russet hair.

"Your granddaughter is going to be a very handsome girl," a lady told grandmother. "She doesn't resemble her lovely mother, of course, but there is something very striking about her face."

"Handsome is as handsome does," said grandmother in a tone which implied that, judged by that standard, Jane hadn't the remotest chance of good looks. But Jane didn't hear it and wouldn't have cared if she had. She knew what dad thought about her bones.

Jane could not send presents to the Island . . . she had no money to buy them. An allowance was something Jane had never had. So she wrote a special letter to all her friends instead. They sent her little gifts which gave her far more delight than the fine ones she got in Toronto.

Min's ma sent her a packet of summer savory.

"Nobody here cares for summer savory," said grandmother, meaning that she didn't. "We prefer sage."

"Mrs. Jimmy John always uses savory in her stuffing and so do Min's ma and Mrs. Big Donald," said Jane.

"Oh, no doubt we are sadly behind the times," said grandmother, and when Jane opened the packet of sprucegum Young John had sent her, grandmother said, "Well, well, so *ladies* chew gum nowadays. Other times, other manners."

She picked up the card Ding-dong had sent Jane. It had on it the picture of a blue and gold angel under which Ding-dong had written, "This looks like you."

"I have always heard," said grandmother, "that love is blind."

Grandmother certainly had the knack of making you feel ridiculous.

But even grandmother did not disdain the bundle of driftwood old Timothy Salt expressed up. She let Jane burn it in the fireplace on Christmas eve, and mother loved the blue and green and purple flames. Jane sat before it and dreamed. It was a very cold night . . . a night of frost and stars. Would it be as cold on the Island and would her geraniums freeze? Would there be a thick white fur on the windows at Lantern Hill? What kind of a Christmas would dad have? She knew he was going to Aunt Irene's for dinner. Aunt Irene had written Jane a note to accompany her gift of a very pretty knitted sweater and told her so. "With a few of his old friends," said Aunt Irene.

Would Lilian Morrow be among the old friends? Somehow Jane hoped not. There was always a queer little formless, nameless fear in her heart when she thought of Lilian Morrow and her caressing "'Drew."

Lantern Hill would be empty on Christmas. Jane resented that. Dad would take Happy with him and the poor Peters would be all alone.

Jane had one thrill on Christmas Day nobody knew anything about. They went to lunch at Uncle David's and there was a copy of *Saturday Evening* in the library. Jane pounced on it. Would there be anything of dad's in it? Yes, there was. Another front page article on *The Consequences of Confederation in Regard to the Maritime Provinces*. Jane was totally out of her depth in it, but she read every word of it with pride and delight.

Then came the cat.

31

THEY had had dinner at 60 Gay and were all in the big drawing room, which even with a fire blazing on the hearth still seemed cold and grim. Frank came in with a basket.

"It's come, Mrs. Kennedy," he said.

Grandmother took the basket from Frank and opened it. A magnificent white Persian cat was revealed, blinking pale green eyes disdainfully and distrustfully at everybody. Mary and Frank had discussed that cat in the kitchen.

"Whatever has the old dame got into her noddle now?" said Frank. "I thought she hated cats and wouldn't let Miss Victoria have one on any consideration. And here she's giving her one . . . and it costing seventy-five dollars. Seventy-five dollars for a cat!"

"Money's no object to her," said Mary. "And I'll tell you what's in her noddle. I haven't cooked for her for twenty years without learning to read her mind. Miss Victoria has a cat on that Island of hers. Her grandmother wants to cut that cat out. She isn't going to have Andrew Stuart letting Miss Victoria have cats when she isn't allowed to have them here. The old lady is at her wits' end how to wean Miss Victoria away from the Island and that's what this cat means. Thinks she . . . a real Persian, costing seventy-five dollars and looking like the King of All Cats, will soon put the child out of conceit with her miserable common kittens. Look at the presents she give Miss Victoria this Christmas. As if to say, 'You couldn't get anything like *that* from your father!' Oh, I'm knowing her. But she's met her match at last, or I'm mistaken. She can't overcrow Miss Victoria any longer and she's just beginning to find it out."

"This is a Christmas present for you, Victoria," said grandmother. "It should have been here last night but there was some delay . . . somebody was ill."

Everybody looked at Jane as if they expected her to go into spasms of delight.

"Thank you, grandmother," said Jane flatly.

She didn't like Persian cats. Aunt Minnie had one . . . pedigreed smoke-blue . . . and Jane had never liked it. Persian cats were so deceptive. They looked so fat and fluffy, and then when you picked them up, expecting to enjoy a good satisfying squeeze, there was nothing to them but bones. Anybody was welcome to their Persian cat for all of Jane.

"Its name is Snowball," said Grandmother.

So she couldn't even name her own cat. But grandmother expected her to like the cat and Jane went to work heroically in the following days trying to like it. The trouble was, the cat didn't want to be liked. No friendliness ever warmed the pale green fire of its eyes. It did not want to be petted or caressed. The Peters had been lapsters, with eyes of amber, and Jane from the first had been able to talk to them in their own language. But Snowball refused to understand a word she said.

"I thought . . . correct me if I'm wrong . . . that you professed to be fond of cats," said grandmother.

"Snowball doesn't like me," said Jane.

"Oh!" said grandmother. "Well, I suppose your taste in cats is on a par with your taste in friends. And I don't suppose there is very much that can be done about it."

"Darling, *couldn't* you like Snowball a little more?" pleaded mother, as soon as they were alone. "Just to please your grandmother. She thought you would be delighted. Can't you *pretend* to like it?"

Jane was not very good at pretending. She looked after Snowball faithfully, combed and brushed him every day, saw that he had the right kind of food and plenty of it, saw that he did not get out in the cold and take pneumonia . . . would not have cared in the least if he had. She liked pussies who went out boldly on their own mysterious errands and later appeared on the doorstep pleading to get in where there was a warm cushion and a drop of cream. Snowball took all her attention as a matter of course, paraded about 60 Gay, waving a plumy tail, and was rapturously adored by all callers.

"Poor Snowball," said grandmother ironically.

At this unlucky point Jane giggled. She couldn't help it. Snowball looked so little desirous of pity. Sitting on the arm of the chesterfield, he was monarch of all he surveyed and quite happy about it.

"I like a cat I can hug," said Jane. "A cat that likes to be hugged."

"You forget you are talking to *me*, not to Jody," said grandmother.

After three weeks Snowball disappeared. Luckily Jane was at St. Agatha's or grandmother might have suspected her of conniving at his disappearance. Everybody was away and Mary had left the front door open for a few moments. Snowball went out and apparently wandered into the fourth dimension. A lost-and-found ad had no results.

"He's been stole," said Frank. "That's what comes of having them expensive cats."

"It's not me that's sorry. He had to be more pampered than a baby," said Mary. "And I'm not of the opinion Miss Victoria will break her heart about it either. She's still hankering after her Peters . . . she's not one to change, and the old lady can put that in her pipe and smoke it."

Jane couldn't pretend any great grief and grandmother was very angry. She smouldered for days over it and Jane was uncomfortable. Perhaps she had been ungrateful . . . perhaps she hadn't tried hard enough to like Snowball. Anyhow, on the night the big white Persian suddenly materialised on the street corner, as she and mother were waiting for the Bloor car amid a swirl of snow, and wrapped itself around her legs in an apparent frenzy of recognition and hoarse meows, Jane yelped with genuine delight.

"Mummy . . . mummy . . . here's Snowball."

That she and mother should be standing alone on a street corner, waiting for a car on a blustery January night was an unprecedented thing. There had been doings at St. Agatha's that night . . . the Senior girls had put on a play and mother had been invited. Frank was laid up with influenza and they had to go with Mrs. Austen. Before the play was half through Mrs. Austen had been summoned home because of sudden illness in her family and mother had said, "Don't think of us for a moment. Jane and I can go home perfectly well on the streetcars."

Jane always loved a ride on a streetcar, and it was twice as much fun with mother. It was so seldom she and mother went anywhere alone. But when they did, mother was such a good companion. She saw the funny side of everything and her eyes laughed to Jane's when a joke popped its head up. Jane was sorry when they got off at Bloor, for that meant they were comparatively near home.

"Darling, how can this be Snowball?" exclaimed

mother. "It does look like him, I admit . . . but it's a mile from home. . . ."

"Frank always said he'd been stolen, mummy. It must be Snowball . . . a strange cat wouldn't make a fuss over me like this. . . ."

"I shouldn't have thought Snowball would either," laughed mother.

"I expect he's glad to see a friend," said Jane. "We don't know how he's been treated. He feels awfully thin. We must take him home."

"On the street car. . . ."

"We can't leave him here. I'll hold him . . . he'll be quiet."

Snowball was quiet for a few moments after they entered the car. There were not many people on it. Three boys at the far end sniggered as Jane sat down with her armful of cat. A pudgy child edged away from her in terror. A man with a pimply face scowled at her as if he were personally insulted by the sight of a Persian cat.

Suddenly Snowball seemed to go quite mad. He made one wild leap out of Jane's incautiously relaxed arms and went whizzing around the car, hurtling over the seats and hurling himself against the windows. Women shrieked. The pudgy child bounced up and screamed. The pimply-faced man's hat got knocked off by a wild Snowballian leap, and he swore. The conductor opened the door.

"Don't let the cat out," shrieked breathless, pursuing Jane. "Shut the door . . . shut it quick . . . it's my lost cat and I'm taking it home."

"You'd better keep hold of it then," said the conductor gruffly.

"Enough is as good as a feast," thought Snowball . . . evidently . . . for he allowed Jane to nab him. The boys all laughed insultingly as Jane walked back to her seat, looking neither to the right nor to the left. A button had burst off her slipper and she had stumbled and skinned her nose on the handle of a seat. But she was Jane victorious . . . as well as Victoria.

"Oh, darling . . . darling," said mother, in kinks of

laughter . . . real laughter. When had mother laughed like that? If grandmother saw her!

"That's a dangerous animal," said the pimply-faced man warningly.

Jane looked at the boys. They made irresistibly comic faces at her and she made faces back. She liked Snowball better than she ever had before. But she did not relax her grip on him until she heard the door of 60 Gay clang behind her.

"We've found Snowball, grandmother," cried Jane triumphantly. "We've brought him home."

She released the cat who stood looking squiffily about.

"*That* is not Snowball," said grandmother. "That is a female cat."

Judging from grandmother's tone it was evident that there was something very disgraceful about a female cat!

The owner of the female cat was eventually discovered through another lost-and-found and no more Persians appeared at 60 Gay. Jane had ticked off December, and January was speeding away. The Lantern Hill news was still absorbing. Everybody was skating . . . on the pond or on the little round, tree-shadowed pool beyond the Corners. . . . Shingle Snowbeam had been queen in a Christmas concert and had worn a crown of scalloped tin; the new minister's wife could play the organ; the Jimmy John baby had eaten all the blooms off Mrs. Jimmy John's Christmas cactus, every last one of them; Mrs. Little Donald had had her gobbler for Christmas dinner . . . Jane remembered that magnificent white gobbler with the coral-red wattles and accorded him a meed of regret; Uncle Tombstone had butchered Min's ma's pig and Min's ma had sent a roast to dad; Min's ma had got a new pig to bring up, a nice pink pig exactly like Elder Tommy; Mr. Spragg's dog at the Corners had bit the eye out of Mr. Loney's dog and Mr. Loney was going to law about it; Mrs. Angus Scatterby, whose husband had died in October, was disappointed over the result . . . "It's not so much fun being a widow as I expected," she was reported to have said; Sherwood Morton had gone into the choir and the managers had put a few more nails in the roof

. . . Jane suspected Step-a-yard of that joke; there was wonderful coasting on Big Donald's hill; her dad had got a new dog, a fat white dog named Bubbles; her geraniums were blooming beautiful . . . "and me too far away to see them," thought Jane with a pang; William MacAllister had had a fight with Thomas Crowder because Thomas told William he didn't like the whiskers William would have had if he had had whiskers; they had had a silver thaw. . . . Jane could see it . . . ice jewels . . . the maple wood a thing of unearthly splendour . . . every stalk sticking up from the crusted snow of the garden a spear of crystal; Step-a-yard was mudding . . . what on earth was mudding? . . . she must find out next summer; Mr. Snowbeam's pig-house roof had blown off . . . "if he'd nailed the ridge-pole firmly on last summer when I advised him to, this wouldn't have happened," thought Jane virtuously; Bob Woods had fallen on his dog and sprained his back . . . was it Bob's back or the dog's that was sprained? . . . Caraway Snowbeam had to have her tonsils out and was putting on such airs about it; Jabez Gibbs had set a trap for a skunk and caught his own cat; Uncle Tombstone had given all his friends an oyster supper; some said Mrs. Alec Carson at the Corners had a new baby, some said she hadn't.

What had 60 Gay to offer against the colour and flavour of news like that? Jane ticked January off.

February was stormy. Jane spent many a blustery evening, while the wind howled up and down Gay Street, poring over seed catalogues, picking out things for dad to plant in the spring. She loved to read the description of the vegetables and imagine she saw rows of them at Lantern Hill. She copied down all Mary's best recipes to make them for dad next summer . . . dad who was likely at this very moment to be sitting cosily by their own fireside with two happy dogs curled up at his feet and outside a wild white night of drifting snow. Jane ticked off February.

32

WHEN Jane ticked off March she whispered "Just two and a half months more." Life went on outwardly the same at 60 Gay and St. Agatha's. Easter came and Aunt Gertrude, who had refused sugar in her tea all through Lent, took it again. Grandmother was buying the loveliest spring clothes for mother, who seemed rather indifferent to them. And Jane was beginning to hear her Island calling to her in the night.

On a wild, wet morning in late April the letter came. Jane, who had been watching for it for weeks and was beginning to feel a bit worried, carried it in to mother with the face of

"One to whom glad news is sent
"From the far country of his home after long banishment."

Mother was pale as she took it and grandmother was suddenly flushed.

"Another letter from Andrew Stuart?" said grandmother, as if the name blistered her lips.

"Yes," said mother faintly. "He . . . he says Jane Victoria must go back to him for the summer . . . *if she wants to go*. She is to make her own choice."

"Then," said grandmother, "she will not go."

"Of course you won't go, darling?"

"Not go! But I must go! I promised I'd go back," cried Jane.

"Your . . . your father will not hold you to that promise. He says expressly that you can choose as you please."

"I *want* to go back," said Jane. "I'm going back."

"Darling," said mother imploringly, "don't go. You

grew away from me last summer. If you go again I'll lose more of you. . . ."

Jane looked down at the carpet and her lips set in a line that had an odd resemblance to grandmother's.

Grandmother took the letter from mother, glanced at it, and looked at Jane.

"Victoria," she said, quite pleasantly for her, "I think you have not given the matter sufficient thought. I say nothing for myself . . . I have never expected gratitude . . . but your mother's wishes ought to carry some weight with you. Victoria . . ." grandmother's voice grew sharper . . . "please do me the courtesy of looking at me while I am speaking to you."

Jane looked at grandmother . . . looked her straight in the eyes, unquailingly, unyieldingly. Grandmother seemed to put a certain unusual restraint on herself. She still spoke pleasantly.

"I have not mentioned this before, Victoria, but I decided some time ago that I would take you and your mother for a trip to England this summer. We will spend July and August there. You will enjoy it, I know. I think that, between a summer in England and a summer in a hut in a country settlement on Prince Edward Island, even you could hardly hesitate."

Jane did not hesitate. "Thank you, grandmother. It is very kind of you to offer me such a lovely trip. I hope you and mother will enjoy it. But I would rather go to the Island."

Even Mrs. Robert Kennedy knew when she was beaten. But she could not accept defeat gracefully.

"You get that stubborn will of yours from your father," she said, her face twisted with anger. For the moment she looked simply like a very shrewish old spitfire. "You grow more like him every day of your life . . . you've got his very chin."

Jane was thankful she had got a will from someone. She was glad she looked like dad . . . glad her chin was like his. But she wished mother were not crying.

"Don't waste your tears, Robin," said grandmother,

turning scornfully from Jane. "It's the Stuart coming out in her . . . you could expect nothing else. If she prefers her trumpery friends down there to you, there is nothing you can do about it. *I* have said all I intend to say on the matter."

Mother stood up and dabbed her tears away with a cobwebby handkerchief.

"Very well, dear," she said brightly and hardly. "You have made your choice. I agree with your grandmother that there is nothing more to be said."

She went out, leaving Jane with a heart that was almost breaking. Never in her life had mother spoken to her in that hard, brittle tone. She felt as if she had been suddenly pushed far, far away from her. But she did not regret her choice. She had *no* choice really. She *had* to go back to dad. If it came to choosing between him and mother . . . Jane rushed to her room, flung herself down on the big white bearskin, and writhed in a tearless agony no child should ever have to suffer.

It was a week before Jane was herself again, although mother, after that bitter little outburst, had been as sweet and loving as ever. When she had come in to say good-night she had held Jane very tightly and silently.

Jane hugged her mother closer to her.

"I have to go, mother . . . I have to go . . . but I *do* love you. . . ."

"Oh, Jane, I hope you do . . . but sometimes you seem so far away from me that you might as well be beyond Sirius. Don't . . . don't let anyone ever come between us. That is all I ask."

"No one can . . . no one wants to, mother."

In one way, it occurred to Jane, that was not strictly true. She had known for a long while that grandmother would like very well to come between them if she could only bring it about. But Jane also knew that by "no one" mother meant dad, and so her answer *was* true.

There was a letter from Polly Garland the last day of April . . . a jubilant Polly.

"We're all so glad you're coming back this summer,

162

Jane. Oh, Jane, I wish you could see the pussy willows in our swamp."

Jane wished so too. And there were other fascinating bits of news in Polly's letter. Min's ma's cow was worn out and Min's ma was going to get a new one. Polly had a hen setting on nine eggs . . . Jane could see nine real live wee baby chicks running round. Well, father had promised her some hens this summer . . . Step-a-yard had told Polly to tell her it was a great spring and even the roosters were laying; the baby had been christened William Charles and was toddling round everywhere and getting thin; Big Donald's dog had been poisoned, had had six convulsions, but had recovered.

"Only six more weeks." It was weeks now where it had been months. Down home the robins would be strutting round Lantern Hill and the mists would be coming in from the sea. Jane ticked off April.

33

IT was the last week in May that Jane saw the house. Mother had gone one evening to visit a friend who had just moved into a new house in the new Lakeside development on the banks of the Humber. She took Jane with her, and it was a revelation to Jane, whose only goings and comings had been so circumscribed that she had never dreamed there were such lovely places in Toronto. Why, it was just like a pretty country village out here . . . hills and ravines with ferns and wild columbines growing in them and rivers and trees . . . the green fire of willows, the great clouds of oaks, the plumes of pines and, not far away, the blue mist that was Lake Ontario.

Mrs. Townley lived on a street called Lakeside Gardens, and she showed them proudly over her new house. It was so big and splendid that Jane did not feel very much interested in it, and after a while she slipped away in the dusk to explore the street itself, leaving mother and Mrs. Townley talking cupboards and bathrooms.

Jane decided that she liked Lakeside Gardens. She liked it because it twisted and curved. It was a friendly street. The houses did not look at each other with their noses in the air. Even the big ones were not snooty. They sat among their gardens, with spireas afoam around them and tulips and daffodils all about their toes, and said, "We have lots of room . . . we don't have to push with our elbows . . . we can afford to be gracious."

Jane looked them over carefully as she went by but it was not until she was nearly at the end of the street, where it turned into a road winding down to the lake, that she saw *her* house. She had *liked* a great many of the houses she had passed, but when she saw this house she knew at first sight that it belonged to her . . . just as Lantern Hill did.

It was a small house for Lakeside Gardens but a great deal bigger than Lantern Hill. It was built of grey stone and had casement windows . . . some of them beautifully unexpected . . . and a roof of shingles stained a very dark brown. It was built right on the edge of the ravine overlooking the tree tops, with five great pines just behind it.

"What a darling place!" breathed Jane.

It was a new house: it had just been built and there was a For Sale sign on the lawn. Jane went all around it and peered through every diamond-paned window. There was a living room that would really *live* when it was furnished, a dining room with a door that opened into a sun room, and the most delightful breakfast nook in pale yellow, with built-in china closets. It should have chairs and table of yellow too, and curtains at the recessed window between gold and green that would look like sunshine on the darkest day. Yes, this house belonged to her . . . she could see herself in it, hanging curtains, polishing the glass doors, making cookies in the kitchen. She hated the For Sale sign. To think that somebody would be buying that house . . . *her* house . . . was torture.

She prowled round and round it. At the back the ground was terraced right down to the floor of the ravine. There was a rock garden and a group of forsythia bushes that must have been fountains of pale gold in early spring. Three flights of stone steps went down the terraces, with the delicacy of birch shadows about them, and off to one side was a wild garden of slender young Lombardies. A robin winked at her; a nice chubby cat came over from the neighbouring rock garden. Jane tried to catch him, but . . . "Excuse me. This is my busy day," said the cat and pattered down the stone steps.

Jane finally sat down on the front steps and gave herself up to a secret joy. There was a gap in the trees on the opposite side of the street through which a far, purple-grey hill showed. There were misty, pale green woods over the river. The woods all around Lantern Hill would be misty green too. The banners of a city of night were being flaunted in the sunset sky behind the pines further down. The gulls soared whitely up the river.

It grew darker. Lights bloomed out in the houses. Jane always felt the fascination of lighted houses in the night. There *should* be a light in the house behind her. *She* should be turning on the lights in it. She should be living here. She could be happy here. She could be friends with the wind and the rain here: she could love the lake even if it did not have the sparkle and boom of gulf seas; she could put out nuts for the saucy squirrels and hang up birdhouses for the feathered folk and feed the pheasants Mrs. Townley said lived in the ravine.

Suddenly there was a slim, golden new moon over the oaks and the world was still . . . almost as still as Queen's Shore on a calm summer night and there was a sparkling of lights along the lake drive like a necklace of gems on some dark beauty's breast.

"Where were you all the evening, darling?" asked mother as they drove home.

"Picking out a house to buy," said Jane dreamily. "I wish we lived here instead of at 60 Gay, mummy."

Mother was silent for a moment.

"You don't like 60 Gay very well, do you, dearest?"

"No," said Jane. And then, to her own amazement, added, "Do you?"

She was still more amazed when mother said, quickly and vehemently, "I hate it!"

That night Jane ticked off May. Only ten days more. It was days now where it had been weeks. Oh, suppose she took ill and couldn't go! But no! God wouldn't . . . couldn't!

34

GRANDMOTHER coldly told mother to buy what clothes . . . *if any* . . . were necessary for Jane. Jane and mother had a happy afternoon's shopping. Jane picked her own things . . . things that would suit Lantern Hill and an Island summer. Mother insisted on some smart little knitted sweaters and one pretty dress of rose-pink organdy with delicious frills. Jane didn't know where she would ever wear it . . . it was too ornate for the little south church, but she let mother buy it to please her. And mother got her the niftiest little green bathing suit.

"Just think," reflected Jane happily, "in a week I'll be on Queen's Shore. I hope the water won't be too cold for swimming. . . ."

"*We* may be going to the Island in August," said Phyllis. "Dad says he hasn't been down for so long he'd like to spend another vacation there. If we do, we'll be stopping at the Harbour Head Hotel and it isn't very far from there to Queen's Shore. So we'll likely see you."

Jane didn't know whether she liked this idea or not. She didn't want Phyllis there, patronising the Island . . .

looking down her nose at Lantern Hill and the boot-shelf and the Snowbeams.

Jane went to the Maritimes with the Randolphs this year and they left on the morning train instead of the night. It was a dull, cloudy day, but Jane was so happy she positively radiated happiness around her like sunshine. Mrs. Randolph's opinion of Jane was the very opposite of what Mrs. Stanley's had been. Mrs. Randolph thought she had never met a more charming child, interested in everything, finding beauty everywhere, even in those interminable stretches of pulpwood lands and lumber forests in New Brunswick. Jane studied the timetable and hailed each station as a friend, especially the ones with quaint, delightful names . . . Red Pine, Bartibog, Memramcook. And then Sackville where they left the main line and got on the little branch train to Cape Tormentine. How sorry Jane felt for any one who was not going to the Island!

Cape Tormentine . . . the car ferry . . . watching for the red cliffs of the Island . . . there they were . . . she had really forgotten *how* red they were . . . and beyond them misty green hills. It was raining again, but who cared? Everything the Island did was right. If it wanted to rain . . . why, rain was Jane's choice.

Having left Toronto on the morning train, they were in Charlottetown by mid-afternoon. Jane saw dad the moment she stepped off the train . . . grinning and saying, "Excuse me, but your face seems familiar. Are you by any chance . . ." but Jane had hurled herself at him. They had never been parted . . . she had never been away at all. The world was real again. She was Jane again. Oh, dad, dad!

She had been afraid Aunt Irene would be there too . . . possibly Miss Lilian Morrow as well. But Aunt Irene, it transpired, was away on a visit to Boston and had taken Miss Morrow with her. Jane secretly hoped that Aunt Irene would be having such a fine time in Boston that she wouldn't be able to tear herself away for a long time.

"And the car has turned temperamental again," said dad. "I had to leave it in the garage at the Corners and borrow Step-a-yard's horse and buggy. You don't mind?"

Mind? Jane was delighted. She wanted that drive to Lantern Hill to be so slow that she could drink the road in as she drove along. And she liked to be behind a horse. You could talk to a horse as you never could to a car. The fact was, if dad had said they had to walk to Lantern Hill it wouldn't have mattered to Jane.

Dad put lean, strong hands under her arms and swung her up to the buggy seat.

"Let's just go on from where we left off. You've grown since last summer, my Jane."

"An inch," said Jane proudly.

It had stopped raining. The sun was coming out. Beyond, the white wave crests on the harbour were laughing at her . . . waving their hands at her.

"Let's go uptown and buy our house some presents, Jane."

"A double-boiler that won't leak, dad. Bootles always did, a little. And a potato-ricer . . . can we get a potato-ricer, dad?"

Dad thought the budget would stretch to a potato-ricer.

It was delightful, all of it. But Jane sparkled when they had left town behind them, going home to all the things they loved.

"Drive slow, dad. I don't want to miss *anything* on the road."

She was feasting her eyes on everything . . . spruce-clad hills, bits of gardens full of unsung beauty tucked away here and there, glimpses of sparkling sea, blue rivers . . . had those rivers really been so blue last summer? It had been an early spring and all the blossom show was over. Jane was sorry for that. She wondered if she would ever be able to get to the Island in time to see the Titus ladies' famous cherry walk in its spring-blow.

They called for a moment to see Mrs. Meade, who kissed Jane and was sorry Mr. Meade couldn't come out to see her, because he was in bed with an abyss in his ear. She gave them a packet of ham sandwiches and cheese to stay their stomachs if they were hungry on the road.

They heard the ocean before they saw it. Jane loved the sound. It was as if the spirit of the sea called to her. And then the first snuff of salt in the air . . . there was one particular hill where they always got the first tang. And from that same hill they caught their first faraway glimpse of Lantern Hill. It was wonderful to be able to see your own home so far off . . . to feel that every step the horse took was bringing you nearer to it.

From there on Jane was on her own stamping ground. It was so exciting to recognise all the spots along the road . . . green wood lanes, old beloved farms that held out their arms to her. The single row of spruces was still marching up Little Donald's hill. The dunes . . . and the fishing-boats sailing in . . . and the little blue pond laughing at her . . . and Lantern Hill. Home after exile!

Somebody . . . Jane discovered later that it was the Snowbeams . . . had made "Welcome" with white stones in the walk. Happy was waiting for them in the yard and nearly ate Jane alive. Bubbles, the new fat white dog, sat apart and looked at her, but he was so cute that Jane forgave him on the spot for being Bubbles.

The first thing was to visit every room, and every room welcomed her back. Nothing was changed. She looked the house over to make sure nothing was missing. The little bronze soldier was still riding on his bronze horse and the green cat kept watch and ward over dad's desk. But the silver needed polishing and the geraniums needed pruning and *when* had the kitchen floor been scrubbed?

She had been away from Lantern Hill for nine months, but now it seemed to her that she had never been away at all. She had really been living here all along. It was her spirit's home.

There was a bunch of little surprises . . . nice surprises. They had six hens . . . there was a small hen-house built below the garden . . . there was a peaked porch roof built over the glass-paned door . . . and dad had got the telephone in.

First Peter was sitting on the doorstone when Jane came downstairs, with a big mouse in his mouth, very proud of his prowess as a hunter. Jane pounced on him, mouse and all, and then looked around for Second Peter. Where was Second Peter?

Dad put his arm closely around Jane.

"Second Peter died last week, Jane. I don't know what happened to him . . . he got sick. I had the vet for him but he could do nothing."

Jane felt a stinging in her eyes. She would not cry, but she choked.

"I . . . I . . . didn't think anything I loved could die," she whispered into dad's shoulder.

"Ah, Jane, love can't fence out death. He had a happy life, if a short one . . . and we buried him in the garden. Come out and see the garden, Jane . . . it burst into bloom as soon as it heard you were coming."

A wind ran through the garden as they entered it and it looked as if every flower and shrub were nodding a head or waving a hand at them. Dad had a corner where vegetables were all up in neat little rows and there were new beds of annuals.

"Miranda got what you wanted from the seedsman . . . I think you'll find everything, even the scabiosa. What do you want with scabiosa, Jane? It's an abominable name . . . sounds like a disease."

"Oh, the flowers are pretty, dad. And there are so many nicer names for them . . . Lady's pincushion and Mourning Bride. Aren't the pansies lovely? I'm so glad I sowed them last August."

"You look like a pansy yourself, Jane . . . that red-brown one there with the golden eyes."

Jane remembered she had wondered if anyone would ever compare her to a flower. In spite of the little pile of shore stones under the lilac . . . which Young John had piled over the grave of Second Peter . . . she was happy. Everything was so lovely. Even Mrs. Big Donald's washing, streaming gallantly out against the blue sky on her hilltop, was charming. And away down by the Watch Tower the surf was breaking on the sand. Jane wanted to be out in that turmoil and smother of the waves. But that must wait till morning. Just now there was supper to be gotten.

"How jolly to be in a kitchen again," thought Jane, girding on an apron.

"I'm glad my cook is back," said dad. "I've practically lived on salt codfish all winter. It was the easiest thing to cook. But I don't deny the neighbours helped the commissariat out. And they've sent in no end of things for our supper."

Jane had found the pantry full of them. A cold chicken from the Jimmy Johns, a pat of butter from Mrs. Big Donald, a jug of cream from Mrs. Little Donald, some cheese from Mrs. Snowbeam, some rose-red early radishes from Min's ma, a pie from Mrs. Bell.

"She said she knew you could make as good pies as she can but she thought it would fill in till you'd have time to make some. There's a goodish bit of jam left yet and practically all the pickles."

Jane and dad talked as they ate supper. They had a whole winter of talk to catch up with. Had he missed her? Well, *had* he now? What did she think? They regarded each other with great content. Jane saw the new moon, over her right shoulder, through the open door. And dad got up and started the ship clock. Time had begun once more.

Jane's friends, having considerately let her have her first rapture over, came to see her in the evening . . . the brown, rosy Jimmy Johns and the Snowbeams and Min and Ding-dong. They were all glad to see her. Queen's Shore had kept her in its heart. It was wonderful to be *somebody* again . . . wonderful to be able to laugh all you wanted to without anyone resenting it . . . wonderful to be among happy people again. All at once Jane realised that nobody was happy at 60 Gay . . . except, perhaps, Mary and Frank. Grandmother wasn't . . . Aunt Gertrude wasn't . . . mother wasn't.

Step-a-yard whispered to her that he had brought over a wheelbarrow-load of sheep manure for her garden. "You'll find it by the gate . . . nothing like well-rotted sheep manure for a garden." Ding-dong had brought her a kitten to replace Second Peter . . . a scrap about as big as its mother's paw, but which was destined to be a magnificent cat in black with four white paws. Jane and dad tried out all kinds of names on it before they went to bed and finally agreed on Silver Penny because of the round white spot between its ears.

To go to her own dear room where a young birch was fairly poking an arm in through the window from the steep hillside . . . to hear the sound of the sea in the night . . . to waken in the morning and think she would be with dad all day! Jane sang the song of the morning stars as she dressed and got breakfast.

The first thing Jane did after breakfast was to run with the wind to the shore and take a wild exultant dip in the stormy waves. She fairly flung herself into the arms of the sea.

And what a forenoon it was, polishing silver and window-panes. Nothing had changed really, though there were surface changes. Step-a-yard had grown a beard because of throat trouble . . . Big Donald had repainted his house . . . the calves of last summer had grown up . . . Little Donald was letting his hill pasture go spruce. It was good to be home.

"Timothy Salt is going to take me codfishing next Saturday, dad."

35

UNCLE David and Aunt Sylvia and Phyllis came in July to the Harbour Head Hotel but could stay only a week. They brought Phyllis over to Lantern Hill late one afternoon and left her there while they went to visit friends in town.

"We'll come back for her around nine," said Aunt Sylvia, looking in horror at Jane, who had just got back from Queen's Creek, where she had been writing a love letter for Joe Gautier to his lady friend in Boston. Evidently there was nothing Jane was afraid to tackle. She was still wearing the khaki overalls she had worn while driving loads of hay into the Jimmy John barn all the forenoon. The overalls were old and faded and were not improved by a huge splash of green paint on a certain portion of Jane's anatomy. Jane had painted the old garden seat green one day and sat down on it before it was dry.

Dad was away so there was nothing to take the edge off Phyllis, who was more patronising than ever.

"Your garden is *quite* nice," she said.

Jane made a sound remarkably like a snort. Quite nice! When everybody admitted that it was the prettiest garden in the Queen's Shore district, except the Titus ladies'. Couldn't Phyllis see the wonder of those gorgeous splashes of nasturtiums, than which there was nothing finer in the county? Didn't she realise that those tiny red beets and cunning gold carrots were two weeks ahead of anybody else's for miles around? Could she possibly be in ignorance of the fact that Jane's pink peonies, fertilised so richly by Step-a-yard's sheep manure, were the talk of the community? But Jane was a bit ruffled that day anyhow. Aunt Irene and Miss Morrow had been up the day before, having returned from Boston, and Aunt Irene as usual had been sweet and condescending, and as usual had rubbed Jane the wrong way.

"I'm so glad your father put the telephone in for you . . . I hoped he would after the little hint I gave him."

"I never wanted a telephone," said Jane, rather sulkily.

"Oh, but, darling, you should have one, when you're so much alone here. If anything happened . . ."

"What could happen here, Aunt Irene?"

"The house might take fire. . . ."

"It took fire last year and I put it out."

"Or you might take cramps in swimming. I've never thought it . . ."

"But if I did I could hardly phone from there," said Jane.

"Or if tramps came . . ."

"There's been only one tramp here this summer and Happy bit a piece out of his leg. I was very sorry for the poor man. . . . I put iodine on the bite and gave him his dinner."

"Darling, you *will* have the last word, won't you? So like your Grandmother Kennedy."

Jane didn't like to be told she was like her Grandmother Kennedy. Still less did she like the fact that, after supper, dad and Miss Morrow had gone off by themselves for a walk to the shore. Aunt Irene looked after them speculatively.

"They have so much in common . . . it *is* a pity. . . ."

Jane wouldn't ask what was a pity. But she lay awake for a long time that night and had not quite recovered her poise when Phyllis came, condescending to her garden. But a hostess has certain obligations and Jane was not going to let Lantern Hill down, even if she did make sundry faces at her pots and pans. The supper she got up for Phyllis made that damsel open her eyes.

"Victoria . . . you didn't cook all these things yourself!"

"Of course. It's easy as wink."

Some of the Jimmy Johns and Snowbeams turned up after supper and Phyllis, whose complacency had been somewhat jarred by that supper, was really quite decent to them. They all went to the shore for a dip, but Phyllis was scared of the tumbling waves and would only sit on the sand and let them break over her while the others frolicked like mermaids.

"I didn't know you could swim like that, Victoria."

"You ought to see me when the water is calm," said Jane.

Still, Jane was rather relieved when it was time for Uncle David and Aunt Sylvia to come for Phyllis. Then the telephone rang and Uncle David was calling from town to say they were delayed by car trouble and wouldn't likely be able to come till late, so could the Lantern Hill folks see that Phyllis got to the hotel? Oh, yes, yes, indeed, Jane assured them.

"Dad can't be back till midnight, so we'll have to walk," she told Phyllis. "I'll go with you. . . ."

"But it's four miles to the Harbour Head," gasped Phyllis.

"Only two by the short cut across the fields. I know it well."

"But it's dark."

"Well, you're not afraid of the dark, are you?"

Phyllis did not say whether she was afraid of the dark or not. She looked at Jane's overalls.

"Are you going in *them*?"

"No, I only wear these around home," explained Jane patiently. "I was driving in hay all the forenoon. Mr. Jimmy John was away and Punch had a sore foot. I'll change in a jiffy and we'll start."

Jane slipped into a skirt and one of her pretty sweaters and fluffed a comb through her russet hair. People were beginning to look twice at Jane's hair. Phyllis looked more than twice at it. It was really wonderful hair. What had come over Victoria anyhow . . . Victoria whom she used to think so dumb? This tall, arms-and-legs girl, who somehow had ceased to be awkward in spite of arms and legs, was certainly not dumb. Phyllis gave a small sigh; and in that sigh, though neither of them was conscious of it, their former positions were totally reversed. Phyllis, instead of looking down on Jane, looked up to her.

The cool evening air was heavy with dew when they started. The winds were folded among the shadowy glens. The spice ferns were fragrant in the corners of the upland pastures. It was so calm and still you could hear all kinds of far-away sounds . . . a cart rattling down Old Man Cooper's Hill . . . muted laughter from Hungry Cove . . . an owl on Big Donald's hill calling to an owl on Little Donald's hill. But it got darker and darker. Phyllis drew close to Jane.

"Oh, Victoria, isn't this the darkest night that ever was!"

"Not so very. I've been out when it was darker."

Jane was not in the least scared, and Phyllis was much impressed. Jane felt that she was impressed . . . Jane knew she was scared . . . Jane began to like Phyllis.

They had to climb a fence and Phyllis fell over it, tore her dress and skinned her knee. So Phyllis couldn't even climb a fence, thought Jane . . . but thought it kindly, protectively.

"Oh, what's that?" Phyllis clutched Jane.

"That? Only cows."

"Oh, Victoria, I'm so scared of cows. I can't pass them . . . I *can't* . . . suppose they think . . ."

"Who cares what a cow thinks?" said Jane superbly. She had forgotten that *she* had once been fussy about cows and their opinion of her.

And Phyllis was crying. From that moment Jane lost every shred of her dislike of Phyllis. Phyllis, patronising and perfect in Toronto, was very different from a terrified Phyllis in a back pasture on an Island hill.

Jane put her arm around her. "Come on, honey. The cows won't even look at you. Little Donald's cows are all friends of mine. And then it's just a walk through that bit of woods and we'll be at the hotel."

"Will you . . . walk between me . . . and the cows?" sobbed Phyllis.

Phyllis, holding tightly to Jane, was safely convoyed past the cows. The little wood lane that followed was terribly dark but it was short, and at its end were the lights of the hotel.

"You're all right now. I won't go in," said Jane. "I must hurry home to get some supper ready for father. I always like to be there when he comes home."

"Victoria! Are you going back *alone*?"

"Of course. How else would I go?"

"If you'd wait . . . father would drive you home when he comes. . . ."

Jane laughed.

"I'll be at Lantern Hill in half an hour. And I love walking."

"Victoria, you're the very bravest girl I ever saw in my

life," said Phyllis earnestly. There wasn't a trace of patronage in her tone. There was never to be again.

Jane had a good time with herself on the walk back. The dear night brooded over her. Little wings were folded in nest homes, but there was wild life astir. She heard the distant bark of a fox . . . the sound of tiny feet in the fern . . . she saw the pale glimmer of night moths and took friendly counsel with the stars. Almost they sang, as if one star called to another in infinite harmony. Jane knew them all. Dad had given her lessons in astronomy all summer, having discovered that the only constellation she knew was the Big Dipper.

"This won't do, my Jane. You must know the stars. Not that I blame you for not being well acquainted with them. Humanity in its great lighted cities is shut out from the stars. And even the country folk are too used to them to realise their wonder. Emerson says something somewhere about how marvellous a spectacle we should deem them if we saw them only once in a thousand years."

So, with dad's field-glasses, they went star hunting on moonless nights, and Jane became learned in lore of far-off suns.

"What star shall we visit tonight, Janelet? Antares . . . Fomalhaut . . . Sirius?"

Jane loved it. It was so wonderful to sit out on the hills with dad in the dark and the beautiful *aloneness* while the great worlds swung above them in their appointed courses. Polaris, Arcturus, Vega, Capella, Altair . . . she knew them all. She knew where to look for Cassiopeia enthroned on her jewelled chair, for the Milk Dipper upside down in the clear southwest, for the great Eagle flying endlessly across the Milky Way, for the golden sickle that reaped some harvest of heaven.

"Watch the stars whenever you are worried, Jane," said dad. "They'll steady you . . . comfort you . . . balance you. I think if *I* had watched them . . . years ago . . . but I learned their lesson too late."

36

"AUNT Elmira is dying again," said Ding-dong cheerfully.

Jane was helping Ding-dong shingle his father's small barn. Doing it very well too, and getting no end of a kick out of it. It was such fun to be away up in the air where you could see over the whole countryside under its gay and windy clouds, and keep easy tabs on what your neighbours were doing.

"Is she very bad this time?" asked Jane, hammering diligently.

Jane knew all about Aunt Elmira and her dying spells. She took one every once in so long and it had really become a nuisance. Aunt Elmira picked such inconvenient times for dying. Always when something special was in the offing, Aunt Elmira decided to die and sometimes seemed so narrowly to escape doing it that the Bells held their breaths. Because Aunt Elmira did really have a heart condition that was not to be depended on, and who knew but that sometime she really would die?

"And the Bells don't want her to die," Step-a-yard had told Jane. "They need her board . . . her annuity dies with her. Besides, she's handy to look after things when the Bells want to go gadding. And I won't say but they're real fond of her too. Elmira is a good old scout when she isn't dying."

Jane knew that. She and Aunt Elmira were excellent friends. But Jane had never seen her when she was dying. She was too weak to see people then, she averred, and the Bells were afraid to risk it. Jane, with her usual shattering insight, had her own opinion about these spells of Aunt Elmira's. She could not have expressed it in terms of psychology, but she once told dad that Aunt Elmira was just trying to get square with something and didn't know it. She felt rather than knew that Aunt Elmira liked pretty well to be in the limelight and, as she grew older, resented more and more the fact that she was gently but inexorably being elbowed out of it. Near dying was one way of regaining the centre of the stage for a time at least. Not that Aunt Elmira was a conscious pretender. She always honestly thought she was dying, and very melancholy she was about it. Aunt Elmira was not at all willing to give up the fascinating business of living.

"Awful," said Ding-dong. "Mother says she's worse than she's ever seen her. Dr. Abbott says she's lost the will to live. Do you know what that means?"

"Sort of," admitted Jane cautiously.

"We try to keep her cheered up but she's awful blue. She won't eat and she doesn't want to take her medicine and ma's at her wit's end. We had everything planned for Brenda's wedding and now we don't know what to do."

"She hasn't died so often before," comforted Jane.

"But she's stayed in bed for weeks and weeks and said every day would be her last. Aunt Elmira," said Ding-dong reflectively, "has bid me a last good-bye seven times. Now, how can folks have a big wedding if their aunt is dying? And Brenda wants a splash. She's marrying into the Keyes and she says the Keyes expect it."

Mrs. Bell asked Jane to have dinner with them, and Jane stayed because dad was away for the day. She watched Brenda arrange a tray for Aunt Elmira.

"I'm afraid she won't eat a bit of it," said Mrs. Bell anxiously. She was a tired-looking, pleasant-faced woman with kind, faded eyes, who worried a great deal over everything. "I don't know what she lives on. And she's so low in her spirits. That goes with the attacks, of course. She says she's too tired to make any effort to get better, poor thing. It's her heart, you know. We all try to keep her cheered up and never tell her anything to worry her. Brenda, mind you don't tell her the white cow choked to death this morning. And if she asks what the doctor said last night, tell her he thinks she's going to be all right soon. My father always said we should never tell sick people anything but the truth, but we *must* keep Aunt Elmira cheered up."

Jane did not join Ding-dong as soon as dinner was over. She hung about mysteriously till Brenda had come downstairs, reporting that Aunt Elmira couldn't touch a mouthful, and had taken her mother out to settle some question about the amount of wool to be sent to the carding mill. Then Jane sped upstairs.

Aunt Elmira was lying in bed, a tiny, shrunken creature with elf-locks of grey hair straggling about her wrinkled face. Her tray was on the table, untouched.

"If it isn't Jane Stuart!" said Aunt Elmira in a faint voice. "I'm glad someone hasn't forgotten me. So you've come to see the last of me, Jane?"

Jane did not contradict her. She sat down on a chair and looked very sadly at Aunt Elmira, who waved a clawlike hand at her tray.

"I haven't a speck of appetite, Jane. And it's just as well . . . ah me, it's just as well. I feel they begrudge me every bite I eat."

"Well," said Jane, "you know times are hard and prices low."

Aunt Elmira hadn't quite expected this. A spark came into her queer little amber eyes.

"I'm paying my board," she said, "and I earned my keep years before I started doing that. Ah well, I'm of no consequence to them now, Jane. We're not, after we get ill."

"No, I suppose not," agreed Jane.

"Oh, I know too well I'm a burden to everyone. But it won't be for long, Jane, it won't be for long. The hand of death is on me, Jane. I realise that if nobody else does."

"Oh, I think they do," said Jane. "They're in a hurry to get the barn shingled before the funeral."

The spark in Aunt Elmira's eyes deepened.

"I s'pose they've got it all planned out, have they?" she said.

"Well, I did hear Mr. Bell saying something about where he would dig the grave. But maybe he meant the white cow's. I think it *was* the cow's. It choked to death this morning, you know. And he said he must have the south gate painted white before . . . something . . . but I didn't just catch what."

"White? The idea! The gate has always been red. Well, why should I worry? I'm done with it all. You don't worry over things when you're listening for the footfall of death, Jane. Shingling the barn, are they? I thought I heard hammering. That barn didn't need shingling. But Silas was always extravagant when there's no one to check him up."

"It's only the shingles that cost. The work won't cost anything. Ding-dong and I are doing it."

"I s'pose that's why you've got your overalls on. Time was I couldn't abide a girl in overalls. But what does it matter now? Only you shouldn't go barefoot, Jane. You might get a rusty nail in your foot."

"It's easier getting round the roof with no shoes. And little Sid got a rusty nail in his foot yesterday although he had shoes on."

"They never told me! I daresay they'll let that child have blood-poisoning when I'm not round to look after him. He's my favourite too. Ah, well it won't be long now . . . they know where I want to be buried . . . but they might have waited till I was dead to talk of grave-digging."

"Oh, I'm sure it *was* the cow," said Jane. "And I'm sure they'll give you a lovely funeral. I think dad would write a beautiful obituary for you if I asked him."

"Oh, all right, all right. that's enough about it anyway. I don't want to be buried till I *am* dead. Did they give you a decent bite of dinner? Nettie is kindhearted, but she isn't the best cook in the world. *I* was a good cook. Ah, the meals I've cooked in my time, Jane . . . the meals I've cooked!"

Jane missed an excellent opportunity to assure Aunt Elmira she would cook many more meals.

"The dinner was very nice, Aunt Elmira, and we had such fun at it. Ding-dong kept making speeches and we laughed and laughed."

"They can laugh and me dying!" said Aunt Elmira bitterly. "And pussy-footing round in here with faces as long as today and tomorrow, pretending to be sorry. What was them dragging noises I've been hearing all the forenoon?"

"Mrs. Bell and Brenda were rearranging the furniture in the parlour. I expect they are getting it ready for the wedding."

"Wedding? Did you say wedding? Whose wedding?"

"Why, Brenda's. She's going to marry Jim Keyes. I thought you knew."

"'Course I knew they were going to be married sometime . . . but not with me dying. Do you mean to tell me they're going ahead with it right off?"

"Well,, you know it's so unlucky to put a wedding off. It needn't disturb you at all, Aunt Elmira. You're up here in the ell all by yourself and . . ."

Aunt Elmira sat up in bed.

"You hand me my teeth," she ordered. "They're over there on the bureau. I'm going to eat my dinner and then I'm going to get up if it kills me. They needn't think they're going to sneak a wedding off me. I don't care what the doctor says. I've never believed I was half as sick as he made out I was anyhow. Half the valuable stock on the place dying and children having blood-poisoning and red gates being painted white! It's time somebody showed them!"

37

HITHERTO Jane's career at Lantern Hill had been quite unspectacular. Even when she was seen barefooted, nailing shingles on a barn roof, it made only a local sensation, and nobody but Mrs. Solomon Snowbeam said much about it. Mrs. Snowbeam *was* shocked. There was nothing, she said again, that child would stick at.

And then, all at once, Jane made the headlines. The Charlottetown papers gave her the front page for two days, and even the Toronto dailies gave her a column, with a picture of Jane and the lion . . . some lion . . . thrown in. The sensation at 60 Gay must be imagined. Grandmother was very bitter . . . "just like a circus girl" . . . and said it was exactly what might have been expected. Mother thought, but did not say, that no one could really have expected to hear of Jane ambling about P.E. Island leading lions by the mane.

There had been rumours about the lion for a couple of days. A small circus had come to Charlottetown and a whisper got about that their lion had escaped. Certainly people who went to the circus saw no lion. There was a good deal of excitment. Once a monkey had escaped from a circus, but what was that to a lion? It did not seem certain that anyone had actually seen the lion, but several were reported to have seen him . . . here, there, and the other place, miles apart. Calves and young pigs were said to have disappeared. There was even a yarn that a short-sighted old lady in the Royalty had patted him on the head and said, "Nice dogglums." But that was never substantiated. The Royalty people indignantly denied that there were any lions at loose ends. Such yarns were bad for tourist traffic.

"I've no chance of seeing it," said Mrs. Louisa Lyons mournfully. "That's what comes of being bed-rid. You miss everything."

Mrs. Louisa had been an invalid for three years and was reputed not to have put a foot under her without assistance in all that time, but it was not thought she missed much of what went on in the Corners and Queen's Shore and Harbour Head for all that.

"I don't believe there is any lion," said Jane, who had been shopping at the Corners and had dropped in to see Mrs. Lyons. Mrs. Lyons was very fond of Jane and had only one grudge against her. She could never pick anything out of her about her father and mother and Lilian Morrow. And not for any lack of trying.

"Closer than a clam, that girl is when she wants to be," complained Mrs. Louisa.

"Then how did such a yarn start?" she demanded of Jane.

"Most people think the circus people never had a lion .... or it died . . . and they want to cover it up because the people who came to see a lion would be disappointed and mad."

"But they've offered a reward for it."

"They've only offered twenty-five dollars. If they had really lost a lion, they'd offer more than that."

"But it's been *seen*."

"I think folks just imagined they saw it," said Jane.

"And I can't even imagine it," groaned Mrs. Louisa. "And it's no use to *pretend* I imagined it. Every one knows a lion wouldn't come upstairs to my room. If I could see it, I'd likely have my name in the paper. Martha Tolling has had her name in the paper *twice* this year. Some people have all the luck."

"Martha Tolling's sister died in Summerside last week."

"What did I tell you?" said Mrs. Louisa in an aggrieved tone. "Now she'll be wearing mourning. I never have a chance to wear mourning. Nobody has died in our family for years. And black always did become me. Ah well, Jane, you have to take what you get in this world and that's what I've always said. Thank you for dropping in. I've always said to Mattie, 'There's something about Jane Stuart I like, say what you will. If her father is queer, it isn't her fault.' Mind that turn of the stairs, Jane. I haven't been down it for over a year but someone is going to break her neck there sometime."

It happened the next day . . . a golden August afternoon when Jane and Polly and Shingle and Caraway and Punch and Min and Ding-dong and Penny and Young John had gone in a body to pick blueberries in the barrens at the Harbour Head and were returning by a short cut across the back pastures of the Corners farms. In a little wood glen, full of goldenrod, where Martin Robbin's old haybarn stood, they met the lion face to face.

He was standing right before them among the goldenrod, in the shadows of the spruces. For one moment they all stood frozen in their tracks. Then, with a simultaneous yell of terror . . . Jane yelled with the best of them . . . they dropped their pails, bolted through the goldenrod, and into the barn. The lion ambled after them. More yells. No time to close the ramshackle old door. They flew up a wobbly ladder which collapsed and fell as Young John scrambled to safety beside the others on the crossbeam, too much out of breath to yell again.

The lion came to the door, stood there a minute in the sunshine, slowly switching his tail back and forth. Jane, recovering her poise, noticed that he was somewhat mangy and lank, but he was imposing enough in the narrow doorway and nobody could reasonably deny that he was a lion.

"He's coming in," groaned Ding-dong.

"Can lions *climb?*" gasped Shingle.

"I . . . I . . . don't think so," said Polly, through her chattering teeth.

"Cats can . . . and lions are just big cats," said Punch.

"Oh, don't talk, " whispered Min. "It may excite him. Perhaps if we keep perfectly quiet he will go away."

The lion did not seem to have any intention of going away. He came in, looked about him, and lay down in a patch of sunshine with the air of a lion who had any amount of spare time.

"He don't seem cross," muttered Ding-dong.

"Maybe he isn't hungry," said Young John.

"Don't excite him" implored Min.

"He isn't paying any attention to us," said Jane. "We needn't have run . . . I don't believe he'd have hurt us."

"You run as fast as us," said Penny Snowbeam. "I'll bet you was as scared as any of us."

"Of course I was. It was all so sudden. Young John, stop shaking like that. You'll fall off the beam."

"I'm . . . I'm . . . scared," blubbered Young John shamelessly.

"You laughed at me last night and said I'd be scared to pass a patch of cabbages," said Caraway venomously. "Now look at yourself."

"None of your lip. A lion isn't a cabbage," whimpered Young John.

"Oh you *will* excite him," wailed Min in despair.

The lion suddenly yawned. Why, thought Jane, he looks exactly like that jolly old lion in the movie news. Jane shut her eyes.

"Is she praying?" whispered Ding-dong.

Jane was thinking. It was absolutely necessary for her to get home soon if she were going to have dad's favourite scalloped potatoes for his supper. Young John was looking absolutely green. Suppose he got sick? She believed the lion was only a tired, harmless old animal. The circus people had said he was gentle as a lamb. Jane opened her eyes.

"I am going down to take that lion up to the Corners and shut him up in George Tanner's empty barn" she said. "That is, unless you'll all come down with me and slip out and shut him up here."

"Oh, Jane . . . you wouldn't . . . you couldn't . . ."

The lion gave a rap or two on the floor with his tail. . . . The protests died away in strangled yelps.

"I'm going" said Jane. "I tell you, he's tame as tame. But you stay here quietly till I get him well away. And don't yell, any of you."

With bulging eyes and bated breath, the whole gang watched Jane slide along the beam to the wall where she climbed nimbly down to the floor. She marched up to the lion and said, "Come."

The lion came.

Five minutes later Jake MacLean looked out of the door of his blacksmith shop and saw Jane Stuart go past leading a lion by the mane . . . "within spitting distance," as he solemnly averred later. When Jane and the lion . . . who seemed to be getting on very well with each other . . . had disappeared around the back of the shop, Jake sat down on a block and wiped the perspiration from his brow with a bandanna.

"I know I'm not quite sane by times, but I didn't think I was that far gone," he said.

Julius Evans, looking out of his store-window, didn't believe what he saw either. It couldn't be . . . it simply wasn't happening. He was dreaming . . . or drunk . . . or crazy. Ay, that was it . . . crazy. Hadn't there been a year when his father's cousin was in the asylum? Those things ran in families . . . you couldn't deny it. Anything was easier than to believe that he had seen Jane Stuart go up the side-lane by his store towing a lion.

Mattie Lyons ran up to her mother's room, uttering piteous little gasps and cries.

"What's the matter?" demanded Mrs. Louisa. "Screeching like you was demented!"

"Oh, ma, ma, Jane Stuart's bringing a lion here!"

Mrs. Louisa got out of bed and got to the window just in time to see the lion's tail disappear with a switch around the back porch.

"I've *got* to see what she's up to!" Leaving the distracted Mattie wringing her hands by the bed, Mrs. Louisa got herself out of the room and down the staircase with its dangerous turn as nimbly as she had ever done in her best days. Mrs. Parker Crosby, who lived next door and had a weak heart, nearly died of shock when she saw Mrs. Louisa skipping across her back yard.

Mrs. Louisa was just in time to see Jane and the lion ambling up Mr. Tanner's pasture on their way to the hay-barn. She stood there and watched Jane open the door . . . urge the lion in . . . shut it and bolt it. Then she sat down on the rhubarb patch, and Mattie had to get the neighbours to carry her back to bed.

Jane went into the store on her way back and asked Julius Evans, who was still leaning palely over the collection of fly-spotted jugs on his counter, to call Charlottetown and let the circus people know that their lion was safe in Mr. Tanner's barn. She found her dad in the kitchen at Lantern Hill, looking rather strange.

"Jane, it's the wreck of a fine man that you see before you," he said hollowly.

"Dad . . . what is the matter?"

"Matter, says she, with not a quiver in her voice. You don't know, . . . I hope you never will know . . . what it is like to look casually out of a kitchen window, where you are discussing the shamefully low price of eggs with Mrs. Davy Gardiner, and see your daughter . . . your only daughter

. . . stepping high, wide, and handsome through the landscape with a lion. You think you've suddenly gone mad . . . you wonder what was in that glass of raspberry shrub Mrs. Gardiner gave you to drink. Poor Mrs. Davy! As she remarked pathetically to me, the sight jarred her slats. She may get over it, Jane, but I fear she will never be the same woman again."

"He was only a tame old lion," said Jane impatiently. "I don't know why people are making such a fuss over it."

"Jane, my adored Jane, for the sake of your poor father's nerves, don't go leading any more lions about the country, tame or otherwise."

"But it's not a thing that's likely to happen again, dad," said Jane reasonably.

"No, that is so," said dad, in apparent great relief. "I perceive that it is not likely to become a habit. Only, Janelet, if you some day take a notion to acquire an ichthyosaurus for a family pet, give me a little warning, Jane. I'm not as young as I used to be."

Jane couldn't understand the sensation the affair made. She hadn't the least notion she was a heroine.

"I *was* frightened of him at first," she told the Jimmy Johns. "But not after he yawned."

"You'll be too proud to speak to us now, I s'pose," said Caraway Snowbeam wistfully, when Jane's picture came out in the papers. Jane and the barn and the lion had all been photographed . . . separately. Everybody who had seen them became important. And Mrs. Louisa Lyons was a rapturous woman. Her picture was in the paper too, and also a picture of the rhubarb patch.

"Now I can die happy," she told Jane. "If Mrs. Parker Crosby had got her picture in the paper and I hadn't, I couldn't have stood it. I'm sure I don't know what they did put her picture in for. She didn't see you and the lion . . . she only saw me. Well, there are some folks who are never contented unless they're in the limelight."

Jane was to go down in Queen's Shore history as the girl who thought nothing of roaming round the country with a lion or two for company.

"A girl absolutely without fear," said Step-a-yard, bragging everywhere of his acquaintance with her.

"I realised the first time I saw her that she was superior," said Uncle Tombstone. Mrs. Snowbeam reminded everybody that she had always said that Jane Stuart was a child who would stick at nothing. When Ding-dong Bell and Punch Garland would be old men, they would be saying to each other, "Remember the time Jane Stuart and us drove that lion into the Tanner barn? Didn't we have a nerve?"

38

A LETTER from Jody, blotted with tears, gave Jane a bad night in late August. It was to the effect that she was really going to be sent to an orphanage at last.

"Miss West is going to sell her boarding house in October and retire," wrote Jody. "I've cried and cried, Jane. I hate the idea of going into an orphanage and I'll never see you, Jane, and oh, Jane, it isn't fair. I don't mean Miss West isn't fair, but *something* isn't."

Jane, too, felt that something wasn't being fair. And she felt that 60 Gay without her backyard confabs with Jody would be just a little more intolerable than it ever had been. But that didn't matter as much as poor Jody's unhappiness. Jane thought Jody might really have an easier time in an orphanage than she had as the little unpaid drudge at 58 Gay, but still she didn't like the idea any better than Jody did. She looked so downhearted that Step-a-yard noticed it when he came over with some fresh mackerel for her which he had brought from the harbour.

"Do for your dinner tomorrow, Jane."

"Tomorrow is the day for corned beef and cabbage," said Jane in a scandalised voice. "But we'll have them the day after. That's Friday anyhow. Thank you, Step-a-Yard."

"Anything troubling you, Miss Lion-tamer?"

Jane opened her heart to him.

"You just don't know what poor Jody's life's been," she concluded.

Step-a-yard nodded.

"Put upon and overworked and knocked about from pillar to post, I reckon. Poor kid."

"And nobody to love her but me. If she goes to an orphanage, I'll never see her."

"Well, now." Step-a-yard scratched his head reflectively. "We must put our heads together, Jane, and see what can be done about it. We must think hard, Jane, we must think hard."

Jane thought hard to no effect, but Step-a-yard's meditations were more fruitful.

"I've been thinking," he told Jane next day, "what a pity it is the Titus ladies couldn't adopt Jody. They've been wanting to adopt a child for a year now but they can't agree on what kind of a child they want. Justina wants a girl and Violet wants a boy, though they'd both prefer twins of any sex. But suitable twins looking for parents are kind of scarce, so they've given up *that* idea. Violet wants a dark complected one with brown eyes and Justina wants a fair one with blue eyes. Violet wants one ten years old and Justina wants one about seven. How old is Jody?"

"Twelve, like me."

Step-a-yard looked gloomy.

"I dunno. That sounds too old for them. But it wouldn't do any harm to put it up to them. You never can tell what them two girls will do."

"I'll see them tonight right after supper," resolved Jane.

She was so excited that she salted the apple sauce and no one could eat it. As soon as the supper dishes were out of the way . . . and that night they were not proud of the way they were washed . . . Jane was off.

There was a wonderful sunset over the harbour, and Jane's cheeks were red from the stinging kisses of the wind by the time she reached the narrow, perfumed Titus lane where the trees seemed trying to touch you. Beyond was the kind, old, welcoming house, mellowed in the sunshine of a hundred summers, and the Titus ladies were sitting before a beechwood fire in their kitchen. Justina was knitting and Violet was clipping creamy bits of toffee from a long, silvery twist, made from a recipe Jane had never yet been able to wheedle out of them.

"Come in, dear. We are glad to see you," said Justina, kindly and sincerely, though she looked a little apprehensively over Jane's shoulder, as if she feared a lion might be skulking in the shadows. "It was such a cool evening we decided to have a fire. Sit down, dear. Violet, give her some toffee. She is growing very tall, isn't she?"

"And handsome," said Violet. "I like her eyes, don't you, sister?"

The Titus ladies had a curious habit of talking Jane over before her face as if she wasn't there. Jane didn't mind . . . though they were sometimes not so complimentary.

"I prefer blue eyes, as you know," said Justina, "but her hair is beautiful."

"Hardly dark enough for my taste," said Violet. "I have always admired black hair."

"The only kind of hair that is really beautiful is curling, red-gold hair," said Justina. "Her cheekbones are rather high, but her insteps are admirable."

"She is very brown," sighed Violet. "But they tell me that is fashionable now. We were *very* careful of our complexions when we were girls. Our mother, you remember, always made us wear sunbonnets when we went out of doors . . . pink sunbonnets."

"Pink sunbonnets! They were blue," said Justina.

"Pink," said Violet positively.

"Blue," said Justina, just as positively.

They argued for ten minutes over the colour of the sunbonnets. When Jane saw they were getting rather warm over it, she mentioned that Miranda Garland was going to be married in two weeks' time. The Titus ladies forgot the sunbonnets in their excitement.

"Two weeks? That's very sudden, isn't it? Of course, it is to Ned Mitchell. I heard they were engaged . . . even that seemed to me very precipitate when they had been keeping company only six months . . . but I had no idea they were to be married so soon," said Violet.

"She does not want to take a chance on his falling in love with a thinner girl," said Justina.

"They've hurried up the wedding so that I can be bridesmaid," explained Jane proudly.

"She is only seventeen," said Justina disapprovingly.

"Nineteen, sister," said Violet.

"Seventeen," said Justina.

"Nineteen," said Violet.

Jane cut short what seemed likely to be another ten minutes' argument over Miranda's age by saying she was eighteen.

"Oh, well, it's easy enough to get married," said Justina. "The trick nowadays seems to be to *stay* married."

Jane winced. She knew Justina hadn't meant to hurt her. But *her* father and mother hadn't stayed married.

"I think," said Violet, kindling, "that P. E. Island has a very good record in that respect. Only two divorces since Confederation . . . sixty-five years."

"Only two *real* ones," conceded Justina. "But quite a few . . . at least half a dozen . . . imitation ones . . . going to the States and getting a divorce there. And likely to be more, from all accounts."

Violet sent Justina a warning glance which Jane, luckily for her peace of mind, did not intercept. Jane had come to the conclusion that she must mention the object of her call now if she were ever going to do it. No use waiting for a chance . . . you just had to make your chance.

"I hear you want to adopt a child," she said, with no beating round the bush.

Again the sisters interchanged glances.

"We've been talking of it off and on for a couple of years," acknowledged Justina.

"We've got along as far as both being willing for a little girl," said Violet with a sigh. "I would have liked a boy . . .

but, as Justina pointed out, neither of us knows anything about dressing a boy. It *would* be more fun dressing a little girl."

"A little girl about seven, with blue eyes and fair curling hair and a rosebud mouth," said Justina firmly.

"A little girl of ten with sloe-black hair and eyes and a creamy skin," said Violet with equal firmness. "I have given in to you about the sex, sister. It is your turn to give in about the age and the complexion."

"The age possibly, but not the complexion."

"I know the very girl for you," said Jane brazenly. "She's my chum in Toronto, Jody Turner. I know you'll love her. Let me tell you about her."

Jane told them. She left nothing untold that might incline them in Jody's favour. When she had said what she wanted to say, she held her tongue. Jane always knew the right time to be silent.

The Titus ladies were silent also. Justina went on knitting and Violet, having finished snipping toffee, took up her crocheting. Now and then they lifted their eyes, looked at each other, and dropped them again. The fire crackled companionably.

"Is she pretty?" said Justina at last. "We wouldn't want an ugly child."

"She will be very handsome when she grows up," said Jane gravely. "She has the loveliest eyes. Just now she is so thin . . . and never has any nice clothes."

"She hasn't too much bounce, has she?" said Violet. "I don't like bouncing girls."

"She doesn't bounce at all," said Jane. But this was a mistake because . . ."

"I like a *little* bounce," said Justina.

"She wouldn't want to wear pants, would she?" said Violet. "So many girls do nowadays."

"I'm sure Jody wouldn't want to wear anything you didn't like," answered Jane.

"I wouldn't mind girls wearing pants so much if only they didn't *call* them pants," said Justina. "But *not* pajamas . . . never, never pajamas."

"Certainly not pajamas," said Violet.

"Suppose we got her and couldn't love her?" said Justina.

"You couldn't help loving Jody," said Jane warmly. "She's *sweet*."

"I suppose," hesitated Justina, "she wouldn't . . . there wouldn't be any danger . . . of there being . . . of her having . . . unpleasant insects about her?"

"Certainly not," said Jane, shocked. "Why, she lives on Gay Street." For the first time in her life Jane found herself standing up for Gay Street. But even Gay Street must have justice. Jane felt sure there were no unpleasant insects on Gay Street.

"If . . . if she had . . . there is such a thing as a fine-toothed comb," said Violet heroically.

Justina drew her black eyebrows together.

"There has never been any necessity for such an article in *our* family, Violet."

Again they knitted and crocheted and interchanged glances. Finally Justina said, "No."

"No," said Violet.

"She is too dark," said Justina.

"She is too old," said Violet.

"And now that is settled, perhaps Jane would like to have some of that Devonshire cream I made today," said Justina.

In spite of the Devonshire cream and the huge bunch of pansies Violet insisted on giving her, Jane went home with a leaden weight of disappointment on her heart. She was surprised to find that Step-a-yard was quite satisfied.

"If they'd told you they'd take her, you'd likely get word tomorrow that they'd changed their minds. Now it'll be the other way round."

Still, Jane was very much amazed to get a note from the Titus ladies the next day, telling her that they had, on second thought, decided to adopt Jody, and would she come down and help them settle the necessary arrangements.

"We have concluded she is not too old," said Violet.

"Or too dark," said Justina.

"You'll love her, I know," said happy Jane.

"We shall endeavor to be to her as the best and kindest of parents," said Justina. "We must give her music lessons, of course. Do you know if she is musical, Jane?"

"Very," said Jane, remembering Jody and the piano at 58.

"Think of filling her stockings at Christmas," said Violet.

"We must get a cow," said Justina. "She must have a glass of warm milk every night at bedtime."

"We must furnish the little southwest room for her," said Violet. "I think I should like a carpet of pale blue, sister."

"She must not expect to find here the excitements of the mad welter of modern life," said Justina solemnly, "but we shall try to remember that youth requires companionship and wholesome pleasures."

"Won't it be lovely to knit sweaters for her?" said Violet.

"We must get out those little wooden ducks our uncle whittled for us when we were small," said Justina.

"It will be nice to have something young to love," said Violet. "I'm only sorry she isn't twins."

"On mature reflection," said Justina, "I am sure you will agree that it is wise for us to find out how we get along with one child before we embark on twins."

"Will you let her keep a cat?" asked Jane. "She loves cats."

"I don't suppose we would object to a bachelor cat," said Justina cautiously.

It was eventually arranged that when Jane went back to Toronto she was to find someone coming to the Island who might bring Jody along with her, and Justina solemnly counted out and gave into Jane's keeping enough money for Jody's travelling expenses and clothes suitable for such travelling.

"I'll write to Miss West right away and tell her, but I'll ask her not to say anything about it to Jody till I get back. *I* want to tell her . . . I want to see her eyes."

"We are much obliged to you, Jane," said Justina, "you have fulfilled the dream of our lives."

"Completely," said Violet.

39

"IF we could only make the summer last longer," sighed Jane.

But that was impossible. It was September now, and soon she must put off Jane and put on Victoria. But not before they got Miranda Jimmy John married off. Jane was so busy helping the Jimmy Johns get ready for the wedding that Lantern Hill hardly knew her except to get a bite for dad. And as bridesmaid she had a chance to wear the adorable dress of rose-pink organdy with its embroidered blue and white spots which mother had gotten her. But once the wedding was over, Jane had to say good-bye to Lantern Hill again . . . to the windy silver of the gulf . . . to the pond . . . to Big Donald's wood-lane . . . which, alas was going to be cut down and ploughed up . . . to her garden, which was to her a garden that never knew winter because she saw it only in summer . . . to the wind that sang in the spruces and the gulls that soared whitely over the harbour . . . to Bubbles and Happy and First Peter and Silver Penny. And dad. But though she felt sad over it, there was none of the despair that had filled her heart the year before. She would be back next summer . . . that was an understood thing now. She would be seeing mother again . . . she did not dislike the idea of going back to St. Agatha's . . . there was Jody's delight to be looked forward to . . . and dad was going with her as far as Montreal.

Aunt Irene came to Lantern Hill the day before Jane left and seemed to want to say something she couldn't quite manage to say. When she went away, she held Jane's hand and looked at her very significantly.

"If you hear some news before next spring, lovey . . ."

"What news am I likely to hear?" said Jane with the terrible directness which Aunt Irene always found so trying.

"Oh . . . one can never tell . . . who knows what changes may come before them?"

Jane was uncomfortable for a few moments and then shrugged it away. Aunt Irene was always giving mysterious hints about something, throwing out wisps of insinuation that clung like cobwebs. Jane had learned not to mind Aunt Irene.

"I've never really been able to make as much of that child as I would like," mourned Aunt Irene to a friend. "She holds you at arms' length somehow. The Kennedys were all hard . . . her mother now . . . you'd think to look at her she was all rose and cream and sweetness. But underneath, my dear . . . hard as a rock. She ruined my brother's life and did everything . . . *everything*, I understand . . . to set his child against him."

"Jane seems very fond of her father now," said the friend.

"Oh, I'm sure she is . . . as fond as she can be of any one. But Andrew is a very lonely man. And I don't know if he will ever be anything else. Lately I've been wondering . . ."

"Wondering if he'll finally work himself up to getting a United States divorce and marrying Lilian Morrow," said the friend bluntly. She had had much experience in filling up Irene's blanks.

Aunt Irene looked quite shocked at such plain speaking.

"Oh, I wouldn't like to say *that*. . . . I don't really know . . . but, of course, Lilian is the girl he should have married instead of Robin Kennedy. They have *so* much in common. And though I don't approve of divorce ordinarily . . . I think it *shocking* . . . still . . . there *are* special circumstances. . . ."

Jane and dad had a delightful trip to Montreal.

"How nice to think we're an hour younger than we were," said dad, as he put his watch back at Campbellton. He said things like that all along the way about everything.

Jane clung to him very tightly in Montreal station.

"Dad darling . . . but I'll be back next summer, you know."

"Of course," said dad. Then he added,

"Jane, here's a spot of hard cash for you. I don't suppose you get a very huge allowance at 60 Gay."

"None at all . . . but can you spare this, dad?" Jane was looking at the bills he had put into her hand. "Fifty dollars? That's an awful lot of money, dad."

"This has been a good year for me, Jane. Editors have been kind. And somehow . . . when you're about I write more . . . I've felt some of my old ambition stirring this past year."

Jane, who had spent all her lion-reward money on things for Lantern Hill and treats for the young fry who had been associated with her in the episode, tucked the money away in her bag, reflecting that it would come in handy at Christmas.

"Life, deal gently with her . . . love, never desert her," said Andrew Stuart, looking after the Toronto train as it steamed away.

Jane found that grandmother had had her room done over for her. When she went up to it, she discovered a wonderful splendour of rose and grey, instead of the old gloom. Silvery carpet . . . shimmering curtains . . . chintz chairs . . . cream-tinted furniture . . . pink silk bedspread. The old bearskin rug . . . the only thing she had really liked . . . was gone. So was the cradle. The big mirror had been replaced by a round rimless one.

"How do you like it?" asked grandmother watchfully.

Jane recalled her little room at Lantern Hill with its bare floor and sheepskin rug and white spool bed covered with its patchwork quilt.

"It is very beautiful, grandmother. Thank you very much."

"Fortunately," said grandmother, "I did not expect much enthusiasm."

After grandmother had gone out, Jane turned her back on the splendour and went to the window. The only things of home were the stars. She wondered if dad were looking at them . . . no, of course, he wouldn't be home yet. But they would all be there in their proper places . . . the North Star over the Watch Tower, Orion sparkling over Big Donald's hill. And Jane knew that she would never be the least bit afraid of grandmother again.

"Oh, Jane," said Jody. "Oh, Jane!"

"I know you'll be happy with the Titus ladies, Jody. They're a little old-fashioned, but they're so kind . . . and they have the loveliest garden. You won't have to make a garden by sticking faded flowers in a plot any more. You'll see the famous cherry walk in bloom . . . I've never seen *that*."

"It's like a beautiful dream," said Jody. "But oh, Jane, I hate to leave you."

"We'll be together in the summers instead of in the winters. That will be the only difference, Jody. And it will be ever so much nicer. We'll swim . . . I'll teach you the crawl. Mother says her friend, Mrs. Newton, will take you as far as Sackville, and Miss Justina Titus will meet you there. And mother is going to get your clothes."

"I wonder if it will be like this when I go to heaven," said Jody breathlessly.

Jane missed Jody when she went, but life was growing full. She loved St. Agatha's now. She liked Phyllis quite well, and Aunt Sylvia said she had really never seen a child blossom out socially as Victoria had done. Uncle William couldn't floor her when he asked about capitals now. Uncle William was beginning to think that Victoria had something in her, and Jane was finding that she liked Uncle William reasonably well. As for grandmother . . . well, Mary told Frank it did her heart good to see Miss Victoria standing up to the old lady.

"Not that stands up is just the right word either. But

the madam can't put it over her like she used to. Nothing she says seems to get under Miss Victoria's skin anymore. And does that make her mad! I've seen her turn white with rage when she'd said something real venomous and Miss Victoria just answering in that respectful tone of hers that's just as good as telling her she doesn't care a hoot about what any Kennedy of them all says anymore."

"I wish Miss Robin would learn that trick," said Frank.

Mary shook her head.

"It's too late for her. She's been under the old lady's thumb too long. Never went against her in her life except for one thing, and lived to repent that, so they say. And anyhow, she's a cat of a different breed from Miss Victoria."

One November evening mother went again to Lakeside Gardens to see her friend and took Jane with her. Jane welcomed the chance to see her house again. Would it be sold? Unbelievably, it wasn't. Jane's heart gave a bound of relief. She was so afraid it would be. She couldn't understand how it wasn't, it seemed so entirely desirable to her. She did not know that the builder had decided that he had made a mistake when he built a little house in Lakeside Gardens. People who could live in Lakeside Gardens wanted bigger houses.

Though Jane was glad to her toes that her house hadn't been sold, she was inconsistently resentful that it was unlighted and unwarmed. She hated the oncoming winter because of the house. Its heart must ache with the cold then. She sat on the steps and watched the lights blooming out along the Gardens and wished there was one in her house. How the dead brown leaves still clinging to the oaks rustled in the windy night! How the lights along the lake shore twinkled through the trees of the ravine! And how she hated, yes, positively hated, the man who would buy this house!

"It just isn't fair," said Jane. "Nobody will ever love it as I do. It really belongs to me."

The week before Christmas Jane bought the materials for a fruit-cake out of the money dad had given her and compounded it in the kitchen. Then she expressed it to dad. She did not ask anyone's permission for all this . . . just went ahead and did it. Mary held her tongue and grandmother knew nothing about it. But Jane would have sent it just the same if she had.

One thing made Christmas Day memorable for Jane that year. Just after breakfast Frank came in to say that long distance was calling Miss Victoria. Jane went to the hall with a puzzled look . . . who on earth could be calling her on long distance? She lifted the receiver to her ear.

"Lantern Hill calling Superior Jane! Merry Christmas and thanks for that cake," said dad's voice as distinctly as if he were in the same room.

"Dad!" Jane gasped. "Where are you?"

"Here at Lantern Hill. This is my Christmas present to you, Janelet. Three minutes over a thousand miles."

Probably no two people ever crammed more into three minutes. When Jane went back to the dining room, her cheeks were crimson and her eyes glowed like jewels.

"Who was calling you, Victoria?" asked grandmother.

"Dad," said Jane.

Mother gave a little choked cry. Grandmother wheeled on her furiously.

"Perhaps," she said icily, "you think he should have called *you.*"

"He should," said Jane.

40

At the end of a blue and silver day in March, Jane was doing her lessons in her room and feeling reasonably happy. She had had a rapturous letter from Jody that morning . . . all

Jody's letter were rapturous . . . giving her lots of interesting news from Queen's Shore . . . she had had a birthday the week before and was now in her leggy teens . . . and two bits of luck had come her way that afternoon. Aunt Sylvia had taken her and Phyllis with her on a shopping expedition, and Jane had picked up two delightful things for Lantern Hill . . . a lovely old copper bowl and a comical brass knocker for the glass-paned door. It was the head of a dog with his tongue hanging waggishly out and a real doglaugh in his eyes.

The door opened and mother came in, ready dressed for a restaurant dinner party. She wore the most wonderful sheath dress of ivory taffeta, with a sapphire velvet bow at the back and a little blue velvet jacket over her lovely shoulders. Her slippers were blue, with slender golden heels, and she had her hair done in a new way . . . a sleek, flat top to her head and a row of tricksy little curls around her neck.

"Oh, mums, you are perfectly lovely," said Jane, looking at her with adoring eyes. And then she added something she had never intended to say . . . something that seemed to rush to her lips and say itself.

"I *do* wish dad could see you now."

Jane pulled herself up in dire dismay. She had been told never to mention dad to mother . . . and yet she had done it. And mother was looking as if she had been struck in the face.

"I do not suppose," said mother bitterly, "that he would be at all interested in the sight."

Jane said nothing. There seemed to be nothing she could say. How did she know whether dad would be interested or not? And yet . . . and yet . . . she was sure he still loved mother.

Mother sat down on one of the chintz chairs and looked at Jane.

"Jane," she said, "I am going to tell you something about my marriage. I don't know what you have heard about the other side of it . . . there *was* another side, of course . . . but I want you to hear my side. It is better you should

know. I should have told you before . . . but . . . it hurt me
so."

"Don't tell it now, if it hurts you, darling," said Jane
earnestly. (Thinking . . . *I know more about it than you
suppose already.*)

"I must. There are some things I want you to understand . . . I don't want you to blame me too much. . . ."

"I don't blame you at all, mother."

"Oh, I was to blame a great deal . . . I see that now
when it is too late. I was so young and foolish . . . just a
careless, happy little bride. I . . . I . . . ran away to be married to your father, Jane."

Jane nodded.

"How much *do* you know, Jane?"

"Just that you ran away and were very happy at first."

"Happy? Oh, Jane Victoria, I was . . . I was . . . so
happy. But it really was . . . a very unfortunate marriage,
dearest."

(That sounds like something grandmother said.)

"I shouldn't have treated mother so . . . I was all she
had left after my father died. But she forgave me. . . ."

*(And set herself to work to make trouble between you
and dad.)*

"But we *were* happy that first year, Jane Victoria. I
worshiped Andrew . . . that smile of his . . . you know his
smile . . ."

(Do I know it?)

"We had such fun together . . . reading poetry by driftwood fires down at the harbour . . . we always made a rite of
lighting those fires . . . life was wonderful. I used to welcome the days then as much as I shrink from them now. We
had only one quarrel that first year . . . I forget what it was
about . . . something silly . . . I kissed the frown on his
forehead and all was well again. I knew there was no woman
in the world so happy as I was. If it could have lasted!"

"Why didn't it last, mother?"

"I . . . I hardly know. Of course I wasn't much of a
housekeeper, but I don't think it was that. I couldn't cook,

but our maid didn't do so badly and Little Aunt Em used to come in and help. *She* was a darling. And I couldn't keep accounts straight ever . . . I would add up a column eight times and get a different answer every time. But Andrew just laughed over that. Then you were born. . . ."

"And that made all the trouble," cried Jane, in whom that bitter thought had persisted in rankling.

"Not at first . . . oh, Jane Victoria darling, not at first. But Andrew never seemed the same after. . . ."

(I wonder if it wasn't you who had changed, mother.)

"He was jealous of my love for you . . . he *was*, Jane Victoria. . . ."

(Not jealous . . . no, not jealous. A little hurt . . . he didn't like to be second with you after he had been first . . . he thought he came second then.)

"He used to say 'your child' . . . 'your daughter,' as if you weren't his. Why, he used to make fun of you. Once he said you had a face like a monkey."

(And no Kennedy can take a joke.)

"You hadn't . . . you were the cutest little thing. Why, Jane Victoria darling, you were just a daily miracle. It was such fun to tuck you in at night . . . to watch you when you were asleep."

(And you were just a darling big baby yourself, mother.)

"Andrew was angry because I couldn't go out with him as much as before. How could I? It would have been bad for you if I'd taken you and I couldn't leave you. But he didn't care really . . . he never did except for a little while at the first. He cared far more for that book of his than for me. He would shut himself up with it for days at a time and forget all about me."

(And yet you think he was the only jealous one.)

"I suppose I simply wasn't capable of living with a genius. Of course, I knew I wasn't clever enough for him. Irene let me see that she thought that. And he cared far more for her than for me. . . ."

(Oh, no, not that . . . never that!)

"She had far more influence over him than I had. He told her things before he told me. . . ."

(Because she was always trying to pick them out of him before he was ready to tell anyone.)

"He thought me such a child that, if he had a plan, he consulted her before he consulted me. Irene made me feel like a shadow in my own house. She liked to humiliate me, I think. She was always sweet and smiling. . . ."

(She would be!)

". . . but she always blew my candles out. She patronised me. . . ."

(Do I know it!)

"'I've noticed,' she would say. That had such a sting, as if she'd been spying on me right along. Andrew said I was unreasonable . . . I wasn't . . . but he always sided with her. Irene never liked me. She had wanted Andrew to marry another girl . . . I was told she had said from the first that she knew our marriage would be a failure. . . ."

(And did her best to make it one.)

"She kept pushing us apart . . . here a little . . . there a little. I was helpless."

(Not if you had had a wee bit of backbone, Mummy.)

"Andrew was annoyed because I didn't like her, and yet he hated *my* family. He couldn't speak of mother without insulting her . . . he didn't want me to visit her . . . get presents from her . . . money . . . oh, Jane Victoria, that last year was dreadful. Andrew never looked at me if he could help it."

(Because it hurt him too much.)

"It seemed as if I were married to a stranger. We were always saying bitter things to each other. . . ."

(That verse I read in the Bible last night, "Death and Life are in the power of the tongue" . . . it's true . . . it's true!)

"Then mother wrote and asked me to come home for a visit. Andrew said, 'Go if you want to' . . . just like that. Irene said it would give things a chance to heal up. . . ."

(I can see her smiling when she said it.)

"I went. And . . . and . . . mother wanted me to stay with her. She could see I was so unhappy. . . ."

(And took her chance.)

"I couldn't go on living with a person who hated me, Jane Victoria . . . I couldn't . . . so I . . . I wrote him and told him I thought it would be better for both of us if I didn't go back. I . . . I don't know . . . nothing seemed real someway . . . if he had written and asked me to go back . . . but he didn't. I never heard from him . . . till that letter came asking for you."

Jane had kept silence while her mother talked, thinking things at intervals, but now she could keep silence no longer.

"He *did* write . . . he wrote and asked you to come back . . . and you never answered . . . you never answered, mother."

Mother and daughter looked at each other in the silence of the big, beautiful, unfriendly room.

After a little mother whispered, "I never got it, Jane Victoria."

They said nothing more about it. Both of them knew quite well what had happened to the letter.

"Mother, it isn't too late yet. . . ."

"Yes, it is too late, dear. Too much has come between us. I can't break with mother again . . . she'd never forgive me again . . . and she loves me so. I'm all she has. . . ."

"Nonsense!" Jane was as brusque as any Stuart of them all. "She has got Aunt Gertrude and Uncle William and Aunt Sylvia."

"It's . . . it's not the same. She didn't love *their* father. And . . . I can't stand up to her. Besides, he doesn't want me anymore. We're strangers. And oh, Jane Victoria, life's slipping away . . . like that . . . through my fingers. The harder I try to hold it, the faster it slips. I've lost you. . . ."

"Never, mother!"

"Yes, you belong more to him than to me now. I don't blame you . . . you can't help it. But you'll belong a little more to him every year . . . till there'll be nothing left for me."

Grandmother came in. She looked at them both suspiciously.

"Have you forgotten you are dining out, Robin?"

"Yes, I think I had," said mother strangely. "But never mind . . . I've remembered now. I . . . I shan't forget again."

Grandmother lingered for a moment after mother had gone out.

"What have you been saying to upset your mother, Victoria?"

Jane looked levelly at grandmother.

"*What happened to the letter father wrote mother long ago, asking her to go back to him, grandmother?*"

Grandmother's cold cruel eyes suddenly blazed.

"So that's it? Do you think it any of your business exactly?"

"Yes, I think it is, since I am their child."

"I did what was right with it . . . I burned it. She had seen her mistake . . . she had come back to me, as I always knew she would . . . I was not going to have her misled again. Don't begin plotting, Victoria. I am a match for you all yet."

"No one is plotting," said Jane. "There is just one thing I want to tell you, grandmother. My father and mother love each other yet . . . I *know* it."

Grandmother's voice was ice.

"They do not. Your mother has been happy all these years, till you began stirring up old memories. *Leave her alone*. She is *my* daughter . . . no outsider shall ever come between us again . . . neither Andrew Stuart nor you nor anyone. And you will be good enough to remember that."

41

THE letters came on the afternoon of the last of March. Jane was not at St. Agatha's . . . she had had a touch of sore throat the day before and mother thought it was wiser for her to stay home. But her throat was better now and Jane was reasonably happy. It was almost April . . . if not quite spring yet, at least the hope of spring. Just a little over two months and she would keep her tryst with June at Lantern Hill. Meanwhile, she was planning some additions to her garden . . . for one thing, a row of knightly hollyhocks along the dyke at the bottom. She would plant the seeds in August and they would bloom the *next* summer.

Grandmother and Aunt Gertrude and mother had all gone to Mrs. Morrison's bridge and tea, so Mary brought the afternoon mail to Jane, who pounced joyfully on three letters for herself. One from Polly . . . one from Shingle . . . one . . . Jane recognised Aunt Irene's copper-plate writing.

She read Polly's first . . . a good letter, full of fun and Lantern Hill jokes. There was one bit of news about dad in it . . . he was planning a trip to the States very soon . . . Boston or New York or somewhere . . . Polly seemed rather vague. And Polly wound up with a paragraph that gave Jane a good laugh . . . her last laughter for some time . . . the last laughter of her childhood, it always seemed to Jane, looking back on it from later years.

"Mr. Julius Evans was awful mad last week," wrote Polly. "A rat got drowned in his cask of new maple syrup and he made a terrible fuss over such a waste. But dad says he isn't sure it *was* wasted, so we are getting our syrup from Joe Baldwin's to be on the safe side."

Jane was still laughing over this when she opened Shingle's letter. A paragraph on the second page leaped to her eye.

"Everybody is saying your dad is going to get a Yankee divorce and marry Lilian Morrow. Will she be your mother then? How do you like the idea? I guess she'll be your stepmother . . . only that sounds so funny when your own mother is still alive. Will your name be changed? Caraway says not . . . but they do such queer things in the States. Anyway, I hope it won't make any difference about you coming to Lantern Hill in the summer."

Jane felt literally sick and cold with agony as she dropped the letter and snatched up Aunt Irene's. She had been wondering what Aunt Irene could be writing to her about . . . she knew now.

The letter told Jane that Aunt Irene suspected that her brother Andrew intended going to the States and living there long enough to get a U.S. divorce.

"Of course, it may not be true, lovey. *He* hasn't told me. But it is all over the country, and where there is so much smoke there must be some fire, and I think you ought to be prepared, lovey. I know that several of his friends advised him long ago to get a divorce. But as he never discussed it with *me*, I have given no advice for or against. For some reason I am at a loss to understand, he has shut me out of his confidence these past two years. But I have felt that the state of his affairs has long been very unsatisfactory. I'm sure you won't worry over this. . . . I wouldn't have told you if I thought it would worry you. You have too much good sense . . . I've often remarked how old you were for your years. But of course, if it is true, it may make some difference to you. He might marry again."

If you have seen a candle flame blown out, you will know what Jane looked like as she went blindly to the window. It was a dark day with occasional showers of driving rain. Jane looked at the cruel, repellent, merciless street but did not see it. She had never felt such dreadful shame . . . such dreadful misery. Yet it seemed to her she ought to have known what was coming. There had been a hint or two last summer . . . she remembered Lilian Morrow's caressing 'Drew" and dad's pleasure in her company. And now . . . if this hideous thing were true, she would never spend a summer at Lantern Hill again. Would *they* dare to live at Lantern Hill? Lilian Morrow her mother! Nonsense! Nobody could be her mother except mother. The thing was unthinkable. But Lilian Morrow would be father's wife.

This had all been going on in these past weeks when she had been so happy, looking forward to June.

"I don't suppose I'll ever feel glad again," thought Jane drearily. Everything was suddenly meaningless . . . she felt as if she were far removed from everything . . . as if she were looking at life and people and things through the big end of Timothy Salt's telescope. It seemed years since she had laughed over Polly's tale of Mr. Evans' wasted . . . or unwasted . . . maple syrup.

Jane walked the floor of her room all the rest of that afternoon. She dared not sit down for a moment. It seemed that as long as she kept moving, her pain marched with her and she could bear it. If she were to stop, it would crush her. But by dinner-time Jane's mind had begun to function again. She must know the truth and she knew what she must do to learn it. And it must be done at once.

She counted the money she had left from father's gift. Yes, there was just enough for a one-way ticket to the Island. Nothing left over for meals or a Pullman but that did not matter. Jane knew she would neither eat nor sleep until she knew. She went down to her dinner, which Mary had spread for her in the breakfast room, and tried to eat something lest Mary should notice.

Mary did.

"Your throat worse, Miss Victoria?"

"No, my throat is all right," said Jane. Her voice sounded strange in her ears . . . as if it belonged to someone else. "Do you know what time mother and grandmother will be home, Mary?"

"Not till late, Miss Victoria. You know your grandmother and Aunt Gertrude are going to dinner at your Uncle William's, meeting some of your grandmother's old friends from the west, and your mother is going to a party. She won't be home till after midnight, but Frank goes for the old lady at eleven."

The International Limited left at ten. Jane had all the time she needed. She went upstairs and packed a small hand grip with some necessities and a box of gingersnaps that were on her bedroom table. The darkness outside the window seemd to look in at her menacingly. The rain spat against the panes. The wind was very lonely in the leafless elms. Once Jane had thought the rain and the wind were friends of hers, but they seemed enemies now. Everything hurt her. Everything in her life seemed uprooted and withered. She put on her hat and coat, picked up her bag, went to mother's room and pinned a little note on a pillow, and crept down the stairs. Mary and Frank were having their dinner in the kitchen and the door was shut. Very quietly Jane telephoned for a taxi; when it came, she was waiting outside for it. She went down the steps of 60 Gay and out of the grim iron gates for the last time.

"The Union Station," she told the taxi-driver. They moved swiftly away over the wet street that looked like a black river with drowned lights in it. Jane was going to ask for the truth from the only one who could tell it to her . . . her father.

42

JANE left Toronto Wednesday night. On Friday night she reached the Island. The train whirled over the sodden land. Her Island was not beautiful now. It was just like every other place in the ugliness of very early spring. The only beautiful things were the slim white birches on the dark hills. Jane had sat bolt upright all the time of her journey, night and day, subsisting on what gingersnaps she could force herself to swallow. She hardly moved but she felt all the time as if she were running . . . running . . . trying to catch up with someone on a road . . . someone who was getting further ahead all the time.

She did not go on to Charlottetown. She got off at West Trent, a little siding where the train stopped when it was asked to. It was only five miles from there to Lantern Hill. Jane could hear plainly the roar of the distant ocean. Once she would have thrilled to it . . . that sonorous music coming through the windy, dark grey night on the old North Shore. Now she did not notice it.

It had been raining but it was fine now. The road was hard and rough and dotted with pools of water. Jane walked through them unheedingly. Presently there were dark spires of fir trees against a moonrise. The puddles on the road turned to pools of silver fire. The houses she passed seemed alien . . . remote . . . as if they had closed their doors to her. The spruces seemed to turn cold shoulders on her. Far away over the pale moonlit landscape was a wooded hill with the light of a house she knew on it. Would there be a light at Lantern Hill or would dad be gone?

A dog of her acquaintance stopped to speak to her, but Jane ignored him. Once a car bumped past her, picking her out with its lights and splashing her from head to foot with mud. It was Joe Weekes who, being a cousin of Mrs. Meade, had the family trick of malapropisms, and told his sceptical wife when he got home that he had met either Jane Stuart or her operation on the road. Jane felt like an apparition. It seemed to her that she had been walking forever . . . must go on walkng forever . . . through this ghostly world of cold moonlight.

There was Little Donald's house with a light in the parlour. The curtains were red, and when they were drawn at night, the light shone rosily through them. Then Big Donald's light . . . and at last the lane to Lantern Hill.

There was a light in the kitchen!

Jane was trembling as she went up the rutted lane and across the yard, past the forlorn and muddy garden where the poppies had once trembled in silken delight, to the window. What a sadly different home-coming from what she had planned!

She looked in. Dad was reading by the table. He wore his shabby old tweed suit and the nice grey tie with tiny red flecks in it, which Jane had picked out for him last summer. The Old Contemptible was in his mouth and his legs were cocked up on the sofa where two dogs and First Peter were sleeping. Silver Penny was stretched out against the warm base of the gasoline lamp on the table. In the corner was a sinkful of dirty dishes. Even at that moment a fresh pang tore Jane's heart at the sight.

A moment later an amazed Andrew Stuart looked up to see his daughter standing before him . . . wet-footed, mud-splashed, white-faced, with her eyes so terribly full of misery that a hideous fear flashed into his mind. Was her mother . . . ?

"Good heavens, Jane!"

Literally sick from fear, Jane bluntly put the question she had come so far to ask.

"Father, are you going to get a divorce and marry Miss Morrow?"

Dad stared at her for a moment. Then, "No!" he shouted. And again, "No . . . no . . . no! Jane, who told you such a thing?"

Jane drew a breath, trying to realise that the long nightmare was over. She couldn't . . . not just at first.

"Aunt Irene wrote me. She said you were going to Boston. She said . . ."

"Irene! Irene is always getting silly notions in her head. She means well, but . . . Jane, listen, once for all. I am the husband of one wife and I'll never be anything else."

Dad broke off and stared at Jane.

Jane, who never cried, was crying.

He swept her into his arms.

"Jane, you darling little idiot! How could you believe such stuff? I like Lilian Morrow . . . I've always liked her. And I could never love her in a thousand years. . . . Going to Boston? Of course I'm going to Boston. I've great news for you, Jane. My book has been accepted after all. I'm going to Boston to arrange the details with my publishers. Darling, do you mean to tell me that you walked from West Trent? How lucky I hung a moon out! But you are just sopping. What you need is a brew of good hot cocoa, and I'm going to make it for you. Look pleasant, dogs. Purr, Peter. Jane has come home."

43

THE next day Andrew Stuart sent for the doctor, and a few hours later the nurse came. The word went around Queen's Shore and the Corners that Jane Stuart was very ill with a dangerous type of pneumonia.

Jane could never remember anything of those first days very clearly. She was delirious almost from the beginning of her illness. Faces came and went dimly . . . dad's in anguish . . . a grave, troubled doctor . . . a white-capped nurse . . . finally another face . . . only *that* must be a dream . . . mother couldn't be there . . . not even if Jane could smell the faint perfume of her hair. Mother was in faraway Toronto.

As for her own whereabouts, Jane did not know where she was . . . she only knew that she was a lost wind seeking some lost word forever. Not till she found that word could she stop being a wind and be Jane Stuart again. Once, it seemed to her, she heard a woman crying wildly and some one saying, "There is still hope, dearest, there is still a little hope." And again . . . long afterwards . . . "There will be a change, one way or another, tonight."

"And then," said Jane, so clearly and distincly that she startled everyone in the room, "I shall find my lost word."

Jane didn't know how long it was after that to the day

when she understood that she was Jane again and no longer a lost wind.

"Am I dead?" she wondered. She lifted her arms feebly and looked at them. They had grown terribly thin, and she could hold them up only a second, but she concluded that she was alive.

She was alone . . . not in her own little room at Lantern Hill, but in father's. She could see through the window the gulf sparkling and the sky so softly, so ethereally blue over the haunted dunes. Somebody . . . Jane found out later it had been Jody . . . had found the first mayflowers and put them in a vase on the table by her bed.

"I'm . . . sure . . . the house . . . is listening," thought Jane.

To what was it listening? To two people who seemed to be sitting on the stairs outside. Jane felt that she ought to know who they were, but the knowledge just escaped her. Fitful sentences came to her, though they were uttered in muted tones. At the time they meant nothing to Jane, but she remembered them . . . remembered them always.

"Darling, I didn't mean a word of those dreadful things I said. . . ." "If I had got your letter . . ." "My poor little love . . ." "Have you ever thought of me in all those years?" . . . "Have I thought of anything else, loveliest?" . . . "When your wire came . . . mother said I mustn't . . . she was terrible . . . as if anything could keep me from Jane. . . ." "We were just two very foolish people . . . is it too late to be wise, Robin?"

Jane wanted to hear the answer to that question . . . wanted to dreadfully . . . somehow she felt that it would be of tremendous importance to everybody in the world. But a wind came in from the sea and blew the door shut.

"I'll never know now," she whispered piteously to the nurse when she came in.

"Know what, dear?"

"What she said . . . the woman on the stairs . . . her voice was so like mother's. . . ."

"It was your mother, dear. Your father wired for her as soon as I came. She has been here right along . . . and if

215

you're good and don't get excited, you can have just a peep at her this evening."

"So," said Jane feebly, "mother must have stood up to grandmother for once."

But it was several days later when Jane was allowed to have her first real talk with father and mother. They came in together, hand in hand, and stood looking down at her. Jane knew that there were three tremendously happy people in the room. Never had she seen either of them looking like that. They seemed to have drunk from some deep well of life, and the draught had made them young lovers again.

"Jane," said dad, "two foolish people have learned a little wisdom."

"It was all my fault that we didn't learn it long ago," said mother. There was a sound of tears in her voice and a sound of laughter.

"Woman!" What a delightful way dad had of saying "woman"! And mother's laugh . . . was it a laugh or a chime of bells? "I will not have you casting slurs at my wife. Your fault indeed! I will not have one particle of the blame taken away from me. Look at her, Jane . . . look at my little golden love. How did you ever have the luck to pick such a mother, Jane? The moment I saw her I fell in love with her all over again. And now we will all go in search of ten lost years."

"And will we live here at Lantern Hill?" asked Jane.

"Always, when we're not living somewhere else. I'm afraid with two women on my hands I'll never get my epic on Methuselah's life finished now, Jane. But there will be compensations. I think a honeymoon is coming to us. As soon as you're on the hoof, Superior Jane, we'll all take a little run up to Boston. I have to see about that book of mine, you know. Then a summer here and in the fall . . . the truth is, Jane, I've been offered the assistant editorship of *Saturday Evening*, with a healthy salary. I had meant to refuse, but I think I'll have to accept. What about it, Jane? The winters in Toronto . . . the summers at Lantern Hill?"

"And we'll never have to say good-bye again. Oh dad! But . . ."

"But me no buts. What is troubling you, dearest dear?"

"We . . . we won't have to live at 60 Gay?"

"Not by a jugful! A house we must have, of course. How you live is much more important that where you live . . . but we must have a roof over us."

Jane thought of the little stone house in Lakeside Gardens. It had not been sold yet. They would buy it. It would live . . . they would give it life. Its cold windows would shine with welcoming lights. Grandmother, stalking about 60 Gay, like a bitter old queen, her eyes bright with venom, forgiving or unforgiving as she chose, could never make trouble for them again. There would be no more misunderstanding. She, Jane, understood them both and could interpret them to each other. And have an eye on the housekeeping as well. It all fitted in as if it had been planned ages ago.

"Oh, dad," cried this happiest of all Janes, "I know the very house."

"You would," said dad.

THE END

ABOUT THE AUTHOR

L. M. MONTGOMERY'S fascinating accounts of the lives and romances of Anne, Emily, and other well-loved characters have
achieved longlasting popularity the world over. Born in 1874 in
Prince Edward Island, Canada, Lucy Maud showed an early flair
for storytelling. She soon began to have her writing published in
papers and magazines, and when she died in Toronto in 1942 she
had written more than twenty novels and a large number of short
stories. Most of her books are set in Prince Edward Island, which
she loved very much and wrote of most beauifully. *Anne of Green
Gables*, her most popular work, has been translated into thirty-six
languages, made into a film twice, and has had continuing success as a
stage play. Lucy Maud Montgomery's early home in Cavendish,
P.E.I., where she is buried, is a much-visited historic site.